NO TIME
TO WAVE
GOODBYE

NO TIME
TO WAVE
GOODBYE

A Novel

JACQUELYN MITCHARD

**Doubleday Large Print
Home Library Edition**

RANDOM HOUSE | NEW YORK

Published in the United States by Random House, an imprint of The Random House Publishing Group, a division of Random House, Inc., New York.

RANDOM HOUSE and colophon are registered trademarks of Random House, Inc.

ISBN 978-1-61523-585-8

Printed in the United States of America on acid-free paper

This Large Print Book carries the Seal of Approval of N.A.V.H.

For the two Annies—
one who came back,
one who never left.

And for Thomas H. Cook
and Susan Terner,
who changed my lonely
life one lucky day . . .

NO TIME
TO WAVE
GOODBYE

CHAPTER ONE

Before dawn on the day she would finally see his first real film, Beth Cappadora slipped into the guest room and lay down on the edge of the bed where her son, Vincent, slept.

Had she touched his hair or his shoulder, he would not have stirred. When he slept at all, Vincent slept like a man who'd fallen from a relaxed standing position after being hit on the back of the head by a frying pan. Still, she didn't take the risk. Her relationship with Vincent didn't admit of nighttime confidences, funny cards, all the trappings of the sentimental, platonic courtship between a mother and her grown boy. Instead, Beth blessed the air around his head, where coiled wisps of dark hair still sprang up as they had when he was a child.

Show them, Vincent, she said softly. Knock 'em dead.

Beth asked only a minor redemption— something that would stuff back the acid remarks that everyone had made about where Vincent's career of minor crime and major slough-offs would end, because it had so far outlasted the most generous boundaries of juvenile delinquency. She wished one thing itself, simple and linear: Let Vincent's movie succeed.

That night, as she watched the film, and recognized its might and its worth, Beth had to appreciate—by then, against her will—that her wish was coming true. What she didn't realize was something that she'd learned long ago.

Only long months from that morning did Beth, a superstitious woman all her life, re-alize she had forgotten that if a wish slipped like an arrow through a momentary slice in the firmament, it was free to come true any way it would. Only fools thought its trajectory could ever be controlled.

Sixteen hours after Beth tiptoed from Vincent's bedside, a spotlight beam shined out over the seat where she sat fidgeting and craning her neck to peek at everyone else taking their seats in the Harrington Community Center Auditorium.

Suddenly, there was Vincent, onstage. He looked up from nervously adjusting the pink tie he wore against his white shirt and twilight gray suit and said, "I have to apologize. We have a little technical glitch we need to fix and then we'll be ready. Thanks for your patience. In just a moment, the first voice you will hear is my sister, the opera singer Kerry Rose Cappadora, who also narrates this film. I'll be right back. I mean, the film will. Thanks again."

Beth leaned forward as if from the prow of a ship. Her husband, Pat, reached out to ease her back.

"Don't jump," he teased. "You can't do this for him. It's high time, Bethie. You have to agree. Vincent's lived *la vita facile* too long."

"I know," Beth agreed. Though she didn't speak Italian, she wanted to poke Pat in the ribs and not gently. Vincent earned his way, after a fashion. Vincent owned a home, after a fashion—two rooms in Venice Beach, California, that had once been a garage. Vincent had made a gourmet chocolate commercial nominated for an ADDY Award. He hadn't asked them for a dime since . . . well, since the last time he dropped out of college. But she said only, "You're right, of course."

"Bethie?"

"Yeah?"

"Why aren't you arguing with me?" Pat asked. "What's the matter with you?" Beth shrugged, battling the urge to drag her fingers through her careful blowout: If you have to mess with your hair, Beth's friend Candy said, shake, don't rake. Pat cracked his knuckles. "Damn it," Pat said then. "Who am I trying to kid? I haven't wanted a cigarette this bad since the grease fire at the restaurant. I want to jump up on the stage and yell at everybody, This is my son's work! You better appreciate this! But we've got to give this over to him."

"Absolutely," Beth said, her heartbeat

now a busy little mallet that must be visible through her pale silk chemise.

"You sound like a robot. Where's my wife? You could object a little," Pat said.

"Too nervous," Beth replied.

It was more than that, of course. Nothing that she could confide, even in Pat. For Beth was in part responsible for her son's brushes with the law and his seeming inability to finish . . . anything. (In part? Was she flattering herself? Once upon a time, Vincent had done everything he could, including selling a few bushels of thankfully low-order drugs, to get his mother's thousand-yard stare to focus on him.) If this film were to be worthy at all— Beth hugged herself, smiling—then this private screening for a hundred people in the rented theater of a community center would also be the long-overdue premiere of her son's life as a man in full.

More than this, in just a moment, Beth would learn the answers to the questions she'd asked herself for months.

What was the documentary about?

Why had Vincent enlisted his sister and his brother to help him make it? Last year, during the filming, had been the busiest time of their lives: Ben had a wife, a full share in the family business, and a baby on the way. Kerry still lived at her parents' house, but her college major was so demanding that some nights she came home from school or the voice studio with dark smudges under her eyes and fell asleep before she could eat the food she'd microwaved.

Was it because the subject was too intimate or incendiary or simply too off the wall to entrust to a stranger, even a fellow professional? Why had Vincent used film instead of video, which probably quadrupled the cost?

Was the obsessive privacy all pride? Did he have to do this all on his own?

With his first documentary, *Alpha Female,* a snapshot of the life of a young farmer's wife and mother of four putting herself through college as a part-time dominatrix, Vincent had turned to Beth, a photographer for nearly thirty years, on everything from how to light someone so blond that her features were nearly achromatic to how to coax an interview out of the woman's stern, disapproving parents. Beth recalled the look on her mother-in-law's face when *that* film had first screened, in the auditorium of the high school from which Vincent had been expelled. Freckle-faced Katie Hubner saddle-soaped her leather garter belt and said, "They don't care anything about sex, poor things! They just want me to treat them like their mean old mamas did!"

Of this film, Beth knew nothing but its title, *No Time to Wave Goodbye.* In her good moments, it seemed almost a private message from her older son. Her own first photo book—a series of black-and-white shots of her own children walking away from her, dragging fishing poles, hurrying toward the blooming pagoda of a fireworks display, each underlined with a tender quotation—was called *Wave Goodbye.*

What other connection could there possibly be?

Beth began to twist her wedding ring round and round. Did no one else notice the minutes that had collapsed since Vincent's introduction? Two, three . . . seven?

No one close to the family would mind. There they all were, chatting, her family, her in-laws, Ben and his wife, Eliza. People were admiring Ben and Eliza's baby, two-month-old Stella, Beth's first grandchild, on her very first outing. Along with Eliza's mother—Beth's beloved friend Candy—the crowd included dozens of business associates and old and new neighborhood friends. They were the cheering section.

But what about the others?

What of the one reviewer invited to this private event? Where was he? The fourth-row seat on the aisle reserved for him was still empty.

And all the guests Beth didn't recognize?

Would they hate the film if they had to wait much longer?

Beth glanced around her. In the same row, across the aisle, sat a perfect Yankee couple, ramrod-straight, their spines an inch from the seat backs—mother, father, impeccably coutured blond daughter. Several rows back, directly behind Beth, a soft, pretty young black woman held hands with her son, a slender young teenager. To the right and near the back door, there was a round-shouldered guy, not heavy but big, who might have been a day laborer with his snap-closure shirt rolled up to the elbows. No one sat beside him; in presence

rather than size, he seemed to fill a row of
his own. A young Latino couple—a sharply
dressed young man and his hugely pregnant wife—patiently tolerated the two
silently rambunctious preschoolers crawling all over them. An older man, who could
have been an advertisement for mountain-
climbing and Earth Shoes, sat just beyond the young couple. Who were these
people? Who were they to Vincent?

The screen went dark.

Then from the darkness, a canvas appeared and, to the sound of Kerry's pure,
sweet soprano singing "Liverpool Lullaby,"
a beautiful sequence of transparent photos
of children was tacked to the cinematic
canvas by an invisible hand. As soon as
each eager face appeared, a name,
height, and date of birth printed below it,
like a Wanted poster, a visual force like a
strong wind tore the picture off the screen.
Beside the photos, words configured to
look like a child's block printing unfurled.
They read: *A Pieces by Reese Production . . . written and produced by Vincent
Cappadora and Rob Brent . . . in conjunc-
tion with John Marco Ruffalo Projects . . .
edited by Emily Sydney . . .*

Then came the last photo.

The last photo was Ben's preschool photo.

Beth gripped the arms of her seat. *What?*

Twenty-two years ago, that very photo had occupied the whole cover of *People* magazine. For almost a decade, it claimed real estate in the center of the corkboard in the office of Detective Supervisor Candy Bliss, as she had searched tirelessly for Beth's kidnapped son, to no avail. Posters made from this photo melted to tatters under the pummeling of rain and snow and sun and more rain and snow on thousands of light poles all over the Midwest and beyond. And they had produced nothing but phone calls from every crazy who wasn't behind bars and some who were, and a single, valid rumor of the sighting of that little boy in Minneapolis with a "white-haired" woman. That white-haired woman turned out to be a dyed platinum blonde—Beth's old schoolmate Cecilia Lockhart. Everyone remembered Cecil as nuts but not *nuts*. Yet, it was she, at Beth's fifteenth high-school reunion, who had taken Ben's hand and strolled with him out of the hotel

lobby and out of Beth's life, for nine unre-
lenting years.

Though she tried, Beth could not stop
her jaw from shuddering. She wanted to
cling to Pat but dared not move. The last
thing she wanted was to draw attention
from the screen to herself.

And yet, she already had.

Bryant Whittier, who sat in a cultivated posture of ease, flanked by his wife, Claire, el-
egant in a St. John knit suit, and his
daughter, Blaine, demure for once in a designer wrap dress, saw Beth's minute gesture of distress. He recognized it from a
dozen holding cells and living rooms. A defense lawyer, Bryant had observed closely
the parents of the accused, particularly the
moment when incredulity gave way to rage
and then despair. Poor woman, he thought.
She hadn't known.

When he interviewed them, Vincent said
that no one but the crew understood the
substance of this documentary, but Bryant
hadn't believed that "no one" included the
Cappadora brothers' close family. The
slender, expensive-looking woman had to
be Vincent's mother. In profile, she was the

exact image of Vincent. He had never shown them a picture of his parents, but Bryant had found old news photos of the case on the Internet. This clearly was Beth, more attractive than Bryant would have imagined she would be by now. Bryant did not like heavyset women. He sometimes reminded his surviving daughter, who rowed in a coxed quad, to watch her prodigious appetite at the training table. He made a covert inventory of Beth, a cultivated professional knack that also had its personal uses. It was unfortunate. Her husband, or the man he assumed was Vincent's father, slouched with his arms hanging at his sides, as though they'd been dislocated.

Who would want to remember, if they didn't have to?

And yet, it was their son, who, for reasons of his own, had made this film that Bryant participated in only against his will. He had talked to Sam—the name Ben used for himself—and Vincent's camera only because Claire and Blaine, who still had hope that Bryant's missing daughter, Jacqueline, was alive, pleaded with him to do so. There was an awful fairness here.

Why shouldn't the filmmaker's family share in the suffering ripped open anew for all the families Vincent had found and featured?

Bryant put his hand on Claire's arm. She glanced at him, biting her lips. Bryant turned his attention back to the people in the three rows roped off by gold cord: The tiny girl whose long black hair swept over the baby swaddled in her arms? She wasn't Italian. Spanish of some kind?

Ah, yes. Bryant was grown forgetful.

This was Ben's wife.

Ben had married the adopted daughter of the detective, Candy, the sainted policewoman—Candy, whom all the family loved so well. To Bryant's mind, being unable to find a child whose kidnapper had moved him to a house blocks from the place where the Cappadoras had grown up meant no genius at sleuthing! From what the Whittiers understood, twelve-year-old Ben had actually found his birth family on his own, rather than the other way around, quite by accident, when he was passing out flyers offering to mow lawns. Bryant gingerly stroked his well-clipped beard. Hadn't Ben admitted that he'd been raised by the innocent man the kidnapper married, whom he thought of as his father? "Adopted" by this man, Ted—or was it George?—who had no inkling that "Sam" wasn't Cecilia's own child? Hadn't Ben said that his "mother" (the only mother he knew) spent most of his childhood in and out of institutions? Was it from Ben, or from a newspaper account, that Bryant had learned that Cecilia, an actor Claire said she'd seen on an old soap opera, finally committed suicide?

Of course. Bryant would have read that. Ben . . . well, Sam, who still, oddly, answered only to the name given to him by the kidnapper, would not have volunteered it. For all his glad-handing humor, Ben was hard to know. Unlike his sister, he kept very definite doors closed.

Where *was* the sister, Kerry, the pretty little singer? Oh, there she was, just visible behind a fold of curtain on the stage, standing beside Vincent, watching the audience. Kerry didn't just wear her heart on her sleeve; she had no sleeve. The ideal juror, Bryant thought. Emotional. Impressionable. Visible. He smiled blandly, the expression cheerful enough to convince anyone who didn't look into his eyes. The woodland path on the screen was familiar. Bryant had told police that his daughter, Jacqueline, had taken that route as she walked to her death.

The camera followed the trail through the greenwood and Kerry's voice began, "When I was six months old, my brother Benjamin Cappadora was abducted in the middle of the day in a hotel lobby crowded with people, nearly in arm's reach of my brother Vincent, my godmother, and my mother. And though Ben came back to us, it wasn't before my parents and my older brother walked through a valley that no one can understand who hasn't walked it."

Beth turned to Pat and threw out her hands, demanding. But he slowly, woodenly, shook his head. "Bethie," he said, "I swear to God. I didn't know a thing about this."

Beth tried to settle the lineaments of her face, to appear as the Cappadora family history obliged her to appear—sweet, gamine, ineffably cheerful. As ever, as part of a family people recognized and watched, she was on guard. There were obligations that redounded to such a family, to people who had been blessed, had been handed—by a preposterous coincidence—the gift of living happily ever after, when their missing child showed up on their doorstep. In the history of abductions, such luck was not unknown but rare to the point of statistical impossibility. Ben lost-and-found was more complicated, by orders of magnitude, than anyone except Candy understood. But it would have seemed a failure of grace to behave in any other way: Even the grown children knew they were expected to offer a firm handshake, a lustrous smile, even keep a normal weight.

It was no use. The best Beth could do for her face was to cover it with her long, pale fingers, the wedding-band ruby on her fourth finger gleaming like a coal in the moody light.

Kerry's voice continued, "So-called stereotypical kidnappings, or stranger abductions, are fortunately far less common than the news media would have us believe." Beth couldn't quite hear Kerry. There was a rushing in her ears, as though she were trying to listen to her daughter from inside a shower stall. ". . . Fewer than four percent of all child disappearances are stranger abductions. . . . most of them involve noncustodial parents or runaways. . . . Although thirteen years ago, my brother was restored to us, through diligent police work and impossible good luck, few families are so lucky. The five families who told us their stories still wait for the children who had no time to wave goodbye."

A banner fluttered across the screen and was again ripped away: *The First Days.*

There they were on-screen. Claire and Bryant Whittier. The Puritan couple who looked to be an advertisement for New England vitality were, in fact, Californians. They divided their time between a tiny suburb of San Francisco, called Durand, and their second home, a vast, rustic lodge they owned, some miles away in the San Juan Diego Mountains.

Filmed in the living room of their primary residence, the Whittiers sat like matching china figurines on matching Queen Anne chairs, their German shorthaired pointer, Macduff, between them, his head on crossed paws.

"At first, I slept in her bed every night. And Macduff slept under it, every night," said Claire Whittier. "He was her birthday puppy when she was twelve. When he gets to the end of the drive up at our summerhouse, he will still start to howl." Claire Whittier compressed her lips. "That's where we found Jackie's shoes, side by side. She just stepped out of them. It was because they were new, very nice ballet flats. She only wore them once, for graduation the day before. She didn't want to ruin them. Bryant says that Jackie left them because she knew she wasn't coming back. Bryant was far better able to cope than our other daughter, Blaine, and I. We were in shock. We didn't know how much at the time. We were no help at all to the police. The worst moment was waking up. I would forget, until I woke up, and then it would be real. I slept and slept and tried to sleep some more. I needed pills to make me sleep, sleep, sleep. I craved them. I don't believe I got out of bed for a month. And when I did, I wore those shoes everywhere. I still do. They make me feel close to Jackie."

The riddle of Jacqueline Whittier's shoes

so perplexed the police and the FBI that, at first, they harbored doubts about the Whittiers. Why wouldn't Macduff have followed the girl he loved so extravagantly down the road that led to a patchwork of woods and river ponds surrounding the Whittiers' vacation lodge? To Bryant Whittier, it was obvious: Jacqueline was practical and logical. Macduff was as well bred and obedient as his mistress. She had told him downstay; Macduff had no choice except to do that until he was released by Jacqueline or another family member. Jacqueline would have known that. She took after her father, Bryant said. He was the only defense lawyer in tiny Cisco County, sought out by families from around the state. Jacqueline, an honor student, the yearbook editor, and a star swimmer who also ran cross-country, hoped one day, Bryant said, to practice law with her dad.

The Whittiers did not dispute that, in the strictest sense, the case of Jacqueline Bryant Whittier remained an unsolved stranger abduction.

But Bryant Whittier quietly asserted that Jackie, who had suffered serious periods of depression since just before her fourteenth birthday, had taken her own life, although no body had ever been found.

Kerry's voice explained, "According to her parents and sister, Jackie was indeed prey to periods of pain so intense, almost physical on rare occasions, that she would have committed suicide long before if she hadn't loved them so much and hadn't been so afraid of dying alone. But that doesn't mean she was really ready to die. Recent months had been kind to Jacqueline. She seemed to have turned a corner. Her mother and sister don't believe that she left her family voluntarily."

"There are these Internet sites," Jacqueline's sister, Blaine, told the camera as it walked beside her, "where kids who are fascinated with suicide talk about it. We found conversations on Jackie's laptop. Personally, to me they sounded just like overheated dramatic teenagers carried away by the romantic idea of dying young. But this one boy, Jordan? Who used a café in San Francisco as his return address? How many guys are named Jordan? If that's even his name? How many Internet cafés?" Blaine wrapped her scarf around her neck and slipped her hands into leather gloves. "Maybe it wasn't even his real name." After walking a few more paces, Blaine sat down on a stump in the woods and said, "Do you know what I really think? I think maybe he took Jackie's ideas too seriously and came to get her and drove her up to our summer place in the mountains. And maybe he helped her kill herself. Maybe it was all him. But the police never found any evidence of . . . that. They went over the whole area up there by our house. You know? No . . . evidence. No Jordan. Nothing." She paused and continued slowly, "It's not impossible Jackie ran away, with no intention of dying. She . . . we . . . she minded all the expectations from our dad more than I did." The camera pictured Bryant Whittier making a tent of his lean, patrician hands, shaking his head, presumably in reaction to his older daughter's words.

Then Kerry's voice read a poem Jacqueline had written: *"I cherish the smallest spear of light / But inside me is a pool of night / For one whose soul longs just for rest / What may be hardest may be best.* Despite her apparent upswing in mood, this was the poem that Jacqueline left behind in observance of her seventeenth birthday, the day before she disappeared, the day after she graduated first in her class, and told her fellow students to embrace their dreams as the purest reality. Two years later, her case remains open. She is still missing."

Beth glanced at her watch. Twenty-four minutes into the film, Beth finally knew what it was about. She simply had no idea why Vincent had chosen to drag this dark river where his whole family had nearly drowned.

CHAPTER TWO

Beth sat immobilized. She now knew the answer to one question but not to the fifty others it raised.

In public, in row three, in her hip-but-modest clothes, she felt her mouth filling with saliva, the way it had when she'd had morning sickness. She tried to breathe slowly through her nose. What a sight it would be for Beth to run from the theater with a handful of bile. Why choose this topic, and why involve her other children in raking her over the coals—along with his father and his elderly grandparents?

Was it some form of payback—
"gotcha"—for the person she no longer
was, the mother that Vincent had endured
after the kidnapping, the skeletal scaffold-
ing of a human being who lived years,
woke and slept in the same clothes until
Pat ran a bath and led her to it?

As Candy used to say, the answer was
usually in the question.

Beth believed that she and Vincent had
reached a kind of peace over the past
years. If they were not jolly pals, they were
not, at least, people with the same blood
type who spoke on the telephone once
every two months.

Beth lowered her hands and grounded
herself to the seat with the grip of her
palms. She stared unblinking at the screen.
There. That was good. She looked calm
and stoic, engaged and thoughtful.

But eyes saw through her pretense.

From a couple of rows back, Walter Hutcheson noticed that the woman he'd observed laughing and chatting earlier had
gone still and grim. He'd first looked at her
because something about Beth's graceful
hands reminded him of Sari just a few

years ago, before Sari armored herself in fat and chopped off her waist-length brown hair, the skein of hair he once slipped over his fingers like the lengths of cashmere Sari carded from her goats and spun for weavers. It was wrong, given everything, for Walter to miss the physical love of his wife. But there were times he shook with longing for the jasmine scent of her freckled private skin. For him, she was still the leggy twenty-one-year-old he'd kissed at Big Sur the summer before senior year. Once, in the dark, he suggested to Sari that they were young enough to have a child still.

After that, she slept in the loft.

That woman was probably as old as Sari.

She must be family to Vincent and Sam, for she sat in the section cordoned off from the rest by gold rope. Vincent had told him that his family's last name, Cappadora, meant "gold hat." They looked like their name. All the people in that section were shiny with health and wealth. Why should the woman cover her face and then slam her hands down on the arms of her seat? Their lost boy was right there, just feet away from them. Their suffering was all over.

Walter's suffering would not end until his eyes closed for the last time. He tried to believe that Laurel was happy, somewhere, in this world or another.

But what had come before? What agonies?

Had the Cappadoras once been the way Walter was now, all bones and overlarge clothes? Walter sometimes thought he would look into the mirror above the sink and see a man whose frame was crumbling like the piecrust earth of an eroded bluff, but the bluff was made from his dreams.

As the camera panned mountain majesty over the crescent of a hazy ocean bay, in a voice growling like a rock tumbler with the echo of ten thousand cigarettes, the man identified as Walter Hutcheson of Spinnaker, Washington, said, "Laurel's a free spirit, like her mom and me. We tried to be upbeat at first and we still try to do that. Of course we miss her all the time and we worry. But she's self-reliant."

Beth realized that this was the Earth Shoes man she'd spotted earlier in the audience. He was alone here in the theater, but on the screen, he introduced his wife, Sari, who nodded along with Walter—but perpetually, nodding and smiling even when there was nothing to nod or smile about. "I'm half sure she's just found a new way of trying out the independence we all want. I mean, what were we like when we were fifteen?" Walter smiled broadly and his wife began to nod again, her smile collapsed like a Halloween pumpkin too soon carved and frozen. "We still think Laurel will come back when she's ready. Maybe . . ."

But Laurel Hutcheson's backpack was found in the trunk when a feral, fox-faced drifter called Jurgen Smote was arrested in Washington State for a traffic violation. He was only eleven miles from what the police called the PSL—the point last seen. The Hutchesons had taken their daughter Laurel to an Equinox Festival near their home, a festival they had attended a dozen times, where they felt comforted and welcomed.

Smote, interviewed by Vincent for a brief segment in a visiting room at the prison where he was doing what Smote described as "a nickel" for statutory rape, said, "I might've met a girl named Laurel. I've met a lot of girls. Some of them . . . don't stay in touch. They disappear. From my life, that is." His slow smile forced Beth to shrink back in her seat.

Another shot was taken in a moment of sepia light, with Walter's face illuminated from below by a coal fire. "There are people who say we let her go on her own too long. Let her go camping with groups of boys and girls, let her hitchhike. Well, I say to that . . . that they're right. Oh, they are right. We never thought it would be anything but safe for her here . . ."

Laurel's friends, doe-eyed, faces plain of makeup, as much like unicorns as Laurel seemed in the photos, had identified Jurgen Smote as having danced with Laurel at the festival. Smote had taken Laurel's hand, a girl named Echo said in her interview. Laurel had pulled her hand away.

As Echo's voice in the film continued, Sari, filmed listening to Laurel's friend, hid her face in her husband's shirt. Hutcheson put his arm around her shoulders but, abruptly, she pulled away. Beth remembered exactly that, wanting Pat's touch desperately—wanting only one thing more, for no one to touch her at all.

How bad would it get? Beth thought.

Would there be footage of her—a crazed, dirty, and sleep-famished Beth from long ago? Would this whole crowd see her telling the glossy, wide-eyed young anchorwoman who'd asked her to film a "plea" to the kidnapper, *I don't expect you to bring Ben back, because you are a sick, heartless bastard. . . . If you could do this thing, you either don't understand the nature of the hell we are going through, or you don't care. . . .* No.

No. Vincent would spare her that at least. Those were nightmare moments that she had shoveled for years to bury deep.

Tonight, coming in, Beth had seen press people outside, including a few she knew to nod to from her newspaper days. Vincent's partner, Rob, a former radio guy who could have sold parkas to people living in

Death Valley, must have dropped choice hints to the press—if not leaflets from a helicopter.

How elated she had been, when she saw those reporters! Now, the possibility of scrutiny made her sick.

Sit still, she thought. Just sit still.

A banner fluttered across the screen: *Searching.*

On the screen, around a young, pretty black woman, sat three children, an older boy reading and two small girls coloring elaborate, large paper dolls. Identified by a caption as Janice Dicksen of Chicago, Illinois, the woman said, "This new playground guy organized dodgeball games, and DuPre loved that game. One day I was in the park by the school, talking to my sister Tanya, about the gifted class DuPre was going to be in, and there was this short white guy in a black hoodie and jeans. And DuPre was calling, 'Hey, hey Coach.'" The lively young woman's face bled into a video clip of a chubby little mustang of a boy high-footing it out of the goal on a city soccer field. "So I told him, you run over and say hi and then we got to go pick up your little sister." Her brown eyes shined with un-spilled tears. "It wasn't more than one minute that I talked to Tanya. Not five like they said." The camera waited in si-lence as Janice Dicksen's face broke open. "I sent my boy to that man."

A Channel Five reporter in flight-attendant blue said, "Police tonight are seeking a man who allegedly abducted a six-year-old boy, DuPre Dicksen, from Hamlin Community Park near Our Savior Baptist Church on Seventy-fifth Street. The boy's mother, Janice Dicksen, says the man who allegedly took her son was a playground supervisor at John F. Kennedy School. But officials there say that this was no official playground helper. The only man seen that day in the park was an unem-ployed carpenter who volunteered to help with after-school activities. That carpenter was identified as Joseph Jackson, but the man's ex-wife knew him by the name Joseph Jackson Plimoth. The whereabouts of the little boy and Plimoth are unknown. This photo of DuPre was taken at the be-ginning of the school year. When he was last seen, he was wearing a red baseball cap, navy blue shorts, and red Converse high-tops."

Like Ben, Beth thought. Ben had been wearing a baseball cap, too.

Ben had worn new red tennis shoes.

"They blamed me," Janice Dicksen said. "One of the officers asked if I was having a relationship with the man who took DuPre. I never even met him!"

Beth thought it might be possible for her heart to fall out of her chest. Putting her hands on her sternum, she pressed hard. Ben was just two seats down. A muscle in his cheek quivered, but he studied the screen as though he'd never seen a movie before. To avoid his mother's hot gaze? Or did all this feel as removed from reality for Ben as it did for Beth? That had been *Ben's own three-year-old face* up there, a face he didn't remember having been his.

She turned slightly in her seat. There was the real-life Janice Dicksen beside an older version of the boy who'd been read-ing while Janice was interviewed. He must be nearly a foot taller, wearing a suit that almost fit him, except for the gap at the end of the jacket cuffs that exposed two inches of shirtsleeves. Would they come later to the reception? Could Beth touch her, hug her—and not seem patronizing?

With a physical tug, Beth forced herself to turn back to the mammoth moving mouths and foreheads above her.

She peered at her watch.

Eighty-one minutes had passed. Vincent had snagged her, pulled her into the heft and tenderness of his images and vistas, his hard-won moments of naked emotion. In silence, a man's big face fell like a crumbling cliff as he stroked a good-luck teddy bear, decked out in a silver gymnastics leotard, that his daughter had dropped when she was taken. DuPre Dicksen's older brother, small and alone against a background of battered tenements, irregular as ruined teeth, was captured sinking shot after shot through a hoop with a single string of metal mesh, the setting sun a fragile orange gauze.

Beth began to forget time, except to wish that the film would not end.

The interview with the Caffertys hit her with maximum force. The Caffertys were . . . they were like Beth and Pat had been, so much like them—not rich, not connected, ordinary working people. She recognized from the audience the big man who took up his own row; his elfin wife had apparently not come. Two wives had chosen to absent themselves from this screening. Their little daughter Alana was only six when she was snatched from a crowded hallway at a gymnastics meet nearly seven years before.

When Beth looked up, Candy had taken the seat beside her. Pat had disappeared. Beth glanced down the row and saw him with his arm around Rosie, his mother. Hey, thanks, Beth thought.

"It's hard for me, too," Candy said. "You holding up?"

"You know, I'm good," Beth said. "He earned it."

They hugged briefly and sat back.

Standing hand in hand with his sister in the wings, Vincent took his first deep breath when he saw his mother hug Candy. The inhalation made him giddy, like his first pull on a cigarette at the age of thirteen. How long had he been holding his breath? He watched her face—the tears she held back by tipping her face upward, the times she pressed her palms to her cheeks or bit her lip. He'd waited for the volcanic leap out of the seat, the flight from the auditorium. Her stillness scared him even more. He had flanked her. He had gone behind her back. Studying her expression, he saw that she hated it but she couldn't help but appreciate it as a film. How would she act, though, when it got to the parts about Candy and about her? Oh Christ. Kerry had let go of his hand. Vincent reached out again and gripped it tighter.

His mother had taught him that the lens was not human; it couldn't lie. Computers could tweak things away. Even the eye could fool the mind about what it saw. But a film camera was the incorruptible witness. His mother had come all this way and not seen the worst of it yet. She had not seen the old footage of their own family.

Would Ma know that these images made him want to put his fist through a wall but that it would have been coy to leave his own family out at the expense of all the others? After all, Ben had been the strangest case of all, the boy who came home but was no longer Ben. What about Ben? Now, after he had seen the

same footage, which, to Vincent's knowledge, he had never in his life watched.
Vincent had looked into Beth's eyes and
seen a pane of green glass. He had seen
mirth and longing and forgiveness, something seething, something pleading. Now
the film was all of a piece, a force.

After this, what would he see in Beth's
eyes?

The last banner, for the final segment,
was bright yellow: It read *Hope's Long
Road.*

A psychiatrist from New York, known for
his research on the ripple effect of losing a
child, described a skip-tracer—someone
who searched for missing people—and
talked about what could work and what
didn't have a prayer.

A therapist spoke of a life lived around
crisis, a unique mourning, an open pit
with no healed place to lay flowers.

Twenty-two years ago, Beth had been
the poster girl for that world of limbo: She
dared not move, not one inch, to the left or
the right. The world-after-Ben would have
buried her. She told Pat that she would go

mad, and leave him to raise the children alone, if he pressed her to be "normal." She had believed that no one else knew what she knew.

But Vincent had somehow found these people, different from her only as a crystal is different from another crystal, at the microscopic level. Vincent's dexterous hands had lifted this subject out of bathos into impassioned gravity.

The sweet, plump Mexican mother, Rosa Rogelio, nursed her newborn and sobbed. Her prayer chain extended around the world, through China and Greece and Wales and even Russia. Rosa sent out a new prayer each morning.

Her son Luis had been three years old on the evening three years ago when someone wheeled his stroller away from the lobby of a chain restaurant, during the instant that Rosa was in the washroom changing one of his younger brothers and Ernest turned his back to give the cashier his credit card. Hiccoughing, Rosa said, "I feel like he wakes up every morning and wonders, why did Mama let this happen? When will Mama come? He's only six now. He would cry for me and his papa. He would not forget us like Ben. We were so close in our family."

Like Ben. Beth breathed deeply, again.

Luis, Beth guessed, would have been the eldest of the family. Since then, they had apparently had another baby, too young to be in the audience with the preschoolers, and were expecting a fifth.

The beautiful Blaine Whittier appeared again, her ivory face literally sculpted downward by sadness, admitting she had been "shrunk" more times than her favorite sweatpants. She was supposed to get over feeling that she was complicit in Jackie's loss. Blaine Putnam Whittier had briefly considered suicide. What if Jackie came back? What if she had been molested or otherwise hurt and Blaine were gone? One family could only bear so much.

One family, thought Beth, breathless with grief for this child, could only bear so much. One child could only bear so much.

Oh, Vincent. . . . Beth believed she had come to witness Vincent's redemption.

Who was it that Beth had really hoped to absolve?

"And our family tried a hundred ways for a hundred days to cope too," Kerry said evenly. "There were a hundred leads, a hundred errors, and one preposterous stroke of luck."

There was Penny Odin, now the national director of Compassionate Circle, a support group for families of missing or murdered children, which had begun in Madison, Wisconsin, where Pat and Beth lived after college, until five years after Ben disappeared, when they moved back to Chicago so Pat and his father could start The Old Neighborhood, the restaurant designed around an Italian wedding theme that now had two locations and was a regular feature in gourmet and in-flight magazines.

The sight of Penny—Beth didn't hear what she said—hurled Beth back to that overbright fluorescent-buzzing church-basement Sunday School in Madison, where crayoned pictures of baby Jesus at play in his sandals and little Jesus-brown robe looked down on couples Beth had nicknamed Murdered by Boyfriend, Stolen by Boyfriend, Stolen by Nanny, Stolen by Father, and Unknown Disappearance. How long had it been since she thought of those names?

Beth knew what must come next and it did: Candy, younger, a rattled but determinedly dignified newly promoted chief of detectives, her "plain clothes" a pale blue silk suit, her composure contradicted only by the bloodless clench of her fingers on the arms of her chair. Yes, Candy admitted, she had interviewed Cecilia Lockhart just three days after the abduction. Yes, Cecilia did lead Candy to look at Ben, asleep in a bunk bed at her mother's house, where she was staying. Cecilia had already dyed the child's hair dark brown and probably had given him some cough medicine to make him sleep. Cecilia Lockhart had identified him as her own son and expressed grief for the Cappadoras. No, Candy had not examined the child or awakened him. Cecilia had not aroused her suspicion. Cecilia was an actor, after all, but this was no excuse, said Candy.

"This is the greatest regret of my career and perhaps of my life," a present-day Candy on the screen said to the interviewer.

So, Beth thought.

So. So . . . she—Vincent's mother—had not known about the film.

But her best friend had.

What could Beth do about this? Her shoulders sagged: The thing was done. What could she do? It was one more betrayal and yes, probably necessary. Had Beth known, she would have tried to talk him out of this part—if she were honest, she would have tried to talk Vincent out of the whole thing. Had she been successful, it would have been one of the big regrets of *her* life.

Now, back on the screen in footage Vincent had shot only a year ago, Candy on the screen said (as Candy in the audience winced and grabbed for Beth's hand) that the world was more limited nearly a quarter century ago—with no Internet, only the police radio band ISPEN in Illinois and the goodwill of volunteers. She had encouraged the Cappadoras to make public statements. So, finally, there was Beth, her former self in a TV clip, part of the interview she remembered entirely, shamefully, like a dream of standing up naked in church—Beth, dreadful, dazed, saying,

"I am not going to appeal to you. But anyone else . . . anyone who sees Ben's face, and who has a heart, you know that whoever is with Ben is not me or Pat. . . . So if you could, what I want you to do is, grab Ben. If you have to hurt the person, that's okay. I will reward you; my family will reward you. . . . We will give you everything we have."

The final words of the film told of plans and new tracing technology and foundations devoted to eradicating the ugly zeal of the feral, the lonely, the desperate, the sick, the hungry, the twisted who preyed on children. . . .

"Why did we make this film?" Kerry's voice asked. "We chose to bear witness to these families, knowing that so-called stranger abductions cannot be eradicated. We chose to do this, as no film ever has, without lurid images or crude exploitation. We chose to be witness to them and to share what the world concerned with missing children has learned since my brother was abducted. We do know that we must teach children that it is the people they trust who will manipulate them most. Last year in the United States, there were two thousand five hundred abductions, only fifty-seven of the rare sort, stranger abductions. But the year that I was born, one of us was one of them. And there is no place like the place where these families stand, nowhere on earth. I didn't know this until I stood beside them. My brother Ben did not know and not even my older brother Vincent knew entirely. The old adage says that it takes a whole village to raise a child. So is a whole village denatured by a child's loss? Shakespeare wrote, 'All days are nights to see till I see thee, / And nights bright days when dreams do show thee me.' We dream of these families whether we wish to or not. We wish they had, at least, time to wave goodbye."

The end credits rolled against one of Beth's photos of her three children walking away from her, on a tiny crescent of beach.

All three of them had exposed her and exposed her to pain.

They had exploited memories they couldn't understand.

They had learned the truth of their lives.

They had honored it and given it form.

As Kerry's voice again began to sing

the final verse of "Liverpool Lullaby," "Oh, you have your father's face. You're growing up a real hard case. . . ." Beth got up and strode toward the back of the theater. The last fifteen feet, she ran, one foot bare, her other shoe still on the floor in front of her seat. She didn't stop to look at any of her children.

Just as she reached the double doors, they sprang open. From the vestibule, Vincent came barreling through the gap so fast he almost clipped Beth, who had no time to put up her hands. Ben slipped through behind his brother.

"Ma," Vincent said. "Ma, listen . . ."

"I am just . . ." Beth said. "I am just so . . ."

"I know," Vincent said, turning up his palms. "Believe me. I know."

"I am just so proud of you both," Beth said, opening her arms. Neither of her sons moved to embrace her. Beth finally let her arms drop to her sides. "What did I do?"

"You never said that before," Vincent told her.

"She has too," said Ben.

"I have too," said Beth.

"No she hasn't. She's said she loves

me. She's said I could do whatever I wanted if I wasn't such a screw-off. But not that."

"I've heard her say that," Ben said. "Why would she lie now?"

"Because it's already done. She knows how much it means to me."

"Can I get a word in? I could have just said it was great," Beth told Vincent. Was he right? Had she never told Vincent that she was proud of him? "Don't talk about me like I'm not here."

"Were you shocked?" Vincent asked.

"Well, yes, but was that the point?" Beth said and then, in the instant he let his face open, she saw how scared he'd really been—more of her than any critic. Shoulders still rigid, Vincent put his arms around his mother. Ben cupped Beth's shoulder.

"No, it wasn't. The point was to shine on the dark corner. My reasons were pure. For once," Vincent said. "I thought for sure you'd hate it. And I had to do it anyhow. For me. To know."

"I started out hating it. But you won me over," Beth said. Her sons held her closer.

All the outer doors sprang open to the sound of applause.

People stopped for a moment when they saw Beth with her sons in the vestibule. Then a flash went off. Their embrace was the photo that appeared the following Sunday on the front of the Arts section—along with a reprint of *Rolling Stone*'s gracious, admiring review of *No Time to Wave Goodbye.*

Janice Dicksen waited until the paper at work was a day old. Then she sliced the picture out with her thumbnail and, for lack of a better place, she slid it into DuPre's baby book. It didn't seem right to throw it away. After she did, she hugged the book close. For the first time, no matter what her minister said about how we must never second-guess God's plan, she knew she would never see DuPre again. She prayed that this movie would help another mother's son.

Bryant Whittier had a blank Levenger's album to hold stills from the shooting of the film. The photo of Beth with her sons was the tenth one that he glued into place, cutting it with the ceramic knife he used to mat black-and-white photos he took up at the piece of undeveloped mountain land he owned. He then slid the book into a shelf and got out one of his files about various child kidnappings, to add the story about the film to one of the thick folders. But he found himself reaching for the album again. He studied the look on Vincent's face and wondered if that was what Jacqueline had felt—at the last moment. Surprise.

Walter Hutcheson sent the picture to his sister, Amy. Before he sealed the envelope, Walter looked again at the photo. How could he have wondered if the woman was Beth Cappadora? Ben . . . well, Sam . . . was her double. He remembered the tears on her face, made incandescent by the light from the screen. Again, an acrid taste sprang into Walter's throat as he remembered Beth toasting her son at the reception afterward, tremulous with joy, exchanging fashion ideas with poor, sweet Janice Dicksen. Her giddy demeanor offended Walter so much that he made his apologies and pleasantries to the Cappadoras after barely an hour. It was better that Sari hadn't come. How dare

Beth laugh, so soon after a movie that explored the agony of his family and four others?

And where was his little darling, his Laurel?

Walter felt his breath come quicker. He tried to wrest the thought away. But it would not leave him. In the dark, he thought.

In the dark.

CHAPTER THREE

The morning after the screening, Beth
went out to pull the heads off her roses
above the three-leaf and wondered which
of her neighbors had finally crossed the
line and became so affected that they actually owned a limousine. The gray car,
idling at the verge of her driveway, pulled
away almost as Beth stepped outside, the
rear window silently closing. I'd want to
hide my face too, she thought. She would
ask Pat if he knew anyone who owned a
limo.

Back inside, she drank three cups of
coffee before eight a.m. and by nine was

peeing so often she was afraid she'd miss Vincent's call. He had spent the night at his grandparents' house. Though Beth'd fallen into bed extinguished by the emotional medley relay of the film and the reception, she'd risen early to clean, only to find the house spotless. Pat had done it all.

Later that day, the cleaner would come and do it all again.

Her consciousness sharpened by caffeine, Beth slowly remembered hearing, through the submerged bubble of her sleep the previous night, the loading of the dishwasher, the storing of the serving pieces, the snare drum strokes of sweeping. It hadn't occurred to Beth to get up and help. Puttering before sleep was Pat's auditory signature, and his father, Angelo's, before him. And this was true not only on busy nights or party nights but every night, no matter what time they got home from work. They circled the rooms, drawer to drawer, cabinet to cabinet, making sure the pencils were in separate bins from the markers and that none of the long roofing nails had got mixed in with the tacks, lining up the cereal boxes in order by height. Beth thought that Pat's sleep requirement per week was roughly the average person's nightly need. Vincent was like him that way. ("Maybe it's because they're Romans," Beth's brother Bick had once suggested, some long-ago Christmas just after she and Pat were married, when Bick spent a night with Beth at her in-laws' house.) They giggled upstairs over the midnight ramblers. Bick was Beth's favorite brother, just a year younger than she. Paul, five years older, who lived in Seattle now, seemed to have always lived in a grown-up world. Beth had even named her second child after her younger brother. Ben's real name was Victor Benjamin, as was Bick's. (The nickname came from two-year-old Beth's rendering of her brother's first name: "Bicker.")

Beth sat down on the lower landing, her favorite place to tuck herself into a corner and think. When she perched on the oversized furniture picked out by the decorator—who looked about twelve years old—Pat brought home to "do" their new house after she "did" the new restaurant, on one of her vast prairie-colored sofas, for example, Beth still felt like the kind of doll grandmothers sat on a bed.

What would Vincent tell her? Beth wondered. The ordinary mom-type inter-rogatory easily with Kerry was almost unheard-of with her sons. Kerry had so little memory of her babyhood, or of the lost years after Ben's disappearance, wrapped in the gray bunting of Beth's self-imposed exile from life. Vincent, only nine or ten, would arrive home to find Kerry happily sit-ting in her own crap, in the diaper he'd put on her that morning, or lying in her play yard with a juice bottle. Beth would be asleep on the sofa. Beth slept like a dog then—sixteen, twenty hours a day.

After Ben was found, and then Ben left them on his own, to go back to George Karras, Cecilia's husband, whom he still considered his real father, the already torn fabric of their lives ignited. She and Pat du-eled, considered divorce; Beth packed to move back to Madison. And then Ben came home again. Finally, he divided his life between his biological family and George, whom he still called his "real" dad.

Everyone was nice to each other, once the decision was made. George and the Cappadoras were like an amicably divorced couple. No one yelled, the way they had before when Pat vocally and fiercely refused to share his boy.

So what did Kerry know of normal?

In Kerry's life, why wouldn't the kindly husband of the crazy woman who had kidnapped your brother give you a cameo for graduation? Why wouldn't George come for Thanksgiving? He was like some crazy kind of uncle to her. Beth supposed their lives' personal prism was no more peculiar to Kerry than her own youth had been: It was normal for Beth's father, Bill, the village fire chief, to come home late at night singing "Red Is the Rose," his arms slung over the shoulders of two rookies. The rookies still worshipped their fire chief. No one looked funny at them at church the next morning.

Beth glanced up at the clock in the kitchen—the clock as big as a wagon wheel. The decorator had found it in a hotel under demolition. Trash that had cost Pat five hundred bucks. Vincent must have waited for the morning traffic to thin out before driving back from Rosie and Angelo's. Beth heard the upstairs shower flip on. Pat would be at the restaurant to unlock the door—before anyone else, as usual.

But where was Vincent? It was late now, the rush hour well under way.

Beth sat back down and reviewed the previous evening. Despite the coffee, she could easily have gone back to sleep. The party had gone well. Pat's nice sister, Teresa (Monica was another story), and her sweet husband, Joey, had never met a stranger. Their quiet, infectious geniality put everyone at ease. Soon most of the people who were in the film were chatting and had dived gratefully into the crab puffs and focaccia. Food was always a great bridge and these people were strangers who had virtually watched each other in the shower. Awkwardly and then with greater ease, the people who'd been interviewed approached Beth and Pat and complimented them on raising such decent young people. Janice Dicksen asked Beth where she'd gotten her wide-legged silk pants and actually laughed when Beth confided that they were from JCPenney. After that, except for Janice Dicksen, whose job started at seven on Saturdays, everyone stayed late. Before they left, Blaine Whittier came back and hugged Beth, her sons, and Kerry, hard.

"You could wait forever for my dad to tell you this. But Jackie would have been proud of the movie," she said.

All the people in the film from out of town stayed in rooms at the Harrington Suites, just a block away. As Ben liked to say when anyone needed anything from a TV to a quick plane flight, Pat always "knew a guy" who had arranged a rate Vincent could, just barely, afford.

The shower stopped. Beth imagined Pat dressing quickly, his shirt crisply tucked over the tiny potbelly he disguised with perfect posture. Hearing him cross their room to the hall, she moved her coffee mug and reached up to touch Pat's trousered calf as he passed her. To her shock, Pat jumped. Beth jumped, too, and screamed, springing to her feet and spinning around. It wasn't Pat at all.

"Vincent!" Beth cried. He nearly turned and ran back up the staircase. "What are you doing?"

"I was, ah, sleeping, Ma," he said. "Now I am walking downstairs. You almost gave me a stroke."

"I thought you slept at Grandpa's."

"No, I just hid out there for a while. My father seemed unpleased."

"Do you blame him? That loan from Charley Seven, Vincent, you knew he'd be furious."

Vincent dodged the comment and said instead, "Can I have coffee? Is Pop still here?"

"I guess he's already gone," Beth said. "He usually wakes up before me and goes outside to check the pool and stuff. I thought it was him in the shower. There's a whole fresh pot. I've been sitting here drinking coffee and waiting for you since the sun came up!" Beth followed him into the kitchen. "Pop must have left early because he missed work last night."

"Jesus, him, Ben, and Grandpa. The way they act. Like, the restaurants probably blew up and Kenny stole everything out of all the registers."

Beth asked, "Do you want eggs or something?" She already knew the answer. Vincent barely ate at all.

"I want cornetti with cream. I didn't get any. Are there some left?"

"Vincent, people ate like locusts."

"And Auntie Monica cut it too close, too. She brought thirty for fifty."

"Hmmmm," said Beth, not wanting to wade into that pit: Monica ran Gold Hat, the catering arm of the family business, and bitched if she had to provide pastry-wrapped asparagus and Asti for family gatherings if there were "real customers" out there. Monica also had no use for Beth and never had. So instead, Vincent thawed a bagel and put it into the toaster, where Beth knew she would later find it, stiffened.

"Where's the bear?" Vincent asked. Both he and Ben had called Kerry Ker Bear since she was born.

"She has a speech coach on Saturdays," Beth said. Kerry was a voice-performance major at Northwestern, whose major professor scolded her for her flat vowels. She spent two hours every Saturday morning literally with marbles in her mouth.

"School on Saturday," Vincent said. "What's this generation coming to?"

"It's her love," Beth told him. "She's auditioning for Suzuki in *Madama Butterfly* next summer with the Atlanta Opera. Can you believe that? At twenty-one years old. Twenty-two by then," Beth said.

"She's pretty amazing. I don't think I'd ever really listened to her sing—I mean, with her voice the way it is now—until the movie."

"Do you want to sit outside?" asked Beth. The morning was exquisite, a bowl of honeyed weather that, in Chicago in the autumn, could collapse into a chill as dull as lead in an instant. They settled on a pillowed iron bench that would soon be put away for the winter.

"I have to ask," Beth began.

"Do I have to answer?" her son replied.

"Yeah," Beth told him, gently giving Vincent an elbow. "What *did* Dad say about Charley Seven loaning you the money for this project?" Beth had learned about the loan only last night, after everyone left. Pat told her in tones so soft even Beth was scared. It was rare for Pat to become outraged, but the quieter he got, the more danger there was of an explosion.

"Mom, I gotta tell you. I don't know what Pop thinks. Hence my staying at Grandpa's until two a.m. I know I'm going to have to find out eventually, but eventually could be a long time, right?"

"He really was, ah, unpleased," Beth said and Vincent smiled at her use of his pet phrase.

Charley Seven (whose name was actually Charley Ruffalo) was the youngest of the seven children of Grandpa Angelo's oldest friend.

In exchange for Vincent's giving Charley's worthless nephew Marco a job on the shoot, Charley Seven had fronted Vincent the money.

Although the real mob era in Chicago had truly ended when Beth and Pat were little more than teenagers, no one had yet told Charley Seven, who didn't really import olives . . . despite what his business card said. He made loans. He also owned a certain interest in a huge, lurid casino. What else he did, no one asked. And though Charley Seven loved Vincent and would never have charged him cruel interest, any loan he made at all to Pat's son would give Pat hives until it was paid off. Pat's fatherly pride over the movie was affronted by Vincent's disregard for him. Vincent had borrowed real money this time, tens of thousands of dollars.

A few years ago, when Charley Seven fronted Vincent three grand for *Alpha Female,* Pat had laid down the law—not that laying down any law ever discouraged Vincent from anything. Just the credit sequence for *No Time to Wave Goodbye* had cost more than all of his first film. And post-production work, before the formal release date in December, was yet to come. Kerry said they'd hired an L.A. editor. Ka-ching!

At the reception, of course, you wouldn't have known that Charley Seven and Pat weren't the best of friends. Despite being a wiseguy, Charley Seven was, after all, a good guy, with a face that looked carved by erosion rather than by the usual passage of a human lifetime. Despite his craggy nose and his bulk, Charley Seven was handsome, commanding, the real heir to Charley Two, the closest friend among Angelo's crew, friends from forever, friends from off the boat—sharp old men who wore black cashmere suits with tiny rose boutonnieres and played seven-card draw in Angelo's backyard. Under their cotton

T-strap undershirts, their shoulders were tufted with soft white hair but still strapped with real muscle.

In fact, Charley Seven's father, who was so close to Beth and Pat that the Cappadoras and the Ruffalos had raised their children nearly as cousins, could walk on his hands, and, after a certain amount of homemade wine, often did. The old man was called Charley Two—although never to his face—because of his habit of saying everything twice (*Pat, Bethie is pretty enough to be your second wife, your second wife*). Between the older Charley's eldest son and Pat, the absolutes of family history made the ice strong but slippery: They were the front and back of a single coin. Charley Two was Pat's godfather; he would have cut off the tip of his thumb before disrespecting the old man. Pat was actually closer to Petey, a year older than Charley Seven. Pat and Beth were, in fact, godparents to Petey's pretty daughter, Adriana, a little doll who had worked summers at the older restaurant until Petey moved the whole brood to California where he was an entertainment lawyer.

"You know, I hate to bring this up, but I

was . . . ah, unpleased also," Beth said. "I didn't like it that a certain police chief of your acquaintance, and mine, knew about this movie and I didn't. Especially since you told me once that Candy was the mother you never had." Vincent examined his hands.

"Ma, when I said that, I was eighteen. And you know why I told her?"

"You needed the interview."

"No," Vincent said, and related how, just after Candy had oiled Vincent's first and last DUI (compounded by a joint in the glove box) down to a simple ticket for doing fifty in a thirty, she poked him in the chest with one perfectly manicured nail and said, "Listen, Spanky. This is the last time. If you spent as much time doing something other than trying to show Mommy what a bad boy you are, you could do something amazing." Six months after that lecture, Vincent, the talent guy, and Rob, the money and advertising half of Pieces by Reese, made their first national commercial. It was for the chocolatier Tutu Amore, and it was still their cash cow. But even chocolate-commercial residuals wouldn't have paid for *No Time to Wave Goodbye.*

"Let's change the subject. Subjects. From Mafia money and mad mothers."

"That could be an acronym," Beth said. "Mad Mothers Against Mafia Money. Okay. How did you get Ben to do it?"

She expected the usual: *Piece of cake,* or *Call me irresistible.*

Instead, Vincent was strangely forthcoming. He said, "Ma, I had to literally get down on my knees. Ask Kenny at the restaurant. It was last winter. I had all the B-roll done and Rob and I did all the pre-interviews with the families. But it still . . . didn't fit. They knew about us. They weren't going to open up to me the way they would to Ben."

"They knew about us?"

Vincent stared at her. Was she kidding?

"Yeah, Ma. Ben is like, one of the great legends of kidnapping, no offense." Either these people knew because they had joined that family of the probably damned no one wanted to join or because the story of "little Ben Cappadora" had captured the affection of glossy magazines for years, with a huge new transfusion of press after Ben was found. That alone opened the door, as Vincent had always known it would, for all the years—and it seemed like a hundred years—he had thought about making the picture. If Ben had never been taken, Vincent would never have conceived of it. Hell, he would never have been a filmmaker. Vincent would have been doing exactly what his brother was doing—unless he was doing time.

"Cappadora," people would say, rolling his last name around in their mouths like a taste. Even girls at college, once they mentioned him to their parents or someone older, would ask, "Are you . . . *that* Cappadora?"

"Actually, I'm the other Cappadora," he would tell them. It was his shtick. "My brother is the miracle boy."

His family minded that people couldn't forget their past—the thing that made them who they were. But more than anything, they minded how Ben treated them, which was totally nice . . . like a good friend of the family or something. He was different with Vincent and Ker, but except for Grandpa Angelo, he sometimes barely gave the rest of them the time of day. Basically, it killed the parents and the grandparents that Ben never gave an inch when it came to his insistence that he was not the same kind of Cappadora the rest of them were. Ben didn't remember. And he wouldn't pretend to.

Vincent remembered . . . probably more than he would admit.

It wasn't the stuff people expected him to remember: All the magazine covers, Kerry cutting off all her hair, his father sitting him on the bar at his uncle Augie's restaurant. He knew all these things only from his ma's forty-two thousand albums of black-and-white pictures with their little black paper corners. A whole wall of identical albums with little labels on the back to show the year, except some years were missing entirely and some didn't match and had hardly any pictures in them and what there were had the oversaturated, loopy carnival quality that proved they'd been reprints given to them by relatives.

His mother's pictures were severe, classical compositions, in which even the shadows were characters: Stairways looked like the inside of shells and a car lot like a mess of gumballs. Beth's were gallery-worthy photography, at least to Vincent's eyes. Ma's head was a lens. One of the pictures of the three of them walking away from her was in the Art Institute, another in the Simi-let Museum of Photography in Boston. He had a print of that one. It was taken on a street back up where they used to live in Wisconsin, on the Fourth of July. He and Ben were holding Kerry's hands and virtu-ally dragging her behind them. Ma caught them just as Kerry went airborne, one of her rubber sandals dangling from a toe. He remembered that day for the fight that Ben had had with their parents because he didn't want to go.

He wanted to stay with George, with "Dad."

Vincent remembered that day entirely. Of the rest, it was just small images. He seemed to have no memory before Pierce Street in Parkside, where they moved when he was about eleven so Dad could start the restaurant with Grandpa.

That was where he'd first spotted Ben, playing street hockey, at the red house two blocks from the house to which Beth and

Pat had moved. And he'd known it was Ben, his brother. Vincent was still uneager to enlighten them on that point. But Ben was happy! Ben was freaking happy— more than Vincent was. You could tell. Why would he want to bring back the kid he'd already done so wrong, the kid that he, *Vincent,* lost when he let go of Ben's hand in the hotel lobby, although his mother carried the guilt for that forever? Why would he want to bring him back to the zombie village at the Cappadora house? Where Vincent, his betrayer, lived.

Maybe, he thought, this film was half Vincent's not knowing about his own stuff. Tom Kilgore, the therapist his parents had forced him to see when they found out he had started a pretty good bookie operation at the age of thirteen, would have told him how to figure it. But Tom had moved to freaking Michigan a couple of years ago. He had a card, somewhere, and a note Tom once sent to him. Where? Maybe he should even interview Tom and tack it on. The psychologist in the film was sort of lame. . . . Tom had been great. No bullshit.

The only real relic of that time was that

he still thought of Ben as Ben even while he called him Sam.

His grandmother called all of them *caro* (Italian for "sweetie"), and his grandfathers both called Ben Champ or Sport or some shit. But you could tell it still ripped his parents up. This one thing about Ben was . . . the worst. And Ben had to know it. Ben, who would no sooner hurt you than burn his own hand.

"Where were you just then?" Beth asked Vincent.

"When?"

"When you were a million miles from here. When you were telling me how you asked Ben to help out?"

"It was the Sunday after Christmas. The only people at the restaurant were the two old ladies."

"Brandy and Alexander."

"Right," Vincent said, of the two-hundred-year-old sisters who came every Sunday to The Old Neighborhood, ordered a Brandy Alexander each, and then giggled about how they were going to be picked up for drunk driving before they got back to La Grange. Kenny, the bartender, who'd worked with Angelo for thirty years, never even put any brandy in their drinks.

That day, Vincent remembered pleading, "Sam, what else have I asked you to do for me in my life? To be *my* best man? No. To teach *me* to play ball? No . . ."

"Uh, who taught who? I'm having trouble remembering."

"Ben, come on. Don't be an asshole," Vincent said. "I get down on my knees." And he did.

"Get up, fool. You're not going to guilt me into it."

"I'm not trying to guilt you. I'm trying to embarrass you," Vincent said. Kenny laughed.

But Vincent started to freak out a little. If the goddamn restaurant got in the way of this . . . The urgency began pounding at the base of Vincent's throat, like when he was a kid and had fucking panic attacks. It was like a thousand seagulls lifting their wings to take off, just like he'd told Tom Kilgore.

He gave Beth an expurgated version of what he said next, which was, "Are you going to let them run you like this all your life?

I mean, it's your fucking life. But did they let you go to the prom? Did they let you drive?"

The restaurant. The restaurant. Always the restaurant. Now, two restaurants for three generations to obsess over.

When Ben graduated from high school, Pat took the family to Rome—they would have taken Vincent to Rome when he graduated as well, except that he never did. It was there, at the original Cappadora's Ristorante, that Ben announced that he'd decided to major in culinary arts. Everyone was so drop-over thrilled they lit a candle at St. Peter's! An heir! Like white smoke from the chimney! Another Cappadora behind the steam tables, fighting with people over tomatoes on the dock downtown, driving a Caddie, wearing a nice dark Italian suit with a blue shirt and a red tie. And, just like the script, once Ben was back from the woodsy-artsy eastern college, Grandpa and Dad immediately demanded their pound of flesh—a hundred and seventy pounds, to be exact. And Ben-good-boy had to forsake his softball team and even his girl to twitch the corners of the tablecloths, take away the one knife that had a spot on it, to lay just one bay leaf on the gravy that didn't need even a single extra grain of salt to be perfect—gravy from Grandma Rosie's recipe made the way it was eighty years ago by her mother, a recipe guarded like the step-by-step plans for a nuclear weapon.

To Beth, Vincent said, "That's when Ben said, I have a surprise for you. You're going to be an uncle."

Kenny brought Vincent a Campari and soda, which Vincent stared at in contempt until Kenny, laughing again in the soundless way he did, replaced it with two flutes of champagne. Vincent felt a huge lump in his throat. He had to chug the bubbly and ask for the bottle to get over the urge to start bawling. Finally, he said, "How long have you been married, Sam? A week?"

"Long enough," Ben said.

"You're a kid."

"I'm a kid whose parents had a kid by the time they were my age. Although the jury's still out. That could have been a mistake."

"We know it was a mistake. Dad was in grad school."

"I mean a lifelong error, Vincent. Not a

failure of technology." They both laughed then.

"Well, fucking congratulations," Vincent said. "Fucking hallelujah. But how does this rule out my movie? And how does Eliza figure to be a mother when she's what? Twenty?"

"She's twenty-one. And Eliza knows how to wash her face and pick up her clothes, Vincent. She's been washing clothes since she was five."

"Right, sure. I know that," Vincent said, penitent. When Eliza's slang made her sound like a born West Sider, they forgot that she'd spent the first part of her life in one of the poorest places in the poorest country on earth. At Saint Francis Orphanage in Bolivia, eight-year-old Eliza had been considered one of the *older* children, expected to take care of the babies.

It wasn't until Vincent got into the car that he started to freaking cry like an asshole. Jesus. Ben was going to be a dad. Ben, married and a father. Ben was like Dad, the marrying kind. Vincent was like nobody. He didn't even resemble anyone in the family as far as he could tell. Kerry looked like their mother, Ben like

Dad. Maybe he was a throwback. Or the milkman's kid.

"Which ones were the hardest?" Beth asked now. "I've had shoots that took five hours before the person got halfway settled down . . ."

"The Whittiers were hard to convince, but they were easier to do. Once we got there. I don't think either of them was really sold on the idea. The guy was totally, totally against it. The girl, Blaine, the one who was so shy at the party? She was great. And the mom was just so sweet and soft. But Bryant Whittier is such a pompous guy. The first thing he asked was what we hoped to accomplish, and while we were talking he made some comment about the footage of earthquake victims. He said that people liked to feel good about themselves but compassion had its . . . I don't know . . . something . . . that those stories gave people who saw them a compassion high or something that they didn't deserve. The Caffertys were willing, but oh wow. . . . We left the Caffertys at six that night, Ma. We got there to set up at eight in the morning."

"Why?"

And so Vincent took a huge breath and told Beth about the Caffertys. From the corner of his eye, Vincent saw a gray limousine glide past and wondered if Charley Seven was making sure he'd drop off a payment before he went back to California.

CHAPTER FOUR

Beth asked him, "First of all, tell me about how you found them. The Caffertys. And all of the families."

"Penny found them. Penny? From Compassionate Circle?"

Beth said, "I remember Penny."

"I couldn't think how I could do it. I couldn't run an ad. I couldn't search police files. I wanted to find people who would want to do this or at least agree to it so I could try to interview them. Now, Ma, it was over ten years ago she last talked to me. And when she came to the phone, she knew right away who it was." She even

called him "Reese," the teenage nickname
Vincent had once adopted to keep older
guys from calling him "Vinny" when an elbow to the gut didn't suffice. He'd told her
he was regular old Vincent now and had
been for more than ten years.

"It's still great to hear from you," she
told him. "How old are you, Vincent?"

"Every year I'm pushing thirty with a
shorter stick," he said. She laughed.

"Wow, that's *old*!" she said. "How can I
help you?"

Penny Odint was Penny Amos now,
mother of two daughters born after the
child who had been murdered by her ex-
husband while Penny was speaking to him
on the telephone. All Penny heard was
"Bye-bye, Mommy," and the handgun
blast. Compassionate Circle now had
sixty-eight chapters with Penny as the
national director. Sixty-eight chapters . . .
that many children, Vincent marveled,
that much grief. And yet, most of them
were presumably safe, or at least whole,
snatched by their noncustodial parent in
the parting salvo of a divorce. But even
with Penny's ex-husband, her child hadn't
been safe.

Her child was a child who fell between the statistics—like Ben—except that Penny's little boy fell on the wrong side of the percentages.

The first thing that Penny asked him was, "Why? Why are you making a movie about families who never found out what happened? Why can't you do a movie about the happy endings? Your family was one of the lucky ones."

Vincent answered as honestly as he could. "Penny, to tell you the truth, I guess it's because we were lucky. It makes you wonder about the others. How their lives go on and what helps them be strong."

"They're not all strong," Penny said.

"I know," said Vincent. "But look. Your story didn't have a happy ending. But your work helps other people." And she had to agree with that.

Vincent told Beth that Grandpa Angelo had asked him the same question. Turning up the collar of his wool cardigan, Grandpa gripped his espresso cup and pushed the glider back as far as it would go. "So much grief, 'Cenzo. Your mama and papa and Nana and I waited so long. Now you would bring the grief back to us? To build a new house of grief? Pain already lives next door. Even now, I see your father's face sometimes and it's all there."

Vincent said, "The best answer is, I won't really know why I need to do this until I do it, Grandpa. I don't think it's going to be fun."

Over a period of months, long before he told even Grandpa Angelo and Candy what he was doing, Vincent and his business partner Rob winnowed down the possibilities. The choices were finally easy: It came down to a combination of the target families' poignant willingness and the chemistry between them and Vincent. Vincent went to Washington State; then to Durand, California, outside San Francisco; to Texas; to Wisconsin's Lake Madrigal; and to Chicago, to make sure he *had* a film, even before he approached Charley Seven for the money. He shot hoops with the Dicksen boy. He ate the Hutchesons' ranch eggs and sourdough and drank the Caffertys' endless cups of coffee— because these families drank more coffee than anyone except people at an AA meeting. He watched their television programs with them, knowing that they forgot the thread of a TV mystery during a commercial for cream cheese. Swallowing hard, Vincent let them show him home videos and family picture albums. He admired first steps and class graduation and candles on a Sweet Sixteen cake. They began to think of him as someone who could walk back in after getting something out of his car without having to knock. Vincent didn't really have as much of a way with people as Rob did. But he had intensity and he had the history.

He and Rob scouted out the best deals on used lights and cameras and found a Canon XL high-def, the boom, and the other mikes, while Rob began setting up a schedule to make sure they had cheap hotel rooms and good pasta. The quality of a film—any film, even *The Godfather*—depended on the quality of the food.

And finally, the last piece fell into place.

To woo Ben, Vincent had to fight the pull of the restaurant, the restaurant, the restaurant—which was almost genetic. Back when his ma was basically living but brain dead, when she forgot what you said about ten seconds after you said it, Vincent's dad also was always gone—he had the restaurant to run to. For a while, an older girl cousin took care of them, and then Dad presumed Ma could, but he presumed wrong. Except for Ben, who was nurtured by George, the good-guy husband of his goddamned kidnapper, the Cappadora kids lived on leftover bracciole and all the creative child care that Vincent could provide—which was not much, given how busy he was building his bookmaking operation.

Still, Kerry turned out to be a good kid and a great woman.

"Did Ben ask why you wanted to do this too?" Beth asked.

"Only about a thousand fucking times," Vincent answered and winced. "I'm sorry, Ma. I apologize for swearing."

"Accepted. What did you tell him?"

Vincent shook his head. How much could he say? Try the truth, Tom used to say; it catches people off guard. "I told Ben, 'What, do you think there's an excess of awareness about missing kids?' I reminded him that Candy looked right at him sleeping in Cecilia's mother's house and that if people thought more, if they knew how nuts Cecilia was, they could have brought him home after a week. A lot of shit would have remained out of the fan."

Beth winced. She looked out over the pristine and absolutely unused pool. Vincent went on, "What I really told him that was most important was that I didn't think every documentary film has to be about politics. I said there was a strong emotional narrative in the reversed life these people have had to live. . . ."

"You were right."

Vincent said, "Thank you."

"Your father will get over the financing thing."

"I couldn't ask you two," Vincent said.

"You could have asked us."

"I'd have had to tell you what it was about."

"You don't get enough from Tutu Amore 'chocolatto for lovers'? I love how they're swimming in chocolate in the commercial."

"That was risqué when we made it," Vincent said. "And no. We don't get enough. Not even close."

Tutu Amore paid for how Vincent and Rob lived, which was decently, "drinking champagne on a beer gut," as Grandpa Angelo said, in a typical expression. When he said something vaguely insulting, he would tell you he didn't mean to "cast assertions." Vincent's house in Venice Beach had once been a garage, but all two rooms were his own. He had a mortgage. So what, he lived in a dump and dressed like a prince? Didn't all Italians do that? Italians in Italy? Didn't they put everything they had on their backs or on their tables?

"Tell me more about the Caffertys," Beth urged him. The past half hour comprised the largest sum total of sentences in sequence Vincent had spoken to her since he was sixteen.

"Ben got weird. He was fine until we got to the Caffertys' house. Then he stayed outside."

He didn't tell her that, half the time, Vincent wished he had stayed outside too. The night before he shot the Caffertys, two Benadryl and an Ambien hadn't made a dent in Vincent's chronic insomnia, which abated only when he slept at his parents' house. It was while he was with the Caffertys that the gut pain that bothered him for the rest of the shoot first began. It was just him and Rob and Ben with Charley Seven's bizarre nephew Marco, called Markey—the precondition for the loan. It wasn't until after they'd finished the interview that Vincent realized he had felt, the whole time, as though he was walking around the house of his early childhood, with the lumpy green sofa and the Wisconsiny checkered curtains, the things Pat and Beth had had before the restaurants got famous and they got what Ben called the Villa Cappadora in WASPville and did everything over in a variation of beige.

"Do you know Markey Ruffalo?" Vincent asked.

"Not really. Just to see. We know his sister, Adriana."

"The pretty girl. With the hair."

"Yes," Beth said. "That one. Who worked at the restaurant."

Beth got up from the bench and snapped a few more blown heads off the roses that circled the pool. She liked her roses, the only flowers she bothered taking care of herself. They'd gone on blooming through the long, warm fall. Then she sat back down.

"So . . . about Markey. . . . What does this have to do with Ben acting weird?"

"He's nineteen. He wouldn't go to school. He wouldn't hold any job. So finally Petey sent him to work for Charley, who sent him to me because, I'm quoting here, Ma, not swearing, the kid's ass was merging into the sofa in the office."

"I've been in that office," Beth said. "The one with nothing in it but a desk, not even any file cabinets . . ."

"Yeah, and a Coke machine with only one kind of Coke?"

"Was Markey awful?"

"No!" Vincent said. "He was great! That was the thing. He never touched a piece of equipment before, but the light and the sound stuff . . . he was like some kind of savant! He followed us into that dark little room with the camera on creepers and he somehow made it look like humans could live there."

Beth said, "Huh."

Vincent went on to describe Markey's bizarre combination of grace and cluelessness. The purpose statement specified a no-smoking-on-set shoot; and so there was Markey, smoking Marlboros one after the other, snapping the filters off and dropping them on the Caffertys' lawn as fast as Vincent could pick them up. He had to wipe the equipment with baby wipes every five seconds . . . but besides that, he was totally invisible. Vincent said, "He didn't talk. Didn't have any facial expressions."

Beth added, "And there's nothing worse when you're trying to get something done and it's sensitive and somebody's standing there like . . . talking on the phone and texting someone. . . ."

"Yeah! Exactly! Do you even know how to text, Ma?"

"Actually, I do," Beth said. "Where was Ben all this time?"

"That was it. He just sat on the porch. And if Rob and I were the hors d'oeuvres, then Ben's the dessert, okay? And so finally I go out there and he gives me the finger. I'm like, 'What the hell is that?'" The telephone rang, repeatedly and insistently, inside the house, but Beth waved away the glance Vincent shot at it.

"What was it?" she asked.

"He said it was the trampoline. He saw

the trampoline and junk. He said it was then that he realized it was real. Like a real little kid. He said, 'It's like me, asshole. Like a copy of our house. As if you didn't know that when you brought me here.'

"And I told him, Sam, you weren't even there. You don't remember the things you had when you were little. And he's like, . . . first of all, you don't have a family, you are not expecting a baby. And second, you don't know what I remember." Vincent paused. He was sweating in the soft air. "So we did atmospheric shots for a while," he said. With the camera on creepers, they followed Eileen Cafferty into Alana's room. "Ma, the clothes in her closet were so little that they barely took up any vertical space."

Beth found herself breathing harder. She remembered savagely tearing down folded little corduroys with Sesame Street characters on them, little dinosaur T-shirts—putting away the few things her friend Laurie had left behind when she came in and boxed up most of Ben's scattered belongings. While Pat and his family watched her in horror, Beth seemed determined to erase Ben after he was abducted.

Vincent told his mother about postcards from Alana's grandma that were stuck around the mirror. Her doll was missing one shoe. She had written down the words to an old Disney song, but written them down wrong: I know you. You walked with me once upon a bridge . . .

"Do you remember how Ben used to sing some old song the wrong way?" Vincent asked.

Beth said, "If a bunny catch a bunny . . ."

"What is it really?" Vincent asked.

"I can't sing but it's really . . . um, if a body catch a body, coming through the rye. Everybody has somebody, nay they say, have I. But all the girls they smile at me when coming through the rye," Beth sang softly. "Why?"

"They said their little girl used to sing some Disney song. Over and over. Like Ben did. That's all. Anyhow, they took us out to the yard with the huge trampoline and told us Alana got it for her sixth birthday, the last birthday before they lost her." Beth was quiet. "They said she always made Adam, that's the little brother, jump too high . . . he was four then."

"I yelled at you for doing that," Beth said.

Vincent played the track in his head, *Ben, don't be a baby! You big baby! I won't let you fall if you jump . . .* and Ma saying, *Vincent! He's too little for that slide! Stop it! You were scared to death of that slide when you were three. . . .*

"Then, we went back to the living room. . . ." The Caffertys had held a picture of the little girl, grinning with big, white teeth that looked oversized in her face. Eileen must once have looked this way. In the photos, Alana's big eyes were touched with eye shadow, her outfits carefully put together. Eileen had herself been a gymnast—first an Olympic hopeful, then a few seasons high on the ropes with Cirque du Soleil, then a coach at her own gym. She didn't coach anymore.

Now, Eileen Cafferty stayed home, writing endless letters in support of early-alert technology for missing-child cases.

Her husband, Al, was as big as she was tiny, a thickly muscled, blond man whose face didn't seem to match his Irish last name. Al's guys did most of the work now at his construction firm. He went to the office twice a week. He worked out at the gym. He slept. Among the decks of photos picturing Eileen with Alana were a few of her brother, Adam. He wore hockey gear, or held a baseball or a big brown trout. But there were no more family Christmas pictures, fireplace or tree-farm snaps of two kids in matching sweaters they must have hated. Something had seeped out of the Caffertys, the Hutchesons, all of the families: It was as though they'd lost some kind of affective pigment. Their lives ground forward only because people had to breathe and eat so that their missing child wouldn't come back to find them dead.

"They didn't come to the screening," Beth said. "Well, she didn't."

"She just had a baby," Vincent said. "Al didn't think she could. Sari Hutcheson just plain didn't come. I was surprised that the Whittiers' girl, Blaine, did. She was . . . it was funny . . . it was like she was worse off than the father when we were there."

Even the Whittiers, though, as self-possessed as they were, still searched Vincent's eyes for hope. At least the mother and sister did. So did Rosa and Ernest Rogelio, Luis's parents. Vincent was once removed from Ben, the full-solar-eclipse being. They didn't know the fine print and didn't care. There was Ben, who came back. That was all they needed to know, forever and ever, amen.

Should he tell his mother more? About his own nightmares, which had come back full-strength—nightmares he hadn't had since he was a teenager? Vincent decided to stick to the facts. His mother was still so fragile, bright and busy but so thin and all on-purpose. He had no idea what Beth really thought. Like, should he tell her about what Al Cafferty said about the phone number, about how people used to call them all the time? He knew she would want to know. But would it turn the knife?

Al told them, "We got sick of the crazies that come out at the full moon. We got ourselves unlisted now. But we still advertise. We still offer a reward for information."

Vincent had remembered his mother slamming down the phone, uttering words that, at age eight, he understood as "You funning buster!" Wearing pajama pants and his father's old shirts, with unwashed hair and greasy skin, she'd occasionally had the *fegato* to tell the cranks off. Other times, she didn't pick up. She sat on the sofa, her green eyes wide, her hands limp around Kerry's little tummy, where Vincent had ritually placed them. He heard one time what they said: *I saw your little boy with a good family. Not like your godless family. He's better off because you left the church, Elizabeth. You're on God's shit list, Beth. You and your Dago husband. You deserve this.*

Who was it who talked about crank callers in the film? Penny? He wasn't about to mention it now. He'd already given his mother worry for ten lifetimes with all he'd done—not just the Ben thing but after Ben came home, for years, up until . . . now. But he longed to ask, how had she hung on to even strings of her mind? How had she forgiven Vincent for being such a prick, for hating her? Vincent had hated her. Dad took a powder for the restaurant—first Uncle Augie's in Madison, then their own. Mom had the phone calls, the psychics, the endless letters, cards decorated with the Holy Cross or puppies or rainbows, the Protestant zealots, and the tipsters. She had Vincent, terrified, jumping up and down like a Jack Russell terrier trying to get her to see him, then stealing lunch cards and pencils, then cash and candy, then booze and cars. And Kerry, a confused and messy little ragamuffin . . . and Candy.

Maybe Candy's friendship, like a lighthouse, was how Vincent's mother had managed not to lose her mind altogether.

"How did you finally get Ben to come in?" Beth asked, interrupting Vincent's thoughts.

"He just did finally. I was about to give up. And I said, Al and Eileen, this is my brother, Sam Cappadora," Vincent said. "And you can imagine how they took that. The name-switch thing."

"Yes," Beth said. Her skin seemed to grow taut. A pause lengthened like a penny dropped into a deep well. "What did they say?"

Vincent answered slowly. "Eileen asked, wasn't your brother Benjamin? And Ben told them he . . . he didn't remember the time he had that name. He was more comfortable with Sam." Vincent watched his mother. "He said . . ."

"Yes," she said. "I know what he said. Ben said his dad called him that."

"And . . . well, you can imagine."

"I bet Mrs. Cafferty said something like, that must break your mother's heart," Beth said evenly. Vincent bit his lip. Eileen had said that, word for word.

"So then we moved on. . . ."

"You don't have to protect me, Vincent," Beth said. "If you wanted to protect me, you shouldn't have made the film at all. I don't mean that as a put-down. I know he told them about George. He must have. And that he calls us Pat and . . ."

"Well, right. Anyhow, Ben ignored the list of questions. Ben asked, was Alana a gymnast? And, wouldn't she be at the perfect age to compete nationally now? And I thought, great! When we leave, these people are going to get out some clothesline and hang themselves in the garage! But Al said that was just what he thought . . ."

"I remember," Beth said, snapping her fingers. "Someone wanted their own little champion. Or maybe they had a child who died . . . like Cecil."

"Ah, yeah," Vincent said, who now

wanted not just to leave, but to sprint across the yard like Carl Lewis. He got up and brushed off his pants. "I'm cold. Are you cold?"

"I'm fine," Beth said. "The pictures of that little girl. You nailed that, Vincent. His face and then that great bit of the little girl performing." She meant the footage of Alana's floor exercise to the old song "Happy Talk," from *South Pacific*.

"Ma, these gymnastics meets and beauty pageants and stuff for kids, they're like a farmer's market for pedophiles. You know? Buy a wristband and pretend you're somebody's uncle, and take your pick. That's what I think happened to Alana. Somebody remembered seeing a white van with some kind of painting on the side." Vincent paused. "White vans. The vehicle of choice for serial killers. And they told us about one time they might have gotten an authentic call. Someone called and they heard the background noise, like a meet, an announcer and all that, and someone said something that sounded like 'Mama,' and they thought it was Alana."

"That must have been hellish. At least that never happened to us."

That you know of, Vincent thought, thinking of the years he'd sat astride his bike, watching Ben whack the puck in his driveway. And he had left out the part about how he couldn't swallow when Eileen told them that Adam, the little brother, used to sneak in and sleep in Alana's bed. He'd left that part out of the film, too. When he heard the Caffertys say that, Vincent nearly lost it. He was eleven years old again, asleep in Ben's bed with Ben's misshapen toy rabbit, Igor, stuffed carefully under his stomach so that Dad wouldn't see it and think he was a sissy or something.

"She said she wouldn't want to be alive, except that they were having the baby, and Ben said, I told my mom once that there were things worse than dying."

"Ben did say that. And he's right. Dying is an answer. That was a question."

Vincent thought of the last moments, of all saying, *One minute we had all the time in the world. Next minute, no time to wave to her.*

That was when Vincent thought of the

title . . . no time to wave goodbye. Or had he always known it? He turned to his mother, but she had silently gotten up and motioned for him to follow her inside.

He wondered if he had gone too far.

He caught up with Beth halfway across the backyard. They began to laugh as they remembered his bagel, which Beth said must have the consistency now of a hockey puck. And casually, as though she did this all the time, Beth took Vincent's hand.

CHAPTER FIVE

"I've spent my life finding creative ways to get *out* of hosting parties," Beth said. "And this will make, what, five in a year? The wedding shower, the baby shower, the movie party. You do it."

"My house is too small," Candy said.

That much was true. Candy had added on to her little Baltis brownstone after she adopted Eliza, but the whole place was still the size of a very austere, timelessly fashionable camper. "I don't see why there has to *be* a reception for everything anyhow."

"Eliza would absolutely kill me if there

was no reception after Stella's christening. She's the queen of receptions."

They both stopped and Beth pictured Eliza at her wedding, in size zero Vera Wang, dancing in her bare feet with Ben to the tarantella, with the flower girls, Candy's twin grandnieces, in copies of the bride's gown, holding the twenty-foot train and spinning in and out like crazy little spools. On a dime, the couple suddenly stopped and the orchestra struck up "Bella Notte," from *Lady and the Tramp,* and Ben and Liza, who had secretly taken ballroom dancing lessons for the occasion, spun around the room like a prince and princess.

Candy recalled Eliza's face as Candy made her toast, about how her friend, Liza's godmother Beth, had given her the courage to dare the one thing she was always too frightened to try to be—a mother—and about how Eliza had been just the kid to prove Candy was right to take the dare.

She asked Beth now if she remembered the little speech.

"Sheesh," Beth finally said. "Guilt much? I want her to have a reception. I just hate it when I'm responsible for people being comfortable."

Candy said, "How nurturing." She paused. "Okay. I'll host it. Or maybe George Karras will have it at his house. He has a big house."

"Shut up! You're so bad! It's a burr under Pat's saddle that we even invite George to these things," Beth said. "I actually like having him. I'm used to him."

"Okay. I'll pay for everything. Even the cucumber sandwiches. On a civil servant's salary."

"You don't have cucumber sandwiches in January," Beth said. "You have meatballs and hot bread. Stuff people can spill on clothes they have to take to the dry cleaners." She got up to fetch Candy more of Rosie's almond cookies. Candy had probably already eaten a dozen, easy. Though she never gained a pound, to Beth's knowledge, Candy had never done a day's exercise in her life that didn't entail the fitness minimals of the job. Season to season, Beth never knew if she'd have to belt her jeans or use a pliers to zip them, and Candy remained as lean and absent of topography as the flawless skinny skirts and wide-legged slacks she wore, summer and winter. At a moment's challenge, she could drop and do thirty guy push-ups.

Katharine Hepburn genes, Beth thought. What a waste not to have passed them on—although if she had given birth to a child, there would have been no Eliza. What a waste for someone like this woman not to have someone she adored to warm up her bed each night. Candy's life had been an arrow pointed at sheltering children from the kind of people who would make beds cold and terrifying places, where no rest would come.

"Don't be a snot," Beth went on, handing Candy the cookie plate. "Gold Hat will do it. You don't have to pay full price. You're family. And fine! I give up! We'll have it here and we'll pay. Happy now?"

"Why, yes I am," said Candy in her best Southern belle voice. She had, after all, grown up in Atlanta. She placidly completed her tenth invitation and held it up to show Beth that she'd already written Beth and Pat's address as the party location. Beth rolled her eyes.

"You take me for granted."

"Ditto," Candy said. "You know what? I once thought . . . I would be writing *Vincent* and Eliza Cappadora."

Beth set her pen down hard. "Get out! Vincent? You thought Eliza would marry *Vincent*? How could you wish that on your child? He's not exactly husband material."

"Don't go telling me what husband material is, Beth. Vincent's . . . an amazing human being. He's entirely heart."

"Not to me. Well, a little better now. Maybe."

"We've talked about this for twenty years, Beth. Vincent worships you."

"Not enough to tell me what his movie was about."

"Exactly."

Beth said, "Why did you think she'd marry either of my sons?"

"She's too good for anyone else."

"I'll be damned," Beth said. "Do you really think this?"

"I don't say things I don't mean," Candy said pleasantly. "But back to the reception. What I'll do is have people to pass the trays around and put the gifts on a table."

"Off-duty cops you'll force to do it," Beth

went on. "Wait! You're changing the subject . . ."

"That's what off-duty cops are for," Candy answered. "That and house-painting. I pay them well."

They finally agreed that the priest from Beth's old parish, Father Cleary, would perform Stella's baptism, before Mass on the second Sunday in January, but he would come to the Catholic church in Harrington, which the Cappadoras sort of attended. It was called St. Lawrence the Grail, although Ben—who thought Harrington wasn't really a town but instead a pretentious cluster of one-acre houses on one-acre lots plopped on some of the best farmland on earth—had renamed the church St. Lucrative the Gas Grill. It was tiny compared to the Lutheran church, which was the size of a Sears store. Pat said the Lutheran church confirmed his belief that there was a WASP plot to take over the world.

Eliza and Ben were staying at Beth's house the night before the christening and the night after as well because Beth's children hadn't seen each other since the screening—Vincent had worked overnight

so many times before the film was finally
released, two weeks late, that he'd literally
slept through Christmas Day. As godfather, he was not only coming to Chicago,
but staying a few days afterward. Beth
couldn't wait for a chance to photograph
all three of them, as well as Eliza and
Stella.

"Who are all these people?" Candy was
asking, holding up the handwritten list
and shaking it.

Beth agreed but asked, "Who would
you leave out? The old people? The Mob
guys? Janice Dicksen from the movie?
She lives on the South Side, right here."

"You invited all of the people from the
movie?" Candy said. Beth shrugged.

"Ben wanted to," she said.

At that moment, Candy's pager went off
and she answered without preamble,
"Where? I am out almost to Rockford. Get
Jimmy to come in. NO. Not Emma
Witcherly or Ray. Jimmy. And I'll be there
by . . . later on. By tonight. If you like the
father anyhow. . . . He is, huh? Well, isn't
that fucking spectacular." Candy snapped
her phone closed. She wrote out two more
invitations in silence. Then she said to

Beth, "It's freezing in here. Do you have a sweater I can use?"

Beth trotted up the stairs and brought back a thick nubbly cardigan. "What's wrong?" she asked. "Do you want to tell me?"

"No," Candy said and went back to addressing the invitations.

"Okay," Beth agreed, as she always did when Candy threw up the shield of her professional life.

"It's a baby. Murdered and thrown in St. Michael Reservoir like a piece of garbage. Dad's an old friend of ours, nice druggie snitch. But he changed his ways recently. Discovering the glories of crystal meth."

"St. Michael Reservoir is the first place . . ."

"We looked for Ben. Uh-huh." Candy covered her face, then glanced up at Beth. "Can you finish these? I have to go. I have to." Beth stood up and tried to hug Candy, who shrugged her off with a repentant touch on Beth's wrist. "I can't bear it. These things drive me nuts. They did since Ben's case. And it was worse when I got Eliza. Now, with Stella . . ."

"Keep the sweater. It's cold today."

"That's how they found her. The creek froze."

Three weeks later, Beth's job was to pick up the Madonna and child (and Ben, too) the night before the ceremony. That meant also picking up about eighty bundles of silver-and-pink-wrapped packages—the trunk overflowed, and there was barely room for Stella in her car seat in the back of Beth's Range Rover. She was glad, for the first time, that she had the bigger car, although Pat had needed to pry the keys of her eight-year-old Toyota out of her hands and give them to Kerry.

"Presents just keep coming, Auntie!" Eliza said, with childish glee. "Some of them are from people who aren't even going to be there. They don't even get food!"

It was at times like these that Beth was reminded that once, Eliza used to line up with thirty other children, by order of height, to receive a single blue cotton shirt and pants, which, after she turned five, she was expected to wash weekly by hand. Candy used to find her daughter in the laundry room, patiently watching the clothes spin in the machine. She worried that Eliza was autistic until Eliza learned enough English to explain that she was trying to look behind the washer at "the lady making it go." In Bolivia, a baby at the orphanage was only another mouth to feed, not a cause for pretty presents.

Beth settled Eliza and the exquisitely chuckling four-month-old Stella. Buckling himself into the front seat, Ben promptly fell asleep. Stella had slept like an angel for six weeks then decided that the night-time world was beguiling. Because Eliza wanted to start taking a few classes beginning next week, they'd begun to supplement the breast with the bottle, so Ben could feed her, which he did—every hour. When he came home from work at one or two a.m., Stella was all smiles.

Tonight, Beth thought greedily, she would do that—the cuddling, the changing, the feeding, carrying Stella in to Eliza only once. Ostensibly, it was to let the young couple have a night to rest. But Beth had not wakened to a baby in so long. . . . Did mothers who'd had the full complement of years with their children yearn in this way? she wondered. Was it even more poignant? From nowhere, at the wedding, Candy had said that she felt like she had only just gotten Eliza and was already losing her. Beth said nothing then but felt this same thing exactly. The years of her motherhood had been cored by the loss of Ben.

"Sam can't wait to see Vincent," Eliza whispered as, next to her, Stella's lashes brushed her cheeks. "They've talked on the phone three times today already. Whenever Miss Eats Every Minute isn't awake, he keeps saying, 'Do you know how well the picture is doing? Do you know it won the star at the Toronto Film Festival?' Sam is so proud." Beth smiled, realizing how it still jarred her to realize that Liza had never known her husband by his given name. Eliza went on, "Auntie? Have you heard . . . any more about the movie? Like today?"

"Just that Vincent said last night they're getting booked into real theaters all over the place. And I'll have all three of my kids together tonight." She paused and grinned into the rearview mirror. "I mean all *four* of my kids . . . and my grandchild. Under the same roof for two whole nights."

"You're lucky my mom let me leave!

When I take Stella outside, Mom wants to wrap her up like we're going dog-sledding in Alaska. . . ."

"It's probably colder here than in Alaska right now," Beth said.

"But Auntie, she's so . . . overprotective. . . . She's always saying, 'Now, Eliza, I don't know. She's barely four months old. Taking her out of her environment . . .' Actually, what my mom would have said is, I think it's goddamn foolish taking a baby out in this goddamn . . ." Both women laughed, Beth feeling an interior crescent of gold unfurl as she always did when Eliza called her "auntie" in the Mediterranean way, the affectionate name for a godmother or any older woman relative.

"You don't get your mom, Liza," Beth said. "You were her . . . um . . . this isn't going to mean anything to you. But once there was a knight called Lancelot . . ."

"The Holy Grail," Eliza said. "*Duh.* I read the myths when I was little."

"Well, this is no myth. That was you for her."

Eliza shook her head. She pointed to Ben's face on Beth's keychain—Kerry's gift of a heart-shaped gold picture frame that enclosed a photo of all three of them when they were small—the one that jangled beside the one Eliza had given her and Candy, with Stella's photo. *"My husband* was that for her."

"Just because she didn't have you yet," Beth said.

Even before she could press the button on the automatic garage-door opener, Vincent threw open the door of the house. As if someone had hit him with an electrical prod, the sleeping Ben sat upright and was out of the car before Beth could put the vehicle into park. Her throat closed when Ben covered the lawn in two steps and practically picked Vincent up with a hug so eloquent she didn't need to hear the words they said, although they evidently had a bunch of words to say. Vincent shouted something to Ben, who nodded and pumped his fist in the air. . . . Beth began to struggle out of the car, carrying a stack of presents. By then, Ben had given Stella to Vincent, who was holding her in the goofy way single guys did and saying that it was a goddamn stroke of luck she looked like her mother. Ben was so lustrous with pride Beth thought he would glow in the dark.

Beth dumped her first load of gifts and went back for more.

Kerry came in from her lesson and started ragging on Vincent that Stella wasn't made of china. Then she added, "Sam. Vincent. Are you crippled? Can you see Ma carrying stuff in from the car? Alone?"

But Vincent ignored Kerry and said, "Ma, remember when I came out here after the movie was screened? And you said, Vincent, I have to ask you something?"

"Yes," Beth said cautiously.

"Well, Ma, I have to ask you. When was the last time you turned on the TV?" Vincent said.

"I don't remember," said Beth.

"Radio?"

"Umm, last Sunday?"

"Look at the answering machine, Ma," Vincent told her.

Beth gasped. There were thirty messages. She had left just a few hours before. "What's going on?" she asked. "What am I not in on?"

"Have you watched the news? Have you read a newspaper?"

"Come on!" Beth said. "No! I've been trying to plan a family event here . . ."

The door to the house slammed open. "Hey!" Pat called. "Where's Martin Scorsese?"

"Pop's worse than Mom! Kenny probably had to tell him," said Kerry, running to hug her father's neck.

"What?" Beth asked again.

Pat came into the room, his tie askew, his face shining with sweat and excitement.

"Ma," Vincent said. "*No Time to Wave Goodbye* was nominated this morning for an Academy Award."

"What do you mean?" Beth asked.

Ben said, "Beth! Did you hear what he said?"

"An Oscar, Ma! An Oscar for Best Documentary Film!" Vincent told her.

Beth sat down on the floor. "Is this a joke?"

Vincent sat down beside her. "I thought it was at first," he confessed. "I asked to call them back. They said I could never guess how many people did that."

"Honey, I don't know what to say. . . . Vincent! Congratulations! I'm . . . floored." Vincent patted the carpet beside the two of them and grinned.

Then Pat pulled Vincent up and swept him into a hug. "Does this mean you're officially reformed?"

"Oh, no way, Pop. It's worse when you succeed," Vincent teased. "Anyhow, it was only nominated. . . ."

The doorbell rang. Pat answered.

"We're looking for Vincent Cappadora?" a cheerful young woman said. A Channel 5 van sat at the curb. Vincent crossed to the door. "We had to track you down here. Your buddy Rob said you were at your parents' house."

Even as she motioned the cameraman forward and Vincent, blushing from the collar up, began, "Nobody was more shocked than we were . . ." a car arrived from Channel 9 and one from the *Herald-Times.* By the time he got back inside, the sun was setting and Vincent—as well as Ben and Kerry, who ran upstairs to change out of her thrashed blue jeans—had been photographed everywhere from the pool deck to the kitchen.

Even Kerry's girlfriends had been "in the neighborhood" and wanted to meet her suddenly cool brother.

About nine, yet another reporter showed up. She was older, but good-looking. Kerry answered the door. Vincent made a throat-cutting motion to his sister. He was exhausted; the baptism was at ten a.m. and the family had finally gathered around the table alone. For the first time in their married lives, the Cappadoras had ordered pizza from somewhere other than The Old Neighborhood.

"Vincent's . . . worn out," Kerry told the woman.

"Well, I'm not a TV reporter. I'm from a magazine."

"Oh! Which one?"

"Well, I work for a number of them," she said, with a huge smile. "Actually, I wanted to meet Ben and his wife and daughter. I would like to talk to them about how they feel about all this excitement. He wasn't at his house and so I figured . . ."

"We have a family event tomorrow," said Kerry. "That's the most important thing to us right now. I'm so sorry." She practically had to close the door on the woman's foot.

"Probably an autograph seeker," Pat teased her.

"But she went to Ben's house. Ben's number is unlisted. Candy makes them do that," Kerry said. "How did she know where Ben and Eliza live?"

"They have their ways," Beth said. "I found out a lot of things when I was a reporter."

There were calls from the Caffertys and the Whittiers and from Sari Weegander. Feeling guilty, Beth and Pat let the machine record them.

They were all so proud.

They all said proud things.

And there were things they didn't say as well. Nobody said a word about the pain that the rebirth of the film cost them, and would cost them in months to come.

The baptism went without a single hitch or glitch. Vincent didn't even trip on his walk up to the baptismal font, as he had been sure he would. Beth had to admit she kept looking around for the celebrity when they exited the church into the cold sunshine to TV cameras and reporters with notebooks. The whole idea of one of

her children being in the news for something wonderful, amazing, was still a
dream.

It was only after the reception at home—
after the guests, family, and reporters finally left—that Beth got her children alone.

In slouchy clothes, they congregated in
the guest bedroom where Vincent was
staying. Eliza laid the baby down. It was
then that Vincent finally brought out his
gift. It was a leather album for the baptism
thick with lined pages for names and memories and special soft sleeves for photos
and a sack with a zip for the little satin vest
that was placed on Stella's chest by the
priest. Tooled in gilt was *Premiere January
22: Stella for Starlight.*

Lithe as a gymnast, Eliza jumped up
and hugged Vincent. Ben simply tightened
his lips and looked away, out the window
above Vincent's head. Beth had to steal
from the room and grab her Nikon from the
table where she had left it. Kerry and Eliza
settled on either side of the baby, their long
lush hair like twin curtains. *Snap.*

Beth backed up to include all of them.

In the eggshell bedroom with its scatter-
ing of throws and pillows in white and pink

and palest beige—with Ben lounging in an Aran vest with his head pillowed on his hands, Kerry barefoot in gray jeans and a pink sweater crouched on her heels like a dancer, Vincent in khakis and a cashmere sweater on the floor with his back against the footboard—they looked like found objects, seashells on a beach. *Snap.*

Eliza transferred the baby to her breast, the corner of a cashmere blanket over her shoulder—the only visible part of her granddaughter a tiny pink fist, displayed on the lemon-colored wool like a jelly confection. *Snap.* Kerry slid down off the bed and nestled between her two brothers, poking both of them. *Snap.*

"Tell Ma what you told us," Kerry said.

"About the phone calls? I got this phone call and the name on it said Al Gore," Vincent said. "So I pick it up, thinking it's, you know, Rob goofing around, and I say, 'Hello, sir. How's the earth holding up?' But it's really *Al Gore.* He says he's proud of this kind of work! And I can't say anything. Then the call-waiting beeps in. He says, fine, just wanted to say hi. It says, Unknown. There's this younger voice but I know the voice. It's Michael Moore! He says, 'I . . . ah . . . just called because I like your movie. Made me glad I didn't make one this year.' I didn't say anything for a moment and finally I said, 'I'm in shock because Al Gore just called me.' And he sort of giggles and says, 'Well, you're not up against him, either.' And that was before ten. Can you believe this is . . . me?"

"Hey," Beth said, and for an instant, all three of them looked at her. *Snap.* They were all alight, jubilant, uplifted in their eagerness—and facing her way.

It would make a glorious portrait, she thought, a birthday gift for each one of them. And it would have, had Beth ever printed it as she planned to do.

When she finally did make a picture of that shot, all of them were years older. But even then, she would recall the light and feel of that moment, one of the only entirely happy moments of her life.

CHAPTER SIX

On the afternoon of Oscar night, before she left for the Independent Filmmakers Dinner, Beth treated herself to a last look in the mirror. She celebrated what the New-Age foundation garments had done to her waistline beneath the thank-God-it-hadn't-sold Carolina Herrera dress she'd found at the Lily Pad Designers Resale a few miles from her house. She marveled at her face, wishing she could somehow have it decoupaged onto herself forever. Her hair had been blown to appear as it looked in recurrent dreams she had of herself in the arms of her old boyfriends.

Ten years younger in two days, Beth decided. Easy.

She and Candy had had Botox. Botox! Just weeks ago, the idea would have knocked Beth off her perch.

But yesterday, all courtesy of Charley Seven—the reason they had tickets to the Oscars at all, and for fifteen people!—Beth and Candy and Eliza had been duck-footing around a suite at the Beverly Hills Hotel that had been made over into a boutique, salon, and impromptu bar and restaurant. They were stabbing lobster-stuffed ravioli and drinking champagne. They wore haute couture jumpsuits and rubber flip-flops encrusted with sassy double rims of Swarovski crystal, which grim and glam attendants pointed out would cost two hundred dollars at retail. Their toenails had been seashelled beige and gold and their faces smelled like sour cherry pies from their Sonya Donye facial masks, rinsed away as they sat at identical sage-green marble sinks that were wheeled up to the banquette.

A long-haired girl in a black tuxedo vest and skinny satin pants had strolled in from another wing of the hotel and approached

Eliza. She asked her if she was "some-body."

"Do you mean an actress?" Eliza said. "No. I'm just the sister-in-law of someone who got nominated for Best Documentary Film."

"But you're going to the ceremony."

"Yes!"

"Would you come with me anyway? Just for a minute? My boss saw you when she passed through and she has a dress she thinks no one else can wear," said the girl. Candy went immediately on guard, like a hunting dog—always alert to the possibility that someone would steal her little Bolivian peanut and sell her into sexual slavery. But Beth poked her in the ribs and whispered something to the effect of asking if Candy was acting crazy and overprotective even for her and that Eliza *was,* after all, a police chief's *grown* daughter.

As she left, Beth and Candy turned to each other again.

"Have we gone through the looking glass?" Candy asked.

Then the skin people took over.

The two women were spritzed with toner and slathered with a layer of grapefruit moisturizer ("Makes a man see you as ten years younger," the slatherer explained).

"I know that much," Beth said. "From photo shoots. The needle biz is uncharted territory."

"I thought it was supposed to hurt," Candy said to the physician's assistant who erased the lines next to her nose and plumped her lower lip.

"It has the numbing substance right in it," the physician's assistant explained, offering Candy more champagne.

As often as Beth proffered her credit card, it was refused with a coffin-maker's smile by one of the identical Nordic supermodel blondes who stood in ranks at dozens of makeshift display cases. In the cases were tiny palettes of eye shadow and pots of lipstick and iPhones encrusted with the names of studios and KeeBee crystal-sprinkled hair bands and Gilson negligees and Lacoste watches with diamonds at three and nine. Eliza shamelessly asked for one of everything as Beth and Candy drew back in what they imagined to be some semblance of taste. But when one of the pale girls asked Beth if she would like the same, or perhaps a

Vicky's bra sewn in real gold, she glanced at Candy, gulped, and said, "Yes. Yes, I do. Watches and . . . and iPhones and bras. Thirty-four B. And one for my friend too. Same size."

And these things were placed into their hands.

Later that day, they played with their treasure on the bed like toys, letting six-month-old Stella giggle at the watches they stacked on her chubby arms.

Adriana, Pat and Beth's godchild, Petey Ruffalo's eldest, had spent the day caring for Stella, making sure she knew the baby's every need. Adriana, Markey's sister, was no longer the too-buxom high-school girl with braces who'd bused tables at the Cappadoras' restaurant, The Old Neighborhood. The rest of her had caught up with her bosom, though she seemed to have no idea that she'd broken out of her chrysalis. A demure pre-law student in the most unlikely place on earth for subtlety, Adriana took immediately to Eliza; the two of them were immediately promising visits back and forth.

But Adriana protested the gifts. "You guys enjoy this. I go to plenty of premieres because of Dad's being the lawyer for so many producers and stuff. I'm just loving all this. And Markey! My brother is over the moon. We're over the moon for him!"

"You're my godchild, too, just like Eliza. You have to take one iPod at least!" Beth insisted. "Take the Lionsgate iPhone! I like the lion." Laughing, Adriana accepted. "So it's law for sure, honey?" Beth asked.

"I'm not like Liza the genius or Kerry the artist. I think I'll be a chip off the old block. Work with Daddy doing bloodless warfare for neurotics."

Beth looked down and watched all the bling turn into so much carnival plush. She thought of Jacqueline Whittier, who had wanted to be a lawyer like her father.

"We'd better pack this up," she told Candy.

"Did I say something wrong, Beth?" Adriana asked.

"No, honey. No. I just never had Botox before. The anesthetic's wearing off!" She felt Candy watching her. "I need some ice!"

Adriana kissed Beth and headed for Pasadena, promising to be back at two the next day. Her apartment wasn't far from her parents' home. Petey and Debbie

Ruffalo had asked the Cappadoras to come for dinner—and failing that, they had said they'd stop by the hotel before the Cappadoras went back to Chicago.

"She's a hero," said Eliza after Adriana left. "She gave her own ticket up to take care of Stella. I have to admit it's nice not to have to worry about the baby. I just wish we'd gotten here for the Vivienne Westwood Boutique. We could have had so much more stuff, Mom. I'm a very materialistic person, Auntie Beth. You know I intend to spend my life making up to God for it by being a doctor. But . . . not yet." She smoothed the jonquil dress with its slash of wine-colored sash, and repeated in awe, "I can't believe she let me keep it. I can't believe I'm wearing it right now! She let me keep this dress and her sewing people just made it to fit me perfectly. And you know who she is, Mom? Her father used to be this famous singer . . ."

"He's still a pretty famous singer," Beth said and laughed.

"It fit you perfectly because you're perfect," Candy said. "You have Vincent to thank."

"No, we all have Charley Seven to thank," Beth replied.

It was at Beth's house, at the party after Stella's baptism, that Charley, towering in green and gray like a cliff with moss on it, kissed Beth on both cheeks and said, *"Congratulazioni sul bambina! Complimenti per tutto! Tutti i vostri bambini!"* For Candy's sake, Beth explained what she understood—congratulations on the baby and all her children.

"Thank you, Charley," Beth said. "Eliza loves the cross you gave Baby Stella."

Charley said, "This little girl, I mean this little mama, Eliza, she was so sweet. She said, *Grazie con tutti i nostri cuori.* Said it perfectly! And I thought she was Jewish or perhaps Mexican."

Beth stared at him, as though Charley had asked her if she walked to school or took her lunch.

"She converted," Beth finally explained, trying to ignore Candy choking on her champagne.

Charley went on, "I'm an old guy, but I still got three at home. Six kids! I hope they turn out as beautiful as Petey's kids.

Adriana is a junior at UCLA, but you are aware of that. But it's my nephew Markey that brings me to you now, Bethie. I have to speak my heart. Frankly, I didn't even think my nephew Markey could get it up enough to pull off a heist of eggs from a chicken coop, you should pardon me. But this camera thing he did with Vincent. The kid was on fire! And now it is nominated for an Oscar!"

One of Candy's overtime rookies passed with a tray carrying flutes of champagne and tiny glasses with two fingers of Scotch in each. Charley picked up two of those. "Salut!" said Charley, draining a glass. By the time Beth and Candy returned Charley Seven's toast with sips of champagne, he had downed the second full shot, the tot of amber liquid disappearing as though it were spring water. "Now Markey has a future. My elderly father is overtaken with joy, Bethie. He has lived to see this boy we had some suspicion was frankly not quite right in the head do something perhaps better than any of the children. Now my father can die happy."

"Charley, Vincent says Markey really has eyes with the lights and the camera . . ."

"That's what I mean! Who could have known this?" Charley accepted and swallowed another two ounces of Scotch without moving from the spot on Beth's granite tile where he seemed to have taken root. With the same amount of liquor in her system, Beth would have been on her knees in the powder room. "In any case, I couldn't think of a way to thank you. I forgave Vincent some minor debt, although he refused this and I had to be in contact with his partner." Oh, Beth breathed, thank heaven. "But I happen to know that these tickets to the Oscar ceremony are extremely hard to come by, not to mention the invitations to the ritual things the ladies like to do, the facials and the hairstyling and such."

"I don't know what you mean, Charley," Beth said.

"He means Oscar week, Beth. Don't you read trashy magazines?" Candy hissed. "Like even daughters of directors have . . . face peels and get their hair

styled by Kevin Lee and Sally Hersh-
berger . . ."

"How would I know about that?" Beth
asked. Candy sighed.

"I hope I'm not being ignorant here or
presumptuous, but so that your honored
father-in-law and mother-in-law, as well
as my family, and of course Candy and
Eliza and Ben . . . I procured such tickets
and if you would accept them, I would be
so much in your debt."

At just that moment, George Karras
stood up and said, "I'd love to say something if I can. A really brief something, if
you'll let me. I just want to add my congratulations to Vincent and Kerry and to my
Spiro, my Sam, not only for giving us all a
beautiful granddaughter but for this amazing achievement. And I want to thank Beth
and Pat for your great hearts. For letting
me have a part in the life of your boy I so
love."

Beth glanced at Pat, ordinarily cool to
George If he spoke at all, who had often
said he would have been happy if Ben had
never spoken to George again. Pat was
dashing a tear from his eye. Would wonders never cease.

"So, Bethie," Charley Seven said again. "I wonder, will you accept this?"

In answer, Beth threw her arms around as much of Charley Seven as she could manage and squeezed. "This is like Christmas morning and . . . and Stella's day rolled into one! Charley, how can I ever thank you?"

"Please," Charley said, the only evidence of what now had to be nine ounces of straight whiskey a few beads of sweat on his forehead that Charley delicately patted away with a pocket square. "The honor is mine. Imagine my father's face seeing Marco Ruffalo's name up there as cinematographer . . . you can't imagine it."

Then Charley Seven said that he and Maria needed to get home now and that he would see himself out. Maria blew a kiss. Pat excused himself from George and watched as Charley walked, stolidly as a pyramid with feet, in a straight line to Beth's front door, which he opened and closed without a sound.

"What did he say?" Pat asked. "He crossed off the debt, right?" Beth nodded. Pat said, "Damn it. Well. We have to let him. God bless him."

"He'll die like a dog on the express-way," Candy said. "How much can a person drink standing up?"

"He doesn't drive his own car, Candy," Pat told her. "There's been a guy sitting out by the pool for an hour. He's wearing a coat but he won't come inside. And Charley's a very big person. In size, I mean. Not influence. Although, that too, apparently. Did he tell you about the tickets?"

"Yes," Beth said cautiously.

"I told him he had to ask you."

"Well, Pat, how do you feel about those tickets?" Candy asked.

Pat said, "Look, I have my problems with Charley Seven. But I'd have taken those tickets from the devil himself."

CHAPTER SEVEN

Beth tried ginger ale to settle the wobbles in her stomach. Waiting for Eliza to finish nursing Stella and put the last touches on her outfit, Beth felt as parched and nauseated as she had when she ran the Police Benevolent 5K with Candy.

Suddenly, the bedroom door banged open.

"Vincent!" Beth said.

"I'm sorry, Ma. Dad let me in. Is it okay?"

"Of course," Beth said. "I haven't seen you since you said you were having lunch with Barry Levinson and you were going to puke. Did you? Have lunch, I mean? Now I feel like I'm going to. I can't believe it's almost time!"

"I didn't puke. Rob and I went from lunch to some meetings."

As the rosy glare from the tall windows slipped away, Beth noticed that Vincent's face was so white she could see the blue vein in his forehead, his hair so wet he might have climbed out of a pool.

Beth jumped up. She asked, "What's wrong?"

"Nothing, Ma."

"What's wrong, Vincent?"

"We . . . sold it," said Vincent. "We decided to sell the movie to a studio we could maybe work with later. In case we don't win. Think of how many formerly Oscar-nominated documentaries you can think of. None, right? We really don't have much of a chance. But we still got . . . a lot of money."

Pat and Candy appeared in the doorway with Eliza and Adriana, holding Stella.

"How much is a lot?" Eliza asked bluntly.

Vincent said. "It's three million."

"Dollars," said Eliza and sat down.

"And a couple points of the future revenue. Less the money we're giving Kerry and Ben."

"Huh," Beth said. "I'm glad *I'm* sitting down." She breathed, "Oh, Vincent. Oh, honey. You're a millionaire. With your second film."

"And I'm a thousandaire," said Ben, coming into the room, adjusting his bow tie.

"You're a hundred-thousand-aire," Vincent said. Ben grinned. Vincent looked around. "Winning would sort of be over the top now. Like . . . too much to ask. Is this me or all the dope I smoked?"

"I'll ignore that," Pat said.

Vincent went on, "It's really not that much . . ."

"In what universe?" Pat asked. "Come here." He held Vincent close and kissed him. "*Buon lavoro,* Vincent. I love you."

"I love you, Pop. I'm shaking."

"Eliza, we're sort of rich," said Ben. "By the way, you look like a million bucks, Beth. You too, Liza."

"Three million bucks. I owe you, bro," Vincent said. "I, Ma . . . I just wanna go to sleep. Can I just camp out here and you tell me how it all comes out?"

Fifteen minutes later, Beth had to practically haul Vincent up to go put on his tux. He still looked as pale as though he'd spent the past five years farming mushrooms.

All of them assembled in the hotel lobby at four p.m.

The Cappadora clan and Beth's relatives, the Kerrys, spun like a human carousel to gape at the sight of Ben Affleck strolling with his two toddlers, nodding to Hugh Jackman who was sipping a tonic at the bar. Cameron Diaz swept past.

The elevator doors opened and Grandma Rosie appeared in a beige and gold Chanel suit with Grandpa Angelo in gray tails with a cravat and a pearl stickpin.

"Where did you find that?" Beth asked her mother-in-law. "It's . . . you look like a model, Rosie!"

"In the closet," her mother-in-law told her. "Grandpa and I wore these after the war. Now they're vintage. And we're vintage."

They were all clustered in the hall when Charley Seven strolled up, rolling side to side like a moving monument, a fat Cuban in his hand in defiance of signs that prohibited smoking on pain of death.

"I thought you didn't smoke," Beth said, without thinking.

"This isn't smoking," he said. "They took the same position at the front door. I don't understand people's thinking."

"Charley, it's been just amazing," Beth told him.

"A thousand thank-yous," said Eliza. "Charl—I mean, Mr. Ruffalo."

"You look like a bouquet of lilies," Charley Seven said. "I guess this worked." He checked his watch. "Eliza, do you want to go check on the baby before we leave?"

"I just came from feeding her and I don't want her to cry. Adriana is the sweetest girl. You won't let us pay her? Or you?"

"It's all taken care of," Charley Seven said. "But I thank you most kindly. The cars are outside." Charley Seven paused. "Oh, Paddy, you can't bring cell phones, even if they're turned off."

His eyes smoldering, Pat pursed his lips and slipped his slender phone from his interior pocket. Parting with his phone made him feel as though he'd been disconnected from life support.

"I have a silent beeper inside my belt buckle if anyone needs me," Charley

Seven said. "Let the world spin without us for a few hours."

Pat laughed. "A belt-buckle beeper. We'll have to call you Double-O Seven now," he said.

Vincent finally arrived, just in time to say goodbye. His parents would join him at the Independent Filmmakers Dinner, but everyone else, cameras in tow, was heading to the Kodak Theater. Vincent carried a telegram from George Karras, which he gave to Ben.

With the exception of the therapist Tom Kilgore and his mother's dad, everyone who had ever played a pivotal role in Vincent's life stood facing him in the lobby of the Paloma Hotel. Ten had come from Chicago. Mom's brother Paul Kerry had come from Seattle with his eldest daughter, Erin.

Some of them had slept on the plane. Some hadn't slept at all.

He looked at Grandma Rosie and Grandpa Angelo, Ben and Kerry, Dad and Mom and Candy and Eliza, as if they had materialized from the dreamless sleep he awoke from that morning. He thought of the others—Rob, the families.

Vincent wouldn't even be here except for St. Markey Ruffalo, the weird kid with the crazy ability for the camera. He remembered Markey waiting for four hours in the rain outside the Whittiers' mountain home until the drops were dappling the surface of the creek in the exact rhythm of Kerry's song, which he was listening to through headphones.

Just then, Beth dropped her fancy little red leather clutch. Lipsticks and brushes and business cards fell out along with an envelope that scattered invitations to the Academy of Motion Picture Arts and Sciences Awards.

Vincent's heart nearly stopped.

"Everybody give all the tickets to the ceremony to Candy, please," he said. "No offense, Ma."

"None taken," Beth said. "I don't know if I'm in town or not." They all gave their tickets to Candy.

"That's Kate Winslet," Kerry hissed, loud enough so that the desk clerk glanced up and smiled. "It looks like she has a sunburn. Who would get a sunburn before the Oscars?" The fine-boned, tawny-haired actor, severe in plain white satin, slipped past them into the dark recesses of the fabled bar. He ought to reprimand them, Vincent thought in some vaguely self-conscious way; but what the real hell, he was doing the same thing, ogling Kate Winslet's rear end. He was a nobody-somebody and to-morrow he would be a former nobody-somebody. But his brother and his sister and his mother and his eighty-year-old grandparents had flown through the dark-ness to rejoice, as it said in the Bible, for their sheep that had been lost and was now found. And damned if he was going to deny that he was a boy from the West Side of Chicago.

"*Buona fortuna,* 'Cenzo," said Angelo.

"I'll see you there, Grandpa," Vincent said, kissing Angelo's soft, ancient cheek.

Beth would never be able to remember later what they ate. Was it Asian or Italian? Chicken or beef? Somehow letting inane details gnaw her, even years later, was satisfying—like using a fingertip to smooth an old scar.

"Why do you care?" Pat asked her, once, as they lay in the dark, face-to-face, neither daring to breathe lest they wake the other, knowing the other was already awake.

"Just to remember something . . . else," she told him.

The award for Best Documentary Film would be the first of the least, following Best Actor in a Supporting Role.

When the Cappadoras arrived, the sun was still shining in California but people in Illinois gathered at the bar in The Old Neighborhood to see *past* Meryl Streep and Robin Williams, trying to catch a glimpse of a restaurant owner's kid from Chicago. Kenny the bartender did see Beth as she slipped her camera out of her red evening bag and shot Harrison Ford signing autographs and laughing out loud at something Julia Roberts whispered to him as she swept past in layers of crinoline.

He didn't see a guard examine Beth's camera and her credentialing letter from *Eye on Chicago* magazine. Her eyebrow arched in triumph, Beth put on a new lens and took a few more shots of the impossibly lovely, impossibly cachectic young women, with thighs like biceps and eyes like the dials of watches, who stopped to drop a shoulder and pose before gliding on. The men were thin, too; but something, perhaps in their clothing, concealed the extent of it. The women's dresses were sewn on, as Eliza's was. They were draped and ruched to hide torsos that were only rib cages and breasts that were only nipples.

Finally, they were led to their seats and sat and waited for Vincent and Rob to approach—freezing like kids playing Statue Tag as Annette Bening and Warren Beatty assured them there was no reason to stand up to make way for them down the aisles to their seats. Like collection dolls come to life, the faces more familiar to Americans than some of their own family members drifted past and kissed and touched each other softly—the exquisite, the legendary, the heartbreakingly gifted, the mad and the reckless, the meticulous and the obsessed.

And then there was Vincent, looking as resplendent as any actor in black on black with an open collar. He slipped into his seat. Like nits, they all applauded so that Vincent almost forgot that his hair was "done" and was about to start clawing it with his open hands when Kerry held them down.

"I feel guilty, Pop," Vincent told Pat. "I feel guilty we got this money because of what the movie is about. I should start a foundation with the money."

"Vincenzo, there are enough foundations," said Grandpa Angelo. "When the time is right, you'll know what to do for good with your money. You're not a fool. Good films are important. And these also cost money."

"Okay, Grandpa," Vincent said. "Okay."

One word from Grandpa was like one word from the Pope, Beth thought. Still, Angelo had the same effect on her. It was as though he'd been thinking over whatever problem you had for years and finally had decided to let you in on the answer.

And then the music rose and golden platforms rose and golden icicles descended and two gigantic gold pillars in the shape of host Ellen DeGeneres appeared, just before the woman herself.

"This is the surprise tonight. It's a new era. Tonight, the people who don't get Oscars will be getting Ellens." She gestured to the pillars. "They'll be chocolate. At least, once they're in the car, they can bite my head off!"

Soon, the names of five identical young men that Beth only dimly recognized were introduced, in snippets of roles as cavalrymen in World War I and the saviors of twelve-year-old girls sold into sexual slavery. Morgan Freeman was nominated for his role in a film about a young basketball star drafted into the NBA out of high school. He played the hero grandfather who helped steer the boy back to some semblance of his lost innocence.

One of the identical young men won.

"Always a bridesmaid, huh Morgan?" Ellen asked. "Except when you aren't? What, do they just put your name down first and then fill in everyone else's? It's like people at the Grammys used to thank Stevie Wonder for not making an album that year."

Then Sissy Spacek took the stage with an actor Beth remembered as a child actor in a series of sci-fi movies—who had grown up to look something like an elongated elf.

"You're young enough to be my son," Sissy Spacek said. "They promised me a hunk."

"You're little enough to be my daughter,"

he replied. "They promised me a curvy Brazilian."

"Movies are supposed to be make-believe," said Sissy Spacek. She laughed. "Don't you bother to put those cards up there because I can't see 'em anyway! I'm too vain to wear my glasses when I'm dressed up! We count on movies to give shape to our dreams and our nightmares and to alter our consciences and always, we hope, make us laugh. But only one of the four nominated documentary films is a laughing matter, and that one is *Scream Queen,* the story of a young woman whose face you've never seen, but whose voice you've heard a dozen times, in some of the hottest horror movies of the past decade. You try it sometime. Just go out in your car and give a good scream. You're not going to sound like Paul McCartney. Screaming is a gift, as you'll see . . ."

It was funny. The girl, Brenda Gelfman, who had a whole repertoire of screams, from little shrieks to death wails, was a chubby brunette from Brooklyn with a mop of black curls.

"Our next nominee," said the elfin actor, "is a story within a story. Twenty-two years ago, a little boy was kidnapped in a hotel lobby. Nine years later, Ben Cappadora returned to his family unhurt. But ever since then, his family, and especially his older brother, has struggled to come to grips with what this particular loss of a child means to a family and to a community, and, I suppose, to all of us. These families still wait and hope. Let's watch a few moments of *No Time to Wave Goodbye,* a film by Rob Brent and Vincent Cappadora." They watched the excruciating, unsparing minute when the camera never wavered as Al Cafferty explained how they had told Alana to wave to them, even if she was with her coach, and of the surveillance cameras at the door that saw nothing, until they recorded a tiny shining thing, Alana's good-luck bear.

As the presenters introduced *One Shot,* the journey of a shot of heroin from its grower to the middlemen to the nude women who stood at long tables and cut the product surrounded by thugs with guns to the Princeton-educated junkie whose own husband didn't know of her addiction, Vincent leaned over to whisper to Beth, "This one is the winner."

Beth tensed muscles in every part of her body.

Then they heard the words "unprecedented access" and "never-before-seen footage." Vincent said, "There aren't very many surprises in this town. It's all over the street. *One Shot* will win. This guy will be the next Spike Lee or something."

The final nominee was *Buffalo Gal,* a raucous and vivid film about young girls who rode the rodeo. A chasm of silent anticipation opened after the last moments of the twangy soundtrack died away.

Pat reached over Beth to cover Vincent's hand with his own. He said, "At Christmas you would have given your front tooth to even be sitting here. We all think you already won. Right? Am I right?"

Vincent nodded. He gazed down at Pat's high-school ring, which he wore for luck.

Beth wanted to jump up and run out of the room when Sissy Spacek picked up the cream-colored envelope.

Ben wished he were back in the hotel room, singing to Stella.

Candy whispered something under her breath that could have been a string of expletives or a prayer.

Sissy Spacek looked up at her moony counterpart and smiled as if to split her face. Then she turned to face the audience. "The winner is *No Time to Wave Goodbye,* by Rob Brent and Vincent Cappadora."

At first, no one moved. The audience broke into the kind of accolade saved for the dark horse. Michael Moore's beautiful wife, Kathleen, stood and made the victory gesture. Vincent sat blinking, as though he'd just been awakened from a sound sleep.

Finally, Candy, with tears streaming from her impeccable Nars front-row eyes, said, "I think that was your name, Spanky. Hey, Vincent. You won?"

Rob bounded away through the crowd. By the time Vincent got up there, Rob had said, "I thought my esteemed partner was crazy to make this picture at all. Especially for our first big one. But Mom, Pop, Rita, I got that thing you were looking for to put on the bookshelf next to the graduation pictures!"

Vincent stared down at the podium. Pat knew he hadn't prepared a single line he could use as an acceptance speech. A second passed, then another.

Finally Vincent said, "Obviously, I want to thank the Academy and question your sanity." Appreciative laughter. "My brother, Sam, and my sister, Kerry, should be standing here. This would be nothing without you. And I would be nothing without these people, my grandfather Angelo, who taught me to love art in all its forms, my mother for teaching me which form of art was mine, and Candy Bliss and my pop, who suggested that filmmaking might be a good alternative to prison." More laughter. "And I have to thank Marco Ruffalo for seeing people and places as I never could." Both the Charleys, Two and Seven, sobbed openly—huge men with bulging red child's faces. Markey himself sat with his face pillowed in his rough, stubby hands. "But mostly, I want to take this moment to remember five people. They are DuPre Dicksen, Jacqueline Whittier, Luis Rogelio, Alana Cafferty, and Laurel Hutcheson. If this statue is really magic, it will bring you home."

The audience applauded wildly. Sissy

Spacek hugged Vincent with a mother's sweetness.

"Dude won the Oscar," Cole Dicksen said to his little sister, Toni Lynn. But she was already asleep. Unexpectedly, Janice had been called to work. All her friends had insisted on turning the TV in the break room on. Janice's work friends surrounded and hugged her.

"Good for him," Eileen Cafferty said, smiling past eyes bright with tears. Al hugged his wife. Their son, Adam, asked, "Can we get his autograph?"

In Washington State, Walter Hutcheson said, "Well, God bless him."

"God bless Laurel," said his wife.

As they watched Vincent make his way back, stopping for a quick photo with Sissy Spacek, Charley Seven shrugged off the urgent tap on his shoulder. "I put it out," he said, without looking back, referring to his single panicked puff on his cigar. There was a roped-off corner for the smokers at the theater but he hadn't dared leave during the most amazing moments.

"Sir, there's an urgent message for you

outside," said one of the ushers. "I believe the man is a police officer."

"What the hell?" Charley Seven suddenly felt his beeper buzzing like a trapped hornet under his belly. Hauling himself to his feet, he told Beth and Pat he would be right back. When he dialed the unfamiliar number, he found himself on the phone with a young woman whose voice was so drowned in hysteria that at first he couldn't understand a syllable. "Calm down," he told her. "What are you saying? Nothing can happen if I can't hear you."

"I saw Eliza sitting right there on TV!" the voice keened. It was his niece. It was Adriana. *What the hell?* Charley thought.

"Yeah, and so? Is the baby sick? Are you okay?" Blinking in the sunlight, Charley Seven nodded to the police officer and held up one finger.

"She called me, Uncle Charley. Eliza called before and said Beth's brother and his wife were coming to pick up the baby and Liza would meet them outside the theater as soon as they found out who won so that the baby could nurse before they went to the party. . . . And she said I could go home because Beth's brother and his wife would take care of Stella for the rest of the night."

"Adriana! Slow down! Who would meet Beth's brother and his wife?"

"Eliza and Sam! Eliza said she was going to come out and get the baby."

"Eliza is inside."

"I know! I just saw her! But on the phone, she said that Beth's brother would come for Stella. As soon as they made the announcement. And they did come. Eliza said she would come out to get Stella the minute they found out. Or else Sam would. But they were right there. I saw them! I waited awhile and they did this little feature story about the family and stuff and they were still there . . ."

"Sam? Who's Sam?" Charley Seven asked.

"It's Ben! It's Vincent's brother. He uses that name."

"Jesus Christ, Adriana! I can't make heads or tails of any of this. Okay, okay. Now, this was Beth's brother . . . Bick?" Bick could have arrived late; Beth's father, Bill, had been too ill to come with the rest of them, so Bick and his wife had stayed behind to be with him. Maybe they had all come ahead. Of course.

"No, Uncle Charley! It was her brother *Paul* and his wife. Sandy. Not Bick. I know Bick. Her name was Sheila. Or something. But then I remembered that Paul brought his daughter Annie, not his wife. Annie's my age! I met her the first day, Annie Kerry. And this lady wasn't her. I was so excited that I forgot! This lady was older, like Beth's age!"

And Paul and Annie are sitting inside there clapping their heads off.

Only a few other times in his life, Charley Seven had encountered a situation beyond his power to salvage.

Once there had been a meeting under the bridge, out by O'Hare Airport, for which three guys scheduled to show up did not and he and his older brother Tory found themselves alone in the dusk, surrounded by Anthony Taliaferro and five of his eight large and jubilantly psychotic brothers, who even as teenagers never bothered with fists or even bats but opted for vehicular mayhem of all kinds. He could feel the way it had been, surrounded in the parking lot of the bindery on Mannheim Road by the wolf-eyed Taliaferros, as they sat on the hoods of their old, long, ruined Ponti-acs, with their arms folded over their chests. Back then, Charley, who was a slow but thorough thinker, had overcome his agitation and found escape not through fleeing but through backing off—assessing his plight from a bird's-eye view. He'd surveyed the area and seen two black-and-whites parked adjacent, next to Alexander's Diner, cops chatting through their windows over coffee. Sliding his hand through the window of Tory's vehicle, Charley laid on the horn until one of the police got annoyed and came to see what was up. The Taliaferro brothers scattered like roaches under a kitchen light.

Now, there surely was a logical explana-tion for what Adriana was saying; he knew that. But when Charley drew back, to scan for the explanation and the key to the lock, he saw only a broken landscape. He scanned the lines of gawkers leaning over the velvet ropes and the long lines of iden-tical, idling black cars that stretched away for blocks.

Information was the best thing. Charley Seven needed more.

"So Adriana, honey, how long ago was this?"

"It really was Eliza who called, Uncle Charley! I recognized her voice!" she screamed.

"How long ago was this, Adriana?" Charley asked in the voice that could make men forget that they had learned to control their bowels when they were four.

"It was maybe half an hour ago, Uncle Charley? I didn't know when they would give the award for those kinds of movies. Documentaries. I thought they might be way near the end. I forgot they sprinkle those kind in with the big ones. I changed Stella and then the phone call came and I turned on the TV and Beth's brother shows up. He kind of looked like Beth. But afterward, I thought, why wouldn't Eliza have told me before if she was going to send her uncle for the baby?"

Slowly, Charley Seven said, "A half hour ago? Half an hour ago you gave Patrick Cappadora's grandchild to a stranger?"

Adriana began to sob. "Uncle Charley! It was Eliza who called me! She said to give Paul the milk she pumped. Who else would know that but Liza?"

Anyone who knew what most six-month-olds lived on, Charley thought.

He told Adriana to sit and wait, not to move. Perhaps a mistake but an innocent one. Jesus, Holy Mother, please let it have been Beth's younger brother, Bick. Charley swiveled his eyes, concealed by his dark D&G sunglasses, back toward the entrance and saw no delighted Eliza, opening her arms to receive her baby.

Charley nodded to the officer. "We are going to need your help," he said.

The officer asked a guard to bring Vincent Cappadora and his family out.

Vincent and Rob had just finished posing for photos with their statuettes while a CNN reporter asked them questions. But when Vincent saw Charley Seven coming toward Ben and Eliza, Charley's face gray as cement, looking as though he'd walked a hundred miles on hot sand beside the tall police officer, Vincent consciously smiled for what he believed, simply from the sense in the air, like burning, would be the last smile for a long time to come.

Vincent could not imagine what could go so wrong it could cause a police officer to walk into the Academy Awards. Was someone ill? Hurt? The officer kept on walking toward them. Then, like a house of cards on fire, he flashed onto the only member of his family who had come to California but not to the awards.

Vincent began to run toward the doors and was close enough that it was he who caught Eliza when her knees buckled under her and her eyes rolled back.

CHAPTER EIGHT

Still clutching his statue, Vincent stalked the lobby, from reporter to reporter, from microphone to microphone, giving interview after interview.

He said he would tell anyone anything. He said that winning the Academy Award was the worst mistake of his life.

He offered the statue to anyone who would give him any information about the couple seen with his niece.

He offered a reward of $50,000.

He offered a reward of $100,000.

"My family is only a family," Vincent said

to the reporters. They saw a handsome young man, made beautiful by grief, with his shirt undone and tears in his eyes—appealing the way Beth used to think that Pat was at that age, like someone who needed a good meal and looking after, someone to wipe the grief from his gray eyes. The female news reporters felt their hearts pound in their stomachs and flubbed their openers. "I am only a guy. I don't care about my movie or my award. I only care about Stella and my family. I'm Stella's godfather. Ben is my only brother. We lost my brother. We . . . you have to understand. We all did this one time and no one can do this more than one time. My family can't stand any more. All our lives, this thing has been like the only thing that made us who we were. We were the family who lost my brother and my brother came back. We hated it but we lived up to it. We shouldn't have to—no one should have to—feel this ever . . . and not twice in one life."

The lead detective, Bill Humbly, finally had to stop Vincent: His appeals were clogging the phone line with crazies who wanted a hundred grand and an Oscar statuette so that legit people were hanging up in disgust. They had eight hundred calls the first hour and one decent tip. It came from the doorman at the Paloma, who'd accepted three dollars from a couple with a baby who said the woman's father was picking them up to let the dad park in the circle long enough to load the baby in. At around the same time, two young women, sisters, who had heard that Angelina Jolie was staying at the Paloma, although she was not, were nursing cocktails when they saw a couple slip into the backseat of a small Toyota SUV, brand-new, driven by an older man in a golf cap or a baseball cap.

Connecting the dots, the police determined that this happened just before Adriana made her call.

All the witnesses described the car as dark in color. They described the driver as white and middle-aged—eliminating two-thirds of the American population and leaving the other hundred million or so.

The only babies in the hotel that night were a starlet's newborn and her ten-month-old son, in the care of her mother, and a nominated actor's one-year-old twin boys.

And Stella.

Detective Humbly had decided to get his partner, Melissa Rafferty, to run purchases and thefts on the auto when he heard someone pounding down the lobby behind him, obviously in pursuit.

"Wait up!" Candy pleaded. "Wait up!" All the uniforms had identified him as the lead detective. "I need to talk to you. I know the girl who was taking care of the baby. . . . I know the whole family!"

"Stay right here," the detective said. He flashed a gold shield. William R. Humbly. A supervisor, then. A detective sergeant, as she had been twenty-two years ago—a token, the first girl in the area and the youngest. The least likely to become chief and yet she had. "I'm going to get someone to talk to you. We have five interview rooms. We'll put you next in line."

As the detective took a step to guide her toward the line of conference rooms where a close-up of Stella in her baptismal gown, looking directly at the camera, was slapped over another placard, Candy stopped. The guy might not care much about what she had to say, but she gambled he would care enough at least to hear it. Simply stopping, she had learned, worked as well with a person as it did with a dog.

The detective in the tee just a little too small, under a cotton-and-linen sport coat, did what she expected. He stopped too and looked back.

"This kidnapping was planned," Candy said.

"It's still not clear that this even was a kidnapping. Are you a member of the media?"

"No," Candy said. "I was involved with the investigation of the kidnapping of Ben Cappadora, the baby's father. I'm Candace Bliss," she said. "I led the investigation . . ."

"I'm not sure what you mean by 'leading' the investigation. Were you . . . part of a team from the Center for Missing and Exploited—"

"They didn't have assist teams on the ground then," said Candy and took her badge out of her jacket pocket.

"You were a police officer," said Humbly.

Candy replied evenly, "There's no 'was'

about it. How many years in are you? Ten?"

"Nearly twelve."

Candy said, "I am twenty-nine years in. I'm the chief of police in Parkside, Illinois."

"I apologize, Chief," Humbly said and smiled briefly. "But I want you to know. We're doing everything at warp speed. We issued an Amber Alert fifteen minutes in, so there's been a preempt of regular broadcasting . . ."

"I'm familiar with the Amber Alert plan. We were one of the states that threw in for it early on. It's magnificent. It doesn't reassure me."

"Pardon me, ma'am, but are you . . . involved in some other way?" Detective Humbly asked.

"I'm her grandmother."

"Her grandmother? I thought her grandmother is the mother of the guy with the movie. . . ."

"That is her father's mother. I'm her *mother's* mother. My daughter is the mother of the baby, Eliza Cappadora. The families became friends and our kids fell in love, long story short."

"I see. I'm so sorry, Chief Bliss. We want

you to know that we'll do everything in our . . ."

"I know you will," Candy said, kindly. "I know it's balls to the wall for a kid. I just want to be kept in the loop. Somehow."

Oh no, Humbly thought, but he said, "Okay. I'll tell you what we've got going. Well, the Amber Alert . . ."

"Do you think anyone will tip to it? On Oscar night?" Candy asked.

"Absolutely," Humbly said. "The Oscar win makes it a double-shot news story. Now they'll be running descriptions of Stella every ten minutes, breaking into whatever else is on TV, especially the awards ceremony. A bazillion people are watching. If it had to happen . . ."

"Don't say it was a good time," Candy said and smiled in case she sounded too harsh. "What's your gut? I think she's still alive."

Candy's hunch was not sentimental. The facts as she understood them from Charley Seven and his niece didn't imme-diately turn her stomach the way the facts that surrounded Ben's kidnapping had. For one, Ben was hauled away with such disdain for his comfort that one of his little shoes was pulled off and left behind. For another, he wasn't the right age to be fake-adopted by someone who wanted a baby. Most babies looked like most other babies. Little boys, older than a year, had distinctive features. They were more likely to be the prey for people who loved little boys in ways that flattened the imagination. So Ben should have been dead by the time Beth and Candy met.

But Adriana Ruffalo described the couple who came to the hotel room to take Stella as relaxed, unhurried, and charming. They knew how to hold a baby. They commented on how big she'd gotten and made her giggle.

Humbly went on. "And we just got a picture of the baby printed up, maybe you saw that, and TRAK will disseminate that through agencies and volunteers to law enforcement and the media. We already have someone analyzing and enlarging stills from the security-cam footage of the couple walking away with her. And that's going to be blasted out as soon as it's in good enough shape, which should be in ten minutes . . . we're trying to trace the car but we only got a view of the rear and the plate was removed."

"You have a picture of the couple who took Stella?" Candy pressed her fingers to the place between her eyes. "Of course you do. The security here would be unbelievable. That's amazing luck." The Paloma had the kind of tony clientele who paid their $650 a night expecting thirsty towels and caviar-laced moisturizer, and it had its own computerized locking system. There was a routine security scan of each floor at two-minute intervals—not only on Oscar night but every night. Pissed-off beauties and beaux in event finery were now lined up behind tourists in pajama pants and Green Bay Packer T-shirts, waiting to be interviewed and released with instructions to remain in the area. No one expected to find the couple among the guests—only to find someone who'd seen them.

Detective Humbly said, "We have a good picture of them standing at the elevator, facing the camera, with her holding the baby. The baby's face isn't visible but the time stamp and the proximity to the room is exactly right, and the baby bag they brought is an unusual design. It has what looks like a fetus on it . . ."

"It's an ultrasound picture," Candy said. "I bought it. It's not an ultrasound picture of Stella but it's somebody's. It's a black patent-leather bag . . ."

"Yes, and there was also a green bag with some squiggles and question marks on it."

"Stella's clothes were in the bag."

"They're both blond and attractive and well-dressed."

"That should narrow it down in California," Candy said, then quickly added, "Actually, I apologize. That level of composure is a good thing in this case . . . so is taking all the baby's gear. It suggests that they want the baby to . . . keep. Not to rape and suffocate."

"Sure. That much is clear but . . ." There was a big "but" that Humbly wasn't going to bring up unless she did.

"And that there were two of them. A team. Like a husband and wife, although I'm sure they weren't. Couples don't kidnap children," Candy went on.

Humbly thought, but didn't say, They do

if they are well paid. Or threatened. "They do, once in a while," he said. "Had a couple stole two kids from the same yard a few years ago. Instant family. We got them before they hit the freeway . . ."

Looking down, searching for her cell phone, Candy noticed that in the process of ripping off her designer dress and pulling on her jeans, shirt, blazer, and holster, she had torn two of her nails deep down to the quick. She couldn't even feel the pain. It was as though she were examining another woman's hand.

Candy and Humbly sat down on a pair of sofas across from the interview rooms. So far, the Amber Alert or a tip from someone who saw one of those photos was their best hope. Some experts griped about the alert system, which was named after Amber Hagerman, kidnapped in broad daylight in full view of a neighbor who heard her screams, and found days later, a few miles from her home, her throat cut. Skeptics said that an Amber Alert brought out more confessors and creeps than tipsters and wasted valuable time. Still, occasionally it actually worked. A caller to a radio talk show had suggested it: Now police issued the same kind of bulletin to the media for a missing child that was issued for severe weather. All fifty states used some form of it. In some places, a tone was played and programming was interrupted while the child's picture was displayed.

Humbly opened his notebook. "So you say you know the girl who was caring for the baby and you've spoken to her . . . before or after?"

"Before and since . . . since we were all moved up to the Frank Sinatra Suite." At the request of the management and the police, who wanted access to the room where Adriana had cared for Stella for two days, the family members had been given a series of rooms in the huge, glass-walled penthouse.

"Was this while she had the baby with her?" Humbly asked.

"Yes. Not the second time, obviously. But for the past two days, repeatedly. To her and her family." Candy watched as nine of ten people who walked past the plainclothes standing around all but tripped to stare at them. They might as well have been uniforms, she thought. They would have attracted less attention wearing clown outfits. Candy believed that detectives in plain clothes should dress like detectives on TV, in slinky tops and tight jeans or leather jackets and khakis, like *people.* Like this Humbly here. But take them out of their blues and police invariably wore black and navy blue together, or shirts tucked in nice and tight or denim skirts with sensible shoes—like nuns without habits. "Why do plainclothes dress so bad?" she asked. Humbly stared at her as though she'd grown a beard. Why had she said that? Why did her mind keep slipping away from her, into weird corridors, and then Stella's face come roaring back out at her, larger than life, larger than death? She took a deep breath.

"I first met Adriana years ago," Candy said. "She was a teenager in Chicago. Ben and his brother, the guy with the movie, they've known her since childhood. Eliza met her only yesterday. But she felt good about Adriana. She still does. My daughter expressed breast milk for the baby before she put on her evening dress and also pur-chased cans of formula as a backup. She put them all in the refrigerator. Stella's extra diapers and clothing were on the tall dresser. The room should be covered with prints . . ."

"It's a hotel room, ma'am. It's probably got prints from Tony Bennett. And for there to be a match, the people who did this would already have to be in the system. But we'll try. Of course," Humbly said.

"What else did you say you were doing?" Candy asked Humbly.

He said, "We're going to use the press to the maximum." News crews had set up— even foreign press, in town for the Academy Awards. Humbly explained that they invited full media cooperation, as well as volunteers who pushed the images of Stella's face in close-up and the blond couple out even onto cell phones and pagers.

Candy finally found her phone in an inside pocket and popped it open. Her gut coiled and nearly bent her double. How could so much time have passed?

Stella had now been missing for the magic number.

Three hours.

Despite the fact that such technology as the Amber Alert had slightly improved the odds, most abducted kids—including the little girl from Texas after whom the system was named—were dead within three hours of being taken. Statistics proved it over and over.

"Are you okay?" Humbly asked.

"I'm not," Candy said. "It's been three hours. Not much has changed since the Lindbergh kidnapping. If a kid is found dead after an abduction, that kid was killed within three hours of being taken."

"I don't go for that," Humbly said. "This is my case and we will find her."

"That's noble, but . . ."

The two looked at each other for a minute that seemed to stretch out between them like a shred of molten glass. Humbly was afraid she could read his mind. The abduction was well organized and timed and the couple had moved down the hall with the ease of vacationers. Stella was pretty, round and cooey and racially desirable, still little enough for whoever got her to pretend that they'd given birth to her. California's adoption laws were so ludicrous that anyone could find a scumbag lawyer with an Internet license who would make everything look tidy. If it weren't for the publicity and if Stella had been brought to L.A. from Mexico—or Kansas—she would grow up as the daughter of some very nice gay couple up in the Swish Alps above Beverly Hills, drive a five-hundred-dollar pink toy Jeep when she was four, and have every lesson known to humankind. Humbly figured the couple was foreign—Canadian, French, Swiss, Dutch, German. Not Mexicans. Mexicans could have their pick of beautiful babies off the streets for what it would cost to buy a good meal in New York. Some shady "family lawyers" dealt exclusively with would-be parents who were Germans. Germans had plenty of money, were nearly neurotically discreet, and readily shelled out a couple of hundred grand to the attorney and ten grand to a couple of other shills for a few days' work. Some of it went to a couple of young people who posed as the birth parents, who were often unrelated and met each other the day before. The real woman who'd given birth got five hundred bucks and a walk back across the bridge to Mexico. The wish to have a child was so huge and overpowering that couples would look the other way in circumstances that stank like five-day-old fish. With a fake certificate from the Ninth Circuit Court, City of Los Angeles, and enough breast milk and formula to get her to Berlin or Zurich or Toronto, Stella could be on a Swissair flight by now, with flight attendants competing to cuddle her. Stella had even come with diapers. Cute, expensive dresses. Like a dolly with a trunk. Full-service deal.

Instead of saying this—he hoped devoutly Candy didn't have the same sense—Humbly switched leads: "We don't have any reason to like Adriana for this. She had no idea who the people were . . . and Charles Ruffalo's business interests are insignificant in this context. That guy just fell apart. Nobody can fake that kind of grief."

"But how could she give the baby to that couple? Even if she did think they were relatives?" Candy asked.

"You said yourself you had a good gut about her," Humbly answered. "She believed it was one of the other people with you. Like your friend, Betty . . ."

"Beth," Candy said. "The other grandmother. The father's mother."

"So it's not implausible. It's Oscar night, worse than Halloween. Put yourself in the mind of a twenty-one-year-old whose brother was just part of the team who won an Oscar. If she believed Eliza called her for real."

"So . . ."

Humbly snapped his fingers. "Wait! You! I just put this together and it embarrasses me that it took me so long! It should have hit me when I caught the call. Ben Cappadora. The Cappadora case. *You found Ben Cappadora.* You're that person. I've been reading about the movie the brother made. I thought I might go see it with my wife. It happened when I was a kid."

"I didn't find him. I talked to the perp, face-to-face, like your guys out here did with the Polly Klaas case, two days after the kidnapper took Ben. It could have ended right there. Instead, it took nine years."

Jesus, thought Humbly, how does she live with that? But he said, "I remember actually your case had some bearing on my wanting to be a cop. It's funny how all the things in your life catch up."

"Kind of," Candy said and asked, point-blank, "They're pros who'll sell her, right?"

"Look," Humbly said. "Look . . . no."

Humbly didn't want to have to say what he had to say. He'd sooner have given up his middle name—Francis; he didn't like it anyway—than tell this nice lady that she needed to stop being a cop and be a grandma starting right now. With her history, it would be like telling her to hold her breath until the little kid was found.

"I intend to stay. I intend to help find her," Candy said.

"That's the thing, though. I can't control where you go, ma'am. But I can't let you be part of the investigation."

"Why not? I have absolutely unique experience here," Candy pressed him. "You'll let an FBI agent in. Some suit! You don't know my daughter. Or Ben. My daughter and my granddaughter are all I have. Just the job. And them. So you see . . ."

Humbly stared at the ceiling. He scrubbed at his face. "That's it exactly. You're too close in. You're way too close in. And ma'am, you know it."

"No!"

"Yes, ma'am. Yes. You do."

Now I will have to go back there, Candy thought. I will have to walk back down the hall to the ornate bank of elevators and whoosh up to the eleventh floor and use the key to let myself into the room where they had tried to film Eliza pleading with the kidnappers to give her back her baby, but failed because, each time, Eliza got ten seconds into the prepared sentences and began to scream, *I want my baby! I want to feed my baby!* A nurse practitioner staying in the hotel had come to put hot compresses on Eliza's breasts and wrap her in bandages, but Eliza pushed her away and insisted on expressing the milk. *Don't you think these people will find my daughter? This is America! They found my husband when he was little. Are you trying to make me act like my baby is dead? Why would you want my milk to go away?*

Ben, handsome and steady and calm, did better.

But although his mouth moved, his eyes looked dead, like posthumous portraits from the 1800s. Would anyone sympathize with a young man who seemed to have no feelings at all? Ben was buried under mattress after mattress of coincidence. There was no way for him to be himself. But perhaps if he were to be the real Ben, he would be like Eliza, a writhing, desperate thing no amount of Valium could bring even close to down out of the tree she had clawed her way up.

Candy would have to pass the room where Charley Seven wept in his wife's arms. He would give his own life, he swore to God. He would give his right arm. And Pat? Pat had walked every floor of the eleven floors in the hotel, opened every door in the kitchen and the pantry. He walked as he had two decades ago, determined to prove that lightning didn't strike twice . . . when it did, all the time. Blue pouches hung from Pat's eyes and his hands and suit stank of the cigarettes he'd given up so long ago.

No.

Candy bent forward over her knees and began to cry. "Please," she said to Humbly. "Please let me be a police officer."

Humbly saw the dark-haired, smaller woman running toward them and almost got up to get between her and Chief Bliss.

"Ma'am," he said, throwing out a hand. "Please wait there . . ." but by then, Candy had heard Beth's voice.

"I found you!" Beth said. "Oh honey."

Beth sat down and all but pulled Candy into her arms like a child. "Eliza needs you." She held out her hand to Humbly. "I'm Beth Cappadora, Vincent and Ben's mother."

"Who would think this could happen twice in someone's life?" Humbly asked.

"No one," Beth said. "No one on earth."

Humbly's partner came back just then. "Humbly," Melissa Rafferty said. "It's freaky but there are no reported stolens of black or dark Toyota SUVs . . ."

"Doesn't mean there aren't any. People might be out of town. Not know their car's gone yet," Humbly said.

"We have a gang of uniforms checking where the newly purchased are with their purchasers. There are about forty zillion of them," said the small, bright-haired officer. "But here's the thing, Humbly. We called all the rental agencies and one at the San Francisco airport has been expecting a return for three days. The kid who rented it thought the driver's license was phony but he rented it anyway because the lady was adopting a baby . . . and he kind of liked her . . ."

"What was the lady's name?"

"Patricia Fellows."

"Did you run her . . . ?" Humbly began.

"I know who Patricia Fellows is," Beth said.

"Me, too," Candy said. "Can we go to a computer?" With a few strokes, she summoned up a photo that had the ink-block print quality of black-and-white photography of thirty or fifty years ago. "Patricia Fellows is dead. She died in Riverton, on the West Side of Chicago, forty years ago."

"I was a little kid then," Beth said. "It happened right near the part of the city where I lived when I was small, before we moved to Chester. It was the most horrifying thing that ever happened. People didn't kill children then. It wasn't part of the news every day . . . no one's boyfriend got hopped up and just . . ."

"Slaughtered some baby or some teenager. Everybody our age knows about the Fellows sisters," Candy said. "But not everyone knows that I didn't grow up in Chicago like Beth and Pat Cappadora did. I've been there so long they probably assume I did."

"What happened to them?" Humbly asked. "The sisters?"

"They were kidnapped and murdered. It can't be a mistake."

"Candy," Beth asked, "why would they use that name?"

Candy said, "Oh, Bethie. I can only think of one reason. It could be to telegraph to us that this is personal."

CHAPTER NINE

If the rental car took one more minute to come, Kerry would scream. Not that she had any confidence that she could make her way to LAX in time if it did: The Los Angeles freeway system fulfilled every exaggerated horror story she'd ever heard about it. But Kerry felt more confident taking a car of her own than a cab.

In fact, for the three days since Baby Stella was taken, Kerry had longed for a car anyway, simply to be able to flee the atmosphere of mourning and tension in the penthouse suites. Once, she'd gone down to the pool and dived in but when she surfaced, a reporter was there, asking, "Is there any news of Baby Stella, Kerry? Are the police questioning your brother and his wife? Were they on the verge of a divorce?"

And before she could stop herself, Kerry answered, "That's crazy!"

The police weren't, in fact, "talking" to Ben and Eliza. After a cursory chat with Ben and Eliza, no one seemed to suspect anyone within the family. But the interview circle was widening like sound waves from a tower, to old friends and the people who'd been filmed for the movie, to Vincent's ex-girlfriends.

And then George arrived, just this morning, overnight on the red-eye from O'Hare.

When the whole atmosphere ignited, when Ben went nuts for no reason at all, and Beth ran from the room, Kerry had no idea that her mother would hop into a cab and head straight to the airport. Kerry hadn't even seen it—had only heard the few things Pop told her. Kerry was asleep, which was how she coped when she couldn't cope, and the rest of them were sitting with Detective Rafferty. George Karras burst into the living room—thankfully without the annoying wife, Elena, he'd married a few years after Cecilia Lockhart died. Eliza was lying on the bed with Beth, half-asleep, but she jumped up and, with Ben, rushed to George, who enveloped them in a huge embrace. In bits and pieces, Vincent told Kerry what happened next.

George said, "This isn't all so bad as it seems, Sam. The guy down there said they didn't look like drug people or, you know, anyone who wants to hurt Stella. The airlines have these people's picture. . . ."

"Dad, I never got it," Ben said. "How you could love someone so much in just six months."

"That's how I loved you," George said. "Oh, my boy. My son. Oh, Sam, try not to give up. It looks like they have people here . . . top notch."

Pat stood up. "Do you want coffee?" he asked the room at large. And everyone nodded. Pat said, "Eliza, you drink like what Bethie does. Vanilla something large with skim. And Candy, a gallon of black with nothing, right? And George . . ."

"Sure, Pat, I'll have a large one with milk . . ."

"And about eight sugars. It's been twenty years, George. I know how you take your coffee."

Then Ben said, "Shut up."

"What?" Pat asked slowly, his voice hoarse. "What? I . . . didn't hear you, son."

"I said shut up. Don't interrupt my dad and talk to him like he's scum. You interrupt him. You act like you let him come to your fancy house and eat your fancy food because you're such a nice guy . . ."

"Sam, all I meant was, I know how he takes his coffee. I've known George a long—"

"That's not what you meant. You always have that sneer, like, in your voice when you talk to him."

Vincent got up and said, "Stop. Stop. Pop. Sam. Stop. Nobody has slept. Everybody's scared to death."

"You should be scared to death," Ben said. "Vincent, you should be scared to shut your eyes in case you die and there really is a hell. I let you talk me into doing this movie and you know why? Because I figured, he's a loser. He's been a loser all his life. I got a wife I'm crazy about. I got a life. I'm having a baby. What's he got?

He's making Internet cartoons and he's almost thirty, so I think, maybe this will do him good. Make him act not so much like an asshole. But what happens instead . . . to me? To Eliza and Candy and your own dear, dear parents? What happens is what always happens when you touch it . . ."

"Oh Ben," Vincent moaned. "Don't. Oh, don't do this. I know I deserve it. But I would never, I swear to God, I would never hurt Stella or Liza or you. You're my brother, Ben . . ."

"Which is that it turns to shit. Everything you touch. Vincent. You and your big hood friends. Your Cosa Nostra bullshit. Every thing. Every person. It all turns to shit. So go away. All of you. Go away and leave me with my father. Give us our privacy," Ben said, taking Eliza's arm.

Vincent said, "I'm sorry! Just listen, please. I'll do anything . . ."

"Don't you think you've done enough for one lousy lifetime?" Ben asked.

"What happened then?" Kerry asked Vincent later.

"And then Ma slapped Ben," Vincent said.

"No she didn't," said Kerry. "No way."

"She said she couldn't hear him whip me like that. Because it wasn't just now. It wasn't just Stella. She said . . ." Kerry grabbed her brother's arm.

"What, Vincent? What?"

"She said that . . . I would die for Stella. Or Ben. And that I thought it was all my fault. As long as I could remember."

"What else?"

"Ma said that what I tried to do was good . . ."

"Did Pop try to help?"

"Everyone tried. George did. Candy did. But Ben just held the door open and I ran out and Pop ran after me. Ma tried to go back but Ben wouldn't look at her and neither would Eliza. And he shut the door." Vincent stopped, his breath ragged, not caring that Kerry saw the tears that dripped off his chin. "It's worse, though."

How could it be worse? Kerry thought. The mockery of March sunlight made sequential pools on the bedroom carpet. "I guess Candy got up and followed Mom."

"She left Eliza?" Kerry gasped.

"She came out and I heard her say, 'Sam, you're going to use words that can't be taken back. That is your mother. And you need her now. And I need her now. You know what you said isn't true. Nothing that happened here was anyone's doing except someone who knows too much about your family. We need to be together on this.' But Ben just sat there. Candy finally said, 'Okay, I'm going, too, pal.' The door was open and I heard Eliza start to cry and say, 'Mommy! Auntie!' And Ben tried to calm her down. He said, 'Your mom can stay.' But Candy kept going."

"Where's Ma?"

"I can't find her, Bear. She ran and Pop and I can't find her. She took her big backpack and . . . crazy stuff like all the iPhones she got."

"Vincent, did you ask downstairs?" Kerry asked, but had pulled a rugby shirt on over her sweats and strappy T-shirt before he could answer.

Mrs. Cappadora had taken a cab to meet a relative, said the doorman.

"Where?" Kerry asked.

"She said the airport," the guy in the black uniform with red piping told Kerry. He was British and a flirt.

"How soon can I get a rental?" Kerry asked.

That was forty-five minutes ago. Now, she stalked back into the scented cool air of the Paloma with her hands grasping the roots of her long auburn hair. "The car that you ordered for me hasn't come! My mom needs me. Can you please call them back?"

"Josh, I'm taking my lunch," said the doorman, pulling off his hat. "Here, I'll run you up there . . ." He took the keys to one of the Paloma vans and hopped in.

"You don't have to do that, and all I have is a credit card," Kerry protested.

"No worries. You've been through enough, you lot."

And so they careered through back roads and down canyons and on and off the freeway, the Brit, who called himself Craig, madly trying to interest Kerry in something other than his driving prowess, while she tried to think of what airline they'd taken out here, five days and a lifetime ago. "United," she said suddenly. "United."

"You go in and I'll park," he said.

"How will I know you?" Kerry asked.

"Me, I'll be the one wearing the black uniform with the brass buttons."

"I'm sorry," Kerry said. "Of course. Of course. I'm so grateful." She ran through the automatic doors and sprinted for the United counter but, before she could engage the attention of the woman herding the departing passengers into the line, she saw Beth, about to put her bag onto the conveyor belt at the security line.

"Mom!" Kerry cried. "Mom!" Kerry began to push past the others in the lines leading to the screening machines.

"Where is your boarding pass, ma'am?" said a brusque woman who, until Kerry slid under the rope, appeared to have been asleep. "You get back here."

"That's my mother," Kerry said. "I have to stop her!"

"I don't care who she is. I need to see your boarding pass."

"I don't have a boarding pass. I'm not boarding!"

"Then you need to get out of this line before I call security," the uniformed woman said, her voice rising.

Kerry yelled, "My mom is out of her mind!"

Everyone stopped then.

Beth slowly removed her bag from the belt and walked back. In instants, mother and daughter were surrounded by security, who whisked them into a glass-walled office. A man with a gold bar ID badge asked Beth's permission to search her bag. Out tumbled her wallet, her Carolina Herrera dress, and eight iPhones. "What are these?" he asked

"They're from the Oscars," Beth explained. The fellow glanced at Kerry.

"They really are from the Oscars," Kerry said. "This isn't what it looks like."

"It never is," the man told them.

"It really isn't. My brother won an Oscar for Best Documentary Film and the same night my baby niece was kidnapped . . ."

"Let me see your ID," the man said, suddenly gentle.

"Look there," Kerry said. "Look at your newspaper." Behind him on the desk was a copy of the *Los Angeles Times* with the headline SEARCH FOR OSCAR BABY ENTERS THIRD DAY and a picture of Eliza and Beth with Stella. There was also a blowup of the security-camera picture of the couple at the elevator.

"That's you?" the man asked, pointing to the photo of Beth's face. Beth nodded. "Why were you getting on the plane to Chicago?"

"Mom, it's a good question," Kerry interrupted. "Were you going to leave Candy and Ben and Vincent and me? Like you did before? Duck out on us? Because it hurts too much?" Kerry began to cry. "It hurts me too, Mom. It's killing Candy. Don't you care? Or is it all about you?" Beth shook her head and let Kerry embrace her.

The security officer held out the newspaper for his colleague to see. "Let's get you two back," he said.

"I'm sorry, Ker," Beth said to her daughter. "It's so bad now. Candy is me now but I'm still me too."

"Wait," Kerry said. "Let me see the newspaper." She hadn't even looked at one. She'd avoided the coverage on TV. For the first time, Kerry took time to study the photo the police had isolated from the hotel video footage. She said, "Mom.

Mom. I think . . . no, I'm sure that was the lady who came to our house."

"What lady?" Beth asked.

"The lady who was a reporter, who I didn't think was really a reporter, who came to our house so late on the night before Stella's christening? The night when everybody found out Vincent was nominated?"

"I don't remember, Kerry," Beth said. "There were so many people there."

"She asked for Ben, Mom! Think. She wanted to see Ben and Eliza. We didn't let her in."

Beth took a deep breath. "I remember now."

"It was late, so she could have come from somewhere else, far away, but it means, if it is her . . ."

"Somebody was planning this even then," said the airport security guard. "You'd better call . . . whoever's on this from one of those phones. No, here, use mine. Sometimes cell phones don't work from inside the airport."

"None of them is charged," Beth said.

"Well, that would make a difference too," the man said.

"Mom, how could they possibly track her down, months later?" Kerry asked.

No one had an answer.

They were pulling into the crescent drive at the Paloma Hotel in a police cruiser when Kerry remembered the cute Englishman who was probably still parked in the van at LAX.

Bill Humbly was worn out.

They had a strange case. Almost too much information and not a blessed thing to connect any of the dots.

For the first time in his life, he was glad to see a guy from the FBI.

"Agent Joel Berriman," he said, his thick trench coat absurd for the weather.

They went over everything Humbly had tried.

Although it was impossible to interview everyone who knew the Cappadoras, anyone who might have had a grudge that was tripped by *No Time to Wave Goodbye* had come under their scrutiny in some way—even Cecilia Lockhart's brother, who had told people he thought Vincent was a pig for raking up old grudges. But when they called him, he choked up and said he was a jerk for saying such a thing. The local detective, one of Candy's, found out also that the brother was alibied from here to eternity . . . that he had, in fact, been at an Oscar party at The Old Neighborhood restaurant, which was where he made the remarks. No one could connect the lady in the photo to any photo of any known perp in Los Angeles or Chicago. This lady had never even gotten a traffic ticket. Humbly's next-in-line, Detective Rafferty, had even called Ruth Fellows, the now ancient mother of the long-dead Fellows sisters. He sent her a picture of the woman using her daughter's name. Ruth Fellows said the woman looked something like Patricia might have looked if she had lived to grow up—Patricia had been only thirteen—which opened a whole other dead-end avenue. At its conclusion, it was established by a former coroner that Patricia and Nancy were indeed Patricia and Nancy and that they had slept side by side for thirty years under an oak tree in Mount Carmel Cemetery.

Together, Humbly and Berriman visited a lawyer famous for those multi-hundred-thousand-dollar "adoption" deals. He was coming out of his mansion in Brentwood when they approached him.

"I know what you're here for and I know why," he said. "In fact, I called some people this morning and I would actually tell you if one of them had said a single thing that made the hair stand up on the back of my neck because this thing stinks, it really stinks. I would never do it. I swear on my mother's grave and I can prove it."

"You're breaking my heart," said Bill Humbly. "You remind me of my Boy Scout leader."

"But here's the truth. I've done some stuff in my life. But I never took a baby away from anyone who loved her baby," the lawyer said. "If I could help those people, I'd pay my last year's profits. Well, half of them."

It was the last sentence that convinced Humbly.

Humbly later told Ben and Eliza, "Even so, that's the kind of avenue where our tip will come from. Maybe not from a couple who thinks they adopted a baby, but from their neighbor. Everyone in the world has seen Stella's face now. What if your neighbor shows up all of a sudden with a baby old enough to crawl?"

Eliza said, "It could be worse."

Ben gasped. "What?"

"If they love her, it could be worse," Eliza said. "In my village, a girl was . . . was forced . . ."

"Raped," Humbly said.

"Which was a sin. And she put the baby in the woods to die. And it ruined the fields and the corn. And so she put her dress around her neck and hung from a tree, far away, across a river from where her parents lived." Where the hell did she grow up? thought Humbly. It sounded like the fourteenth century. "Adopted babies are the most loved babies. I could almost stand it with knowing someone loved her as much as we do."

"That's crazy!" Ben said. "Honey! She's my daughter. Our flesh and blood."

"What am I?" Eliza asked simply, her tiny hands folded on the table. "What is George?"

"That isn't what I mean."

"But it's what you said," Eliza continued.

"You threw your mother, your flesh and blood, out the door."

"Eliza! They're going to start saying you killed her!"

"You're a fool, Sam."

"Liza, you don't know what you're talking about. Even if they care about her, they'll never be her parents."

"Candy is my mother. She loves me. She cares for me. George loves you. Beth and Pat love you. You just never had anything bad happen in your life, Sam. You had an easy life." She made a sign with two fingers on her cheeks like two tears running down. "I know what you went through. But Mother Superior used to say that a few tears isn't drowning."

Humbly excused himself before Candy could get back from the quick run she'd made to buy everyone sweatshirts and underwear and pajamas. Candy would know that what Humbly was saying added up to sum zero shit.

On the fourth day, a freak snowstorm in the San Juan Diego Mountains trapped a young couple camping with a two-year-old and a four-year-old.

Idiots, Humbly thought. Who took kids

who could barely even eat on their own up a narrow pass to do a little mountain camping? Everyone knew it could snow in March on a dime up there.

Stella slipped below the fold as rescue workers from the U.S. Forest Service searched frantically through ten inches of powder in a featureless wilderness. It was a fast and very bad find: The mother was delirious; the baby was dead, fifty feet from the tent. The father's hands were frozen. Only the four-year-old was basically fine.

But then, to Humbly's relief, the strange story of the kidnapping made the cover of *People,* a six-page story under the head-line FALLING STARS: OSCAR WINNER'S NIECE KIDNAPPED, TWENTY YEARS AFTER HIS BROTHER with eight pictures that chronicled the abductions, in successive generations, of Ben Cappadora and his daughter, Stella. Bill Humbly was relieved that it pumped life into the story again, even if on the cheesy cable stations with blond starlets playing news-caster.

With Humbly's permission and an officer listening in, Vincent made his own calls.

After Vincent had called and Blaine

Whittier had consoled him, she was shocked when the phone rang again and it was her father, who called her twice a year. Blaine asked, "Is Mom okay? Have you spoken to Vincent Cappadora?"

Bryant said, "I haven't spoken about it with Mother . . . or certainly Vincent. I'm very busy. Mother and I are going to Italy as you know, and I have a good deal of business to tie up. Just things about the office."

"Oh Dad, it's so horrible," Blaine said softly.

"They have no leads at all," Bryant answered. "It savors more of planful professionalism than of psychopathology, don't you think?"

"Gee, Dad," Blaine said. "Always the lawyer. All I can think of is that poor family. On the happiest day of their lives."

"Well, I'd look for some individual who wants to draw attention to how easy it really is to abduct a child. Perhaps this can do some good. The issue is not addressed or resolved by 'awareness' or 'compassion.' It takes more, much more. In a sense . . ."

"But that's what Vincent was trying to say," Blaine interrupted.

"In a treacly way that brought glory to him but no real change. And now, much, much more trouble."

"Dad! Let me talk to Mom. I can't believe you said that! Whoever did this was insane, Dad. Or the most evil person on earth."

"I don't think either is necessarily the case, Blaine," Bryant said. "Insane people would hurt the child."

"I hate what you said about Vincent."

"Now, Blaine, calm down. I believe Vincent was sincere. Just naïve. I'll have Mother call you later."

Blaine stood in her room, looking out at the early, snow-tipped buds in the Massachusetts snow and thought, What is he saying? Not only is this the most my father has ever said to me, what he's saying is gobbledygook.

"Well, have fun in Italy, Dad," Blaine said. But Bryant had already hung up, as he customarily did, without saying goodbye. Where was her mother? Except to the screening and then not willingly, Mom hadn't gone farther than the mailbox since Jackie disappeared. Immediately she called home and Claire picked up.

"Blaine, darling," she said. "I'm beside myself."

"I am too. Is there anything at all we can do? I just talked to Dad. I forgot to ask him if there was anything he could suggest . . ."

Claire paused. "You talked to your father?"

"He wanted to tell me all these theories about who did this . . ."

"Where did he call from?"

"From his office, I assume," Blaine said. "Why?"

"Bryant left home four days ago. I'm leaving tomorrow by car to meet him in Los Angeles. He's at a conference. I haven't been able to reach him to talk about Stella Cappadora. I must have called him ten times."

"He said he was tidying things up in the office. But he might have meant finishing business there."

"Darling," Claire said. "Of course, you're right. I'll call you on my mobile, from the car. Is that okay? The doorbell just rang. I think Laura from next door is here to get the key to bring in our mail."

"I love you, Mommy," Blaine said.

"I love you, B," said Claire and hung up.

Claire sat down on the hard Quaker bench near the door. Her chest thudded as though she had fallen and had the wind knocked out of her.

No one was ringing the doorbell at all.

That evening after work, Eileen Cafferty asked Al, "Do you think they did just get too lucky and somebody wanted to punish them?"

Al nearly shouted but lowered his voice because the baby was asleep. "Eileen! The Cappadoras? How can you say anything about this is lucky!"

"They got their boy back and the boy grew up and the people who had him didn't rape him or torture him and his brother won an Oscar. Look on TV. They run this over and over." There was a brief moment of news footage of the Cappadora family on their feet, cheering and crying, at the Oscar ceremony. "They thought they'd be happy forever."

"You sound like you don't like that," said Al.

"Vincent's even profiting off that poor baby. Oprah went out there to California.

Vincent's everywhere you look. He couldn't have arranged it better if he tried . . ."

"Eileen, listen," Al said. "I love you and I loved Alana as much as you did. In fact, maybe I loved her more because you saw yourself in the little star she was going to be. I've never said a cross word to you. But I don't like this. Would you let their little baby die or stay lost forever if we could have Alana back?"

"Yes, of course," Eileen said. "Wouldn't you?"

"God forgive you, Eileen," Al said. "This is foolish talk."

She began to sob then, and so did the baby, Alyssa, a sound like bleating, as though Eileen and their daughter were little lamed animals. "Al, I'm sorry. I don't mean any of that. I have no idea why I said such a thing. Please forgive me."

"Eileen, I know. I know. But think of Beth. Think of what she's going through. Twice in a lifetime."

That night, Al rocked Alyssa, while Eileen slept. As the hour grew late, he dialed the number on the card he found pinned to the corkboard. It went directly to a chirrupy British voice that said, "Congratulations! You've reached the offices of Pieces by Reese, Film and Video Productions. You might think we have your phone number. But really, we don't keep anybody's. So repeat it a couple of times, do."

"I'm so sorry, Ben and Eliza, Beth and Pat," he said. "This is Al, Al Cafferty. And Alana and I . . ." Oh, God, Al thought and nearly put down the telephone. "*Eileen* and I want you to know we'll do anything. Anything. Anything in the world to help."

At that moment, Vincent was speaking to Walter Hutcheson's sister, Amy.

She said, "All those towns in Mexico sound the same to me. Flora del Rita. Rita del Flora. I'm just really happy for Walter and Sari. Happened all at once, suddenly, a baby in Mexico. They thought they would have to wait forever because they're over forty. The residence requirement is only ten days but they said they'd be gone probably three weeks. You know how it is in Mexico . . . Mañana, mañana. I'll tell them you called, though," said Amy. "I'm here taking care of Jerry Garcia and her kittens. Jerry they named her, right? And she has five kittens a month later."

"Tell them I'm really happy," Vincent said. "Do they have their cell phone with them?"

"They don't believe in cell phones. Gave that one Republican guy cancer."

"Oh. Yeah. Okay." Vincent turned to his father, who was awkwardly stretched out on the bed, looking about as uptight in the tracksuit Candy had bought for him as most people looked in a tux. "The Hutchesons are in Mexico. Adopting a *baby*. Pop, it's Mexico. They might never come back."

"Vincent, that's way too easy," Pat said.

Detective Humbly said, "We'll check it out but I have a feeling your dad might be right. These were the people who weren't happy about the movie but weren't hostile, right?" Vincent nodded. "And they haven't been in touch? I know a woman who monitors that stuff in Mexico. A good cop. And for every person I know there, Mr. Joel Berriman, FBI, will know ten."

Vincent lay down on the bed beside Pat. He said he would not sleep but didn't even finish the sentence before he was snoring.

Humbly called two hours later. The Hutchesons were not in Mexico, but in San Antonio, staying with the Rogelios until the interstate compact would allow them to bring home their five-day-old daughter, Annalee. She was the birth child of a twenty-year-old Mexican-American girl, a married student at the University of the Incarnate Word and the mother of a two-year-old. Her husband had just lost the use of his legs in the war. The Rogelios, with their new baby born right after the premiere—their third since losing Luis— were overjoyed about their new baby. They sent their love and concern to the Cappadoras. The Hutchesons apologized for not calling.

Pat considered waking Vincent. He knew that he should go look for Beth instead, but Sister Bartholomew used to tell them to let each day's evil be sufficient unto that day. Pat found a thick blanket on a shelf and lay down next to his son. Morning would come soon enough.

CHAPTER TEN

Later that night, when she and Pat and Kerry arrived at Vincent's house, filling it to more than capacity, Beth tried to make herself useful. She experimented, with the limited repertoire of cooking skills of a restaurateur's wife, to make an omelet that no one ate although it looked pretty good. She wiped the counters and put in the obligatory loads of laundry before realizing she was washing clothes that had never had the sales tags removed. She read a stack of *Variety*s, although Vincent's subscription evidently had stopped in 2007.

Finally, her limbs heavy as water balloons, she sat on the mattress where Pat slept. She lay down next to Pat, who had cocooned himself in a thick blanket, covered herself with two beach towels, pulled Pat's arm across her, and fell into a gray and intermittent sleep.

In the little box of a living room and kitchen, Vincent turned on the TV, finally finding a station that featured nothing about him or his family. It was a Marx Brothers movie. The hour grew late. Finally, without really meaning to, Vincent picked up and dialed the number on the card he'd had in a pocket of one of his blue-jean jackets for so long it was barely legible. The phone rang once.

"Tom?" Vincent said.

"Yes."

"This is Vincent Cappa—"

"Vincent! I wanted to call you but I didn't know if that would be an intrusion. And I don't have a home number for you," said Vincent's therapist. It was ironic that Vincent, a resident of California, had had his only counseling experience as an adolescent Chicagoan.

"I don't have a home number, Tom.

This is my business number and that's it. I wanted to call you but I didn't want you to think I would only call you if I was in trouble."

"I know you'd have called eventually, either way, about stuff."

Vincent said, "I'm in the worst trouble."

"I know, Vincent." There was a settling sound, a rustle and a soft, brief puppy whimper as Tom obviously got out of bed. "Do you want to talk about it?"

"Who's that?"

"It's my daughter. We let her sleep in the bed. Horrible father. Love her too much, I guess. We waited too long and now she's going to be this spoiled . . ."

"How old is she?"

"She is six months old, Vincent."

"Oh, shit," said Vincent, and the tears began to slip down his face and into his mouth. "Oh, shit."

"Yeah," said Tom. "Now, let's see. What time is it where you are, Vincent?"

"It's like . . . oh Jesus, Tom, it's one in the morning. That would make it like four in the morning where you are? Is Michigan in Central?"

"Eastern. But I get up early," Tom said.

"I'm sorry. But if I wanted to crack up a car before, when I lost Ben? This time, I'm not a kid who didn't know better. I did this. I did this and I cost my brother his kid and I'm fucked. My life is fucked. Which I don't care about. *Their* life is fucked. And they're innocent."

"So that would make you guilty."

"No. Yes."

Tom said, "No." He asked then, "Why did you make this movie, Vincent?"

"I don't know!"

"Did you do it for world peace?"

"No."

"Did you do it because you were sorry for what happened to Ben and wanted to make it better for someone else?"

"I guess. And it turned out worse."

Tom said, "Yeah, and that's bad. Life owes you an apology. But you're not going to get one. It doesn't work that way." Tom's voice softened. "And hey, guess what. You don't get to blame yourself for this one, either."

Vincent carried the phone out onto the porch, where the extravagantly benign California night bathed his face, as if to say, *nothing matters . . . nothing but you, remember that . . . nothing but you.* He said, "I wish you hadn't moved to goddamned Michigan."

Tom said, "It's not bad, here in goddamned Michigan. I knew my wife in high school, although she wouldn't look at me then. She's lowered her standards over twenty years. We live on a lake. Do you live near the ocean?"

"A block. I live in Venice. The crummy artist part, not the minor-movie-star part. You can hear the waves. They call it 'ocean sounds' in real-estate ads. I swear to God." He added, "I can't live with myself. No one in my family can."

"I think they can. Better than you know. Take it easy, Vincent."

"They'll hate me forever. They'll think I did this for me."

"Having a personal reason for doing something well doesn't negate the purer reasons, Vincent. Just think of Olympic athletes. They say they did this for their mom who loved to skate but she got macular degeneration . . ."

"What?"

"She went blind."

"Oh."

"And the thing that happened. It's not cause and effect. It's not *ad hoc ergo propter hoc.* It wasn't like you made a movie, therefore your niece . . ."

"Look, I'm not entirely illiterate, but I don't know what the hell that means either."

"It's a legal term. It means 'from which, therefore because of which.' Remember I went to law school for a year. You're not alone, are you?"

"No, my mom and dad are here."

"Good. Take care," Tom said. "I gotta run. My daughter's an early riser too." He added after a moment, "Vincent, try to do this. Just keep one thing in the front of your mind, okay? When Ben was kidnapped, you were a child, which presumes you were innocent. And now, you're an adult. But that doesn't make you automatically responsible for the actions of every nut on earth who sees your work. I watched your face on TV that night. You were glowing like the guy who discovered religion. And it wasn't that you had a big head about what an artist you were. It was about Kerry and

Ben and you having done this thing together. And about those children in the
film."

"And now," Vincent said.

"And now, you do your best. Ben will
need you. Count on it."

"Tom, who would do this thing?"

"I think, someone who had needs, like
the woman who kidnapped your brother.
I think they should be checking hospitals
for people in the area who recently lost
babies. Stillbirths. Or crib death or menin-
gitis. Young children."

"That's what my mother thinks. And they
are. They have been."

"And also people who have been somehow complicit in the loss of their children.
Accidents."

"Someone would steal another person's
baby because their baby got killed in a car
accident?" Vincent asked. "You say I'm
crazy . . ."

"People often feel guilty about things
that aren't their fault."

"Tom."

"Be good, my man."

Don't hang up, Vincent wanted to
scream. The pulse just above his sternum

began to beat and he tried to breathe out slowly before he spoke. *Don't leave me!* Finally, he said, "I'll give you a call again. Soon."

Vincent crossed his arms and watched the first of the insane California joggers set out on their endless runs to nowhere.

When his phone rang, at five a.m., he nearly fell out of the deck chair. It was Candy, telling him to brace himself for what she had to say. She told him, "There's a letter, Vincent."

"To us?"

"From the kidnapper. Sent to *The New York Times*."

"Is it real?"

"Either it's real or I'll turn in my shield," Candy said. "Wake your mom and dad up. Turn on the TV."

CHAPTER ELEVEN

The letter read:

The minor child Stella Bliss Cappadora is unharmed and well. She is being cared for gently. As proof that she indeed is the child in question, we point out that she has a pale brown birthmark on the back of her neck, roughly the shape of the State of Florida. She will be restored to her parents very soon at a place soon to be evident—a designated "safe place" such as a hospital emergency room. This deliverance will occur within hours.

The taking of Stella Cappadora is to be considered a demonstration. It intends to point out the fact that, while the world gazed fatuously on the acclaim given to a film exploiting the feelings of five families of abducted children, a child from the film-maker's own family was abducted without violence.

"Caring" is not enough. It changes nothing. It advances no knowledge of causes or solutions—merely provides those who vicariously experience grief the phenomenon known by some as "contact compassion," which allows them the sense of having done good merely by understanding the "issue." It is no more than satisfying the voyeurism of the masses who feed on pain.

This demonstration, however painful, was a direct result of the acclaim accorded to what was essentially a dishonest bid for attention. *Ad hoc ergo propter hoc,* in essence. It redirects the focus, in a way that could not be achieved without a certain level of sensationalism.

Any temporary distress caused to the Cappadoras is unintentional.

Along with the letter was a package containing Stella's little satin shoes—embroidered with stars on the toes and her name on the heels by Candy's sister, the baby's great-aunt. It was mailed from Vancouver by priority mail and the security footage in the post office seemed to show a pleasant-faced woman, dressed like a grandmother in her fifties or sixties, wearing an oversized wool hat, smiling at the postal worker. She signed the register "Patricia Fellows" and gave her address as 1060 West Addison Street in Chicago—which was Wrigley Field. There were no fingerprints. The woman, said a Vancouver police officer, could have been anyone. In any books in Canada, or any computer files, there was no trace of her under any name. And, they added, after analyzing the tape, despite her cloth coat and old-fashioned orthopedic shoes, the woman actually walked like someone in her twenties.

Although the false name of the murdered child in Chicago was used again, that proved nothing to Detective Humbly except that Candy might be right: This was personal.

The letter itself was strange. Although it was obviously written by someone with a brain—which was some comfort—it was convoluted and drew no real conclusions, which was no comfort at all. Smart people could snap their caps as easy as vagrants.

"The letter is goofy," Candy said, as Humbly drove her, Ben, and Eliza to a little guesthouse in Venice, near where Beth and Pat were staying with Vincent. Beth and Pat had come back to help, offering the trunk of their rental, which Ben had used to stow a couple of garment bags, without saying a word.

Rosie and Angelo had gone home that morning.

"Bethie, my daughter," Angelo said. "I am an old man but I never wanted to be old enough to see this. We thought life might be kind now." For the first time, Beth saw her vital, mischievous in-laws as truly old, even frail. They leaned on Pat as he escorted them to the car that Charley Seven had summoned by phone call. There was nothing she could say to comfort them, nothing to soften the splinter wedged hard into the contentment of their age. Angelo was right. They had seen too much, all of them. More than was possible to comprehend or intellectualize.

The only one who chose to stay at the Paloma was George, whose wife and six-year-old son had flown out to join him.

"Pat," George said as the Cappadoras left. "You'll let me know. . . ."

"Of course, everything, George," Pat said. "No hard feelings. I know that what Ben said didn't have anything to do with you."

Ben said nothing. He said nothing on the ride, although because of the dimensions of the squad car, he had to ride in the backseat of his father's rental car.

The management of the Paloma had offered to put the Cappadoras up . . . forever if need be; but no one wanted to stay anymore.

At the end, that morning just before they left, Candy and Beth were lost in skeins of memory as they watched the command center in the hotel dismantled, as the command center in the Tremont Hotel lobby in Chicago had been dismantled after the first few days following Ben's kidnapping—when it became apparent that they were in for a long haul rather than a short and ugly solution.

Hauling Eliza's things, along with Ben's few things, into the guest house gave Pat and Candy something to do.

Alone with Vincent, who was inert, Beth was frantic. Hope seemed close at one hand. Destruction seemed to have the other hand pinned. She decided to arrange her son's home—since rearranging it would have been a misnomer. Vincent had basically moved some elements of furniture into his cinder-block space, which was maybe twenty by twenty feet divided into two cubes, and shoved everything against the wall. The living room was basically a futon and a huge table—the table holding a laptop surrounded by at least ten stacks of paper three inches thick and a corkboard covered with thicknesses of slides and still photos. In the kitchen portion of the "big" room, a sink and stovetop stood like bookends on either side of the refrigerator. A piece of Formicaed planking jutted out into the room. Beth supposed this was counter space.

On the floor and against the wall were a

large 7UP sign and a huge yucca plant beyond the sincerest hopes for survival. Behind the screen in the bedroom were a mattress with clean sheets and one pillow, a few transparent plastic storage bins labeled SOCKS and SWEATS, and a dentist's chair pointed at two TVs and two stereos.

There was a bag containing an unopened shower curtain. Beth strung that together with the rings and put it up. Trolling through the refrigerator then, Beth threw out a bulging trash bag filled with grisly Styrofoam boxes of takeout and dumped some milk that was on the verge of cottage cheese.

She folded the sleeping bag where Kerry had lain and topped it off with the pillow. Kerry, who'd said she needed to move, had walked the mile or so to see Candy.

Finally, there was nothing left for Beth to do.

"No one wants to eat, but we can go get a few things," said Vincent. "Maybe coffee and bread and milk and bologna and frozen pizza." Beth fought the urge to gag at the mention of lunch meat. "I can't believe that Pop went in there with them given what Ben said."

"You will someday," Beth told him quietly.

As they drove along in Vincent's ancient Citroën, Vincent said, "Ma. It's bugging me. Something about that letter. I have this sense of something about it. But I don't know what. If I could talk to Rob or Emily . . ."

"Emily?"

"The editor, Emily Sydney. . . . I know something's in the film. A link. Somewhere."

The telephone in the office vibrated, like some kind of little insect trapped in Rob Brent's hand. He dropped it and nearly hit the floor after it: He had been asleep in his desk chair and his leg was numb.

For so many hours, it had toned the old Blondie song "Call Me" nonstop, with other calls breaking in on the first calls, which, when he switched over, were interrupted by other calls, until his jaw literally ached from answering questions he had no answers for. No one knew Vincent's number but Pieces by Reese was listed for both of them, two lines. Finally, Rob had switched off the tone and set the phone to vibrate.

He sat up and rubbed his stubbled jaw. He was going to put this phone down, once and for all, take a long shower, and fall in his bed for eight or fourteen deep ones. There was nothing he could do. Nothing.

He laid the phone on the table. It brrred again, spinning in its insistence. At the same moment, the fax machine erupted with a waterfall of sheets that spilled onto the floor. Rob picked up the first. It said the same thing as the second and the third and all twenty that came after.

PICK UP PICK UP PICK UP IT IS VIN-CENT I NEED TO FIND EMILY WE WILL COME TO THE STUDIO IT'S A LEGAL TERM IT'S A LEGAL TERM.

CHAPTER TWELVE

"They'll check it out, thoroughly," Candy said. "They'll go through the whole film. Humbly and the FBI guy."

"Thoroughly enough for you?" Vincent pressed her.

"Vincent, it's never thoroughly enough for me," Candy said. "Not ever and especially not now."

"Let's make sure, then," Vincent said. "Then we'll call Humbly. It'll take what . . . a few minutes to find the exact place he said something like that?"

It took eleven hours. And that was after

Vincent got Emily to California from Canada.

Vincent called everyone he knew and it was finally the production company that had purchased *No Time to Wave Goodbye* that found a charter to fly Emily the editor down from Vancouver. By 6 p.m., she was in Venice. Candy and Vincent drove to the studio, the majority of which was in Rob's house, with Beth and Pat following. Vincent's genial partner, Rob, met them there. They all went into the studio with Emily and watched as, with absolute efficiency, the small, quiet girl pulled her dark hair back into an elastic band without a thought for how many ends poked out. As Pat watched, he thought, This is definitely not a Hollywood chick.

"Where do you want to start?" she asked.

"Well, of course with the Whittiers. Like I told you, the kidnapper used legal language. The part about Jackie's depression or Blaine's perspective before and after . . . I don't think those could have any bearing," Vincent said. Where exactly had Bryant Whittier mentioned the fixation on the tragedy of others as a form of something . . . something bad, like pornography, but that wasn't the word? Was it Bryant for sure?

Or had it been Walter Hutcheson? Hutcheson too was articulate. He had a degree. He resented intrusions on their privacy in Laurel's name. . . .

But no. It had to be Whittier: No one else was so pompous or verbose. No one else had used that phrase about cause and effect. But when? Where in the film?

Slice by slice, they searched the rough cut. Vincent's head ached, and the little room seemed to fill with a mist of exhaled anxiety.

There was an extraordinary amount of footage. The Whittiers had been first; Vincent had had no idea how much film they would need for each segment, so they'd spent the most on the Whittiers—nine hours. After Emily had set up her own programs, she and Vincent were able to search by references to what was pictured on the screen or, using another strategy, to spoken words. After an hour of searching, they couldn't find "contact compassion" or "sensationalism."

"What if he used another word?" Emily asked.

"Are you sure it was that word?" Candy asked. "That was in the letter. In the movie, it was 'voyeurism.' I think it was."

"I don't remember him saying that when we interviewed him, though. And even more, I don't remember that whole sequence. Maybe it was out of sequence. It has to be at the beginning or the end. It sounds like a wrapping-up thing—you know, 'in conclusion. . . .' I could never have imagined that I'd ever forget a word anyone said," Vincent marveled. "Now it all seems like a lifetime ago."

"Excellent illustration of the theory of relativity," Emily murmured. "Time really is flexible." She downloaded a larger thesaurus. She tried other words—"lasciviousness," "obscenity," "voyeurism"—straining the words, one by one, through the opening and closing segments. They found nothing.

"Try them all in segment four," Vincent suggested. "The one tagged Social Responsibility."

Emily plugged in each of the key words. On "voyeurism" they got a hit.

"Is this it?" Pat asked and began to cough.

"I hope so, Pop," Vincent said. "What's the matter? Did you choke?"

"No, I, uh, I forgot to breathe."

"Don't have a heart attack, Pop. It's rush hour in Southern California. You're dead two hours before an ambulance gets here."

Pat said, "I'm fine."

"Turn it up," Vincent told Emily.

They heard Bryant Whittier say, "For one thing, people have compassion fatigue. The instant dissemination of every piece of tragic footage, worldwide, has worn out genuine personal concern. We're a global society. Our eyes can't be on every sparrow. A child is safe in a hospital after an earthquake but then is stolen by a sexual slavery ring. It batters the mind. It's not like it was with Ben. Do we weep for the child who drowned on the beach in the tsunami or the one who was saved and abducted?"

"Shit," Vincent interrupted, as Emily hit pause. "Does he ever stop yakking?"

"Shhhh," Emily told Vincent.

Bryant went on, "Or the child left in the

car while her mother went into the store to buy diapers, who died of heat exhaustion? Her mother was a client of mine. Responsible for the death, yes, but criminally negligent? No, simply a young, very young woman left holding the bag by her simpleton boyfriend. The only people who stay obsessed with these things are people who are awake far too late at night or in front of the television far too . . ."

"Where is it?" Vincent asked.

"Wait," Emily said. "Be patient."

"I'm not."

"Right," she replied.

Bryant Whittier continued, "For them, it's a form of addiction. It's like people who chase tornadoes. They think knowing about something can change it—after which, therefore because of which, *ad hoc ergo propter hoc* . . ."

"That's the thing Tom said. The phrase in Latin. . . . That was what it was," Vincent said.

Rob looked up from his laptop. "*Ad hoc ergo* whatever. Play it again, Emily, please." Emily did.

Then, on Emily's screen, Bryant went

on. And on. "People who like to get excited over other people's triumphs, like sports fans, or weep for the tragedies of people they will never meet . . . it's almost voyeurism."

"Bingo," Emily breathed.

"So it has to be him," Vincent said. "He said both things. He said they were voyeurs and that just caring didn't influence or change anything. He said the same thing that was in the letter. There's a legal term . . . *Ad hoc* something something . . ."

Vincent continued, "I never heard the phrase until last night. I wouldn't have even thought of it if Tom hadn't mentioned it. And it's the connection."

"You talked to Tom, your old therapist?" Pat asked. "That's good."

"I'm glad you were listening when you talked to him," Emily said. "So we know that this footage wasn't in the final cut. And it can't be something a person could pick up from watching the movie."

Vincent asked, "But was it in the first cut? The one that was screened in Chicago? Oh, Jesus."

"Search the term," Rob suggested, squeezing his bulk into the group surrounding Emily.

"I would, but I won't know the exact phrase until I hear it or even something like it," Vincent said. Backing away, Rob sat down on the floor against the wall and opened his own laptop.

"No," Emily said, her fingers flying over the keys. "Wait. Let's be sure. Let me check." She reached out for a cup of coffee on which the milk had gone to greasy film and looked down at it doubtfully. Pat replaced it with a fresh cup.

"Beth bought new milk," said Pat. "It's safe, Emily."

Emily said then, "Thanks, Mr. Cappadora. It's good coffee. You make good coffee. Not like Vincent."

"He doesn't measure it," Pat said. "He just eyeballs what looks like it should make the right number of cups."

Emily asked, "You *measure* it?"

Pat nearly laughed and said, "Are you kidding or serious?"

"I'm serious," Emily said. "I never knew people measured coffee."

Pat smiled, the crooked, boyish look

awakening a face that seemed to have aged twenty years in just days. Looking at his father, Vincent was reminded of Walter Hutcheson's frosty-gray ponytail. How could Vincent have suspected Walter, the simple, good-hearted old hippie? Bryant Whittier must dye his hair, Vincent thought then. He was between the ages of Vincent's parents. He had to have some gray, not a full head of chestnut cut like old pictures of Ronald Reagan.

That didn't mean he was a psycho, though.

"It's a teaspoon of grounds for every cup," Pat told Emily. "And you have to make sure the water's ice cold and if you really want it good, you rinse out some eggshells and put them in with the grounds."

"Why?" Emily asked.

"I have no idea," his father admitted. "My ma said to."

"Here. Here it is!" Emily said suddenly. "Now we know for sure. No part of that phrase or those words was in the first or final cut."

"Emily, let's get married," Vincent said.

"Okay. Let's see how this works out first." She stood up and kissed Vincent on the cheek.

"Emily, when I call his wife, Claire, can we tape it somehow?" Vincent asked. "Will you stay, like a witness? You don't have to be back in Vancouver till like . . . tonight?"

"Tomorrow is good."

"I'll get you the best hotel room in town."

"It's okay. I can just stay here if you have a sleeping bag or a futon. Your dad can teach me to make coffee."

Vincent said, quietly, "Okay."

"The recording. Like a wiretap?"

"Sure."

"You don't have equipment. All you can do is put a regular microphone with a cup on the receiver. I think it's illegal."

"Not if you have the consent of one of the parties in the conversation," said Rob.

"How do you know that?" Vincent asked.

"Former life," Rob said, rummaging for one of his dozen tiny digital recorders. "Here. Just press the button when she picks up. Use my phone. All it says is Robert Brent."

"I can't call her right now," Vincent said. "The sun is barely up."

"Aw, go ahead," Rob told him.

The rain dripping from the evergreens outside the house was the consistency of a child's slush drink. Claire Whittier wondered if she'd be warm enough. She wore trousers with a pair of tights under them and her travel raincoat and Jackie's black ballet flats, with her walking shoes in her small satchel. Because Bryant was so thrifty and the cost of flying out of Los Angeles was less than from San Francisco—at least for this trip—Claire would take a car service all the way from Durand to L.A., saving, from what Bryant had said, the cost of two more nights in Tuscany. It would also save him the trouble of coming back from his meeting to their home. Bryant said he would not live in California if there were no San Francisco and would not live near San Francisco if there were not a civilized small town such as Durand; he loathed the southern part of the state. Still, it was a long drive for Claire, even though she wouldn't be at the wheel. She had two novels in her carryall. She might sleep. Claire had not slept well lately. Not even her customary pills had helped.

When the phone rang, Claire jumped, startled.

It was her neighbor, Laura Pool, who would be caring for the dog, Macduff, and bringing in the mail while they were in Italy. Claire had been unable to tell her friend Laura exactly how long they would be away; Bryant hadn't been specific. But he was rarely able to be absent from the office for more than two weeks. Claire had asked Gary, their longtime caretaker, to drive up to the summerhouse. If the weather turned nice in the coming weeks, as it surely must, Gary would air it out and check for any winter damage or bats in the eaves. Bryant would be eager to go up there when they arrived home, perhaps at Blaine's spring break.

"Claire, did you turn on the television this morning?" Laura said. "*The New York Times* has a story about this kidnapper's letter. It's online."

Claire asked, "The kidnapper? Of the Cappadora baby?"

"Yes," Laura told her. "It might be real or

it might not. I know how you are with computers. I'll just print it out and pop over."

Shivering, Claire decided to drape a
black shawl she had left up in her bedroom
over her trench coat. Running back down,
she opened the door for her neighbor,
noticing, as she did, a postcard that had
fallen through the mail chute with a few
business envelopes and catalogs.

"Brrr," said Laura. "I moved to California
for the sunshine. This is not what I was
promised."

"Don't be a simp," Claire told her. "By
now, most years, it's beautiful. This is the
longest winter I can remember."

"Anyhow, here's the story." Laura stood
beside Claire as Claire read the article
and the text of the letter. "I think the person sounds intelligent. But so did the Un-
abomber," said Laura.

"I think it's interesting that he says, or
she says, that the baby will be returned
safe. And that what the person wants is to
make a point."

"In a pretty roundabout way," Laura
said.

Not for a lawyer, Claire thought.

At that moment, a cold drop landed in

the dark cradle of her stomach. "Thank you, Laura, for everything," said Claire.

The women hugged. Then Laura stroked Claire's hair. "This must make you think of . . . Jackie. All the police questioning and the false leads. People are writing in online that they think this is a confessor, too. Probably works at the library. But I do hope what he says is all real."

After Laura left, Claire looked at the postcard. It pictured the underwater state park in La Jolla. But it had been mailed three days earlier, from Chicago.

What a fool he thought she was, so unobservant as to miss a postmark. She got out her mobile phone to call him, knowing that in ordinary times, he'd be up, doing a brief workout with his workout cords. But his voice mail picked up.

Claire left the phone anchoring the slip of paper from Laura's printer on the front hall table and walked down the hall to Bryant's office.

She had gone into Bryant's office before, of course, but not often.

It had been one of Mother Whittier's admonitions—which, according to Bryant's sister-in-law Jeannie, amounted to a manual of operating instructions—that the two best things a woman could do to preserve a long marriage to a Whittier man were never to work outside the home and always to honor the man's private space.

Claire braced herself hand to hand in the doorway, scanning Bryant's rows of glass-fronted barrister's bookcases, his costly but austere displays of photos of Jacqueline and Blaine and of the four of them together—up at their summerhouse in the San Juan Diego mountains.

There were others of Bryant and Jackie alone, skiing up at the few acres of vacant land that were once owned by Bryant's lumber-baron grandfather, where Claire had never gone, where he and his brothers went to hunt.

There was a photo of them here, at home in Durand, outside the front door, under the very eaves that were dripping now, next to the lilacs, on the day of Blaine's high-school graduation. All of them were arranged in neat and matching silver frames.

Bryant's personal files were in a walnut cabinet. His desktop computer was turned off; his tray of fountain pens and sharpened pencils was set perpendicular to the hinges. An enormous weight seemed to force Claire back, toward the safety of the rest of her calm and familiar house, to her neatly packed suitcase in the foyer and her umbrella at the ready. Back where things were manageable and familiar. Her breath came in gasps and she thought she might become light-headed if she did not sit down.

But she went on. She went inside.

Slowly, she drew open the center drawer of Bryant's massive kidney-shaped desk, which had been his father's. The key to the filing cabinet was labeled, one of several keys hanging from small tassels on a flat holder built into the drawer's commodious interior. With freezing hands, she picked up the key and opened the filing cabinet and then, quickly, before she could change her mind, she extracted the file of American Express statements for the past six months and other files—two labeled KIDNAPPINGS. These were both stuffed with clippings from newspapers and computer printouts describing cases that dated back two or more years. All of the cases had ended badly, Claire noticed, as she skimmed. Some were horrifying. She gathered them up and placed them one on top of the other in stacks.

She looked back at anything that might interest her and found another curious file. It was labeled MALAYSIA, WORKING AND LIV-ING. Still another had a tab that read MALAYSIA, RETIREMENT.

Claire smoothed the credit-card state-ments out on the desk in front of her.

There was a payment in early February to something called Small Shelters, a sub-stantial charge, $9,600. Bryant had made many purchases from a website called ChildFair, which were enumerated on the bill from last month and the previous month as Supplies, Equipment, and Notions. He had purchased a true off-track vehicle, a big one, made by Land Rover, a car that cost $85,000. On Bryant's desk, in a stur-dier cardboard, was an amended copy of their will, leaving the houses and their con-tents to Blaine and/or her descendants. Claire's stomach churned audibly, the slice of toast and cup of tea she'd consumed two hours earlier suddenly threatening the base of her throat. The document be-fore her on the desk transferred both the houses and their contents to Blaine immediately if Bryant or Claire should relocate outside the United States or otherwise be incapacitated by illness, institutionalization, or any circumstance that would prevent their administration of their home and finances. A sum of money had been transferred to an account in Blaine's name to complete her college and set her up for the first year afterward. The balance was in trust.

The vacant mountain acreage, higher up and deeper into the San Juan Diego range than their second home, would be donated to the Nature Conservancy. Some years earlier, Bryant had bought his brothers' share of the inherited and undeveloped land.

Bryant had forged Claire's spidery signature.

On everything.

From the second long drawer, to her left as she sat in Bryant's chair, Claire pulled out the big leather-bound checkbook. There were many checks made out to cash over the past month, in sums that Claire believed were unlike Bryant's usual prudence—$35,000, $25,000, $14,000—

and the notations in the margins were "services rendered" and nothing more.

She stood to reach for a leather binder embossed with the initials JBW. In it was a single sheet of paper. It read, *Jacqueline, my bird, my angel, Jacqueline, my hope, my heart, my prism, my mirror. I avenge you with my every breath.*

Claire's cell phone rang and again she jumped. Suddenly, it seemed that she was part of an alien landscape, a child in a haunted house.

The ID said Rob Brent. She didn't know a Rob Brent.

Claire said, "Hello?"

"Claire, it's Vincent."

"Vincent."

"I hoped I could talk to Bryant."

"He's . . . not here, Vincent. He's at a business meeting in Los Angeles."

"Claire . . ."

"I was to meet him at the airport."

"Which airport?" Vincent asked.

"LAX."

"Are you going on a trip?"

"Vincent, I assume this is about the letter to *The New York Times.* I'm sure that's good news. I know it is. I hope it is."

"Claire," Vincent asked gently, "where are you and Bryant going?"

"It's our twenty-fifth-anniversary trip. To Italy. We went there on our honeymoon. I'm not sure what to do now. I haven't left home." Claire's voice trembled; her stomach was now rampaging, like an empty cage with a wild bird released into it blinded—whirling and crashing against the sides. "Vincent. I've found some . . . things."

"What things?"

"I don't think I should really talk about this without Bryant."

"Claire, I need to talk to you in person."

Claire said, "Yes. But Vincent, you must know, Stella is really fine. She is fine. I am sure of it."

"Did he tell you?"

"No," Claire said. "I'm afraid I can't speak anymore now, Vincent." Claire put down the phone and when it began to ring again, she turned off the ringer and absently opened her novel. The words might as well have been the katakana that Blaine studied in her Japanese class. Claire's eyes blurred with tears she wiped at with the heels of her hands. *My bird, my angel,*

my prism. . . . Claire phoned the car service and canceled. She turned back on the
heat that she had lowered because they
would be gone and wrapped herself in a
thicker shawl that was tucked on her closet
shelf.

She thought of the gladsome childhood
she had known and how, sadly, there was
no love lost between her husband and her
father, who considered Bryant pretentious. Bryant no longer permitted Claire to
invite the Putnams to her home. She had
believed that, after Jacqueline was lost,
there would be a thaw born of a family's
mourning. It had not yet happened. But
Claire cherished her single trip each year
to Chicago. She played game after game
of cutthroat bridge with her quiet brother,
who taught creative writing at the University of Illinois. Each time she witnessed
how erudite and jovial, active and com-
panionable, her parents still were in their
eighties, she thought of how she and
Bryant might have been . . . if life had
taken a different turning.

Now forty-four years old, Claire had
never had a major illness, not even a
twinge of arthritis.

She had years of hours and days and months that would gradually accrete . . . become years, and decades. What was to become of her now? She went into the kitchen and turned on the electric kettle.

Claire heard a soft knock at the door. Passing to the front door, she glanced out the window and was not surprised to see Sarah Switch, the young woman who was the sheriff of Cisco County.

"Come in," Claire said, putting out her hand. "Hello. I think we've met."

"Yes. At the library ball. I'm afraid I wasn't the belle of the ball, but I tried. I'll bet you know why I'm here," said Sheriff Switch.

"Yes, I do. It's about my husband and the Cappadora baby. Are you going to arrest me?"

"Of course not. Mrs. Whittier, I'm just here to wait for the others to get here so we can talk this all out. They'll be here on a flight from Los Angeles that arrives in a few hours."

"Yes, but it's important, before we do, to call Vincent Cappadora. I don't think I told him that I know where Bryant would take the baby, if he has her. And it's important that he know now."

"How do you know?"

"From things Bryant purchased. I went through our credit-card statements. He would take her to our summer house in the mountains. It's remote and sort of off the grid. Well, it's not really remote. It's just twenty miles from here. There are other people, mostly from farther away, who have homes up there. But Bryant always liked to keep the place really basic, like a cabin. A cabin with a gourmet kitchen and five bedrooms. But we have our own generator and so on if the power goes off . . ."

"Why would you think he would take her there? Why not a hotel or a house with whoever helped him . . . take her away?"

"I don't know for certain. It's a hunch. But I know Bryant. He's very predictable in his routines."

"Why wouldn't he just go to Mexico with her? You were going away. The baby's a dark-haired little girl who wouldn't look out of place. He has his passport if you were going on an international trip anyhow," Sheriff Switch argued.

"No, he wouldn't do that. The letter said he was going to leave Baby Stella in a safe place. I'm sure that he was, or is, going to do that and then he'll meet me at the air- port as we planned. He bought provi- sions . . . things. For a baby. All that is on our American Express bill. He wouldn't have needed a Land Rover to drive around Los Angeles or San Francisco, and I mean a true Land Rover, not one of those street vehicles. But he used to drive up to our summer house in a big pickup truck. It was big enough for the four of us. But not for a baby and her gear. Do you see?" Claire said urgently.

"You have a point, but he could as eas- ily go somewhere else. . . ." Sarah Switch said.

"Bryant doesn't intend to keep Stella Cappadora! His plan would be to drop her off somewhere safe, maybe a hospital right here in San Francisco. Why would he go to another state or another country? He'd go to our summer place. It's close and it would be a place to keep her safe until he was ready to drive down to Los An- geles. Maybe he's already on the way. I'm sure he knows that the weather says that

it's going to snow again up there. Tonight
and at least for the next few days. Our
flight to Rome isn't until late, very late tonight. Bryant is very skillful, but I'm worried
he might not be able to get out if he waited.
So he won't wait."

"We will call Vincent, Mrs. Whittier."

"Please call right now," Claire said. "I'm
sure Stella is already at a safe place. Have
you called the hospitals?"

"The state police and the volunteers are
doing that now. Everyone in every church
or ER or home health care agency in California, at least all the ones we can find, will
be on alert and have a copy of Stella's picture within the hour," said the sheriff.

"Are you afraid of your husband?"

"No, I'm not," Claire said. "But whoever
walks up to Bryant should be. Especially in
our summerhouse in the mountains. He
has at least three rifles. He's strong and fit
and he's not . . . in his right mind."

CHAPTER THIRTEEN

They arrived in Durand, the Whittiers' tiny hometown just outside San Francisco. With relative ease, they found the Whittiers' spare but palatial stone house on Paramount Street. Vincent's gut guess, combined with Claire Whittier's account of the bizarre contents of her husband's office, had pushed all of them out of the face-off poses they'd held since the ugly scene at the hotel between Beth and Ben.

Ben still would not speak to his brother except to answer yes-or-no questions, but to Candy, who watched the two with the semidetached eye of an aunt rather than a mother, his silence seemed to savor more of shame than aggression. Ben acknowledged his parents, his eyes downcast. Eliza was eager to hug Beth and Pat at the least opportunity, as if to apologize for her husband. Kerry shuttled between her brothers like a human viaduct, trying to heal with soft words. Eliza was busy doing something that Beth remembered doing herself—trying not to know what was going on for fear she might learn something that would devastate her.

Ben and Vincent were straining at the bit, eager to try something. Anything.

But having flown north from L.A. and been rushed from San Francisco International Airport to a forest ranger's station, they were now all standing around a room the size of an apartment kitchen, listening to what Candy thought amounted to a territorial pissing match.

"Because it would be suicide to go up into those mountains on foot in this weather," Sarah Switch told Bill Humbly and Agent Joel Berriman. The predicted snow had already begun to fall, steadily and then heavily. "There's not enough snow for a snowmobile and it's too slushy to ski. If we take a big vehicle, we might as well drive five feet and park it because it's going to go down up to the wheel wells. The snow and frozen muck are deeper up there than down here."

Berriman kept pacing back and forth between the young, stern sheriff and Humbly, announcing himself over and over as "from the Bureau"—as though the blond-haired Sarah Switch, who towered over both of them, was not only exasperated but ignorant. If Berriman said one more thing about "the Bureau," Humbly had decided, he would trip him.

"We have good reason to believe that this baby is in danger," said Bill Humbly. "This guy could be really unstable. You heard what his wife said. We don't know how taking care of a baby would fit in with his obsession. And the baby's health could be in danger . . ."

"Why do you think that? He was specific about saying she was in good health," said the sheriff. The woman must be six-two easy, Humbly thought. Humbly imagined someone trying to say her name three times fast. On second thought, she was very good-looking, sort of a beach-volleyball-type lady, maybe no more than thirty-five years old, if that. Switch had driven herself up from her office in a small brick building on Center Street in Durand, a few miles outside town, to the ranger's building. She wanted the police and the Cappadora family to get a look at the country they were so eager for her rescuers, mostly volunteers, to go bounding into—and how forbidding it was in this state of weather. She wanted to tell them how merciless it could be. On a dry day in summer or fall, or even with a nice packed-down snow in winter, driving up to the Whittiers' summer home, just twenty miles north and east of Durand, would be nothing to worry about. The house, like other hunting cabins and bigger family homes, lay up a very gradual mountain road. In summer or fall, there would be others around, if anyone did get a flat tire or break an axle. But that would likely not happen. The trip would be nothing more than a bumpy little ride. A good truck would ignore the rocks and the damage winter storms left. An off-road recreation vehicle would make it smooth sailing.

But early spring was tricky. The temperatures in Durand, and even farther south, in the city of San Francisco, could be deceiving. The mountain canyons were colder. They held on to the winter longer. This year, the combination of the wet snow and temperatures that let conditions alternately freeze and thaw made it treacherous. A friend of Sheriff Switch's who was as experienced a hiker as Sarah was herself had put a ski wrong in one of the lower meadows the previous week and snapped an ankle. There was that crazy, tragic case of the family with the little kids who decided to take them camping—from the very trailhead where the ranger station stood—and gone only about five miles in.

Which had been enough for a tragedy.

In her car, she'd brought Claire Whittier and her daughter, Blaine, who'd come home in the early afternoon, courtesy of a company jet volunteered by the father of one of her roomies. The Whittier women sat silent, hands clasped. On the way, Switch had spent time worrying about the officers she'd meet from Los Angeles and how they would try to boss her around, just as they were doing. But Switch knew her territory. Cisco County covered half a million acres geographically but was home to only six thousand full-time inhabitants. Despite all that country, Switch's experience with kidnapping amounted to zero. The thought that the baby might be in danger from the creepy guy who Claire Whittier had described turned her guts to water. She would later tell Bill Humbly that her experience with homicide amounted to one event—a domestic between a lovely half-Miwok woman and her Anglo husband that had been bubbling in a slow cooker for as long as anyone could remember: There was a sort of bet about who would get in the fatal blow and who would get in the way of it. It turned out to be the husband who went down, the weapon a large-sized can of tomato paste.

There had been deaths. Mountain deaths over the years. Stupid hikers and backpackers, five or six, who'd done the equivalent of going deep-sea diving alone. There were harder types who said fools like that deserved what they got.

Switch thought nobody deserved a slow and terrifying death.

But the people who did rescues for her

were as important as the Cappadora baby. Except that she was a baby.

Humbly tried to appeal to Sarah Switch's womanly instincts.

"Here's just one example. What if there was enough formula in those bags for three or four days, no more? This is the sixth day. But more than that, he very likely has no idea how to care for a baby on his own . . ." Humbly said. "And I don't think he would take the chance of having the people who took her along with him. I don't think they'd put themselves in that kind of harm's way, if they were the type who'd do this to begin with."

Berriman said, "We think that that so-called couple were either paid by Whittier or owed him something because of a defense he did, probably for someone close to them, since they're not in the system . . ."

"Or if they are," Humbly put in, "it's not with current names or hair color or birthdays. You heard what we found out about the car rental. That it was under the name of a girl who was kidnapped and murdered in Beth Cappadora's neighborhood when Beth was a young girl too? That was how we knew it was someone who knew the family . . . how we knew for sure, that is."

"I read the fax you sent over before you came up," said Switch. "But I don't see why Whittier would have any need to take care of the baby himself. Why wouldn't he just keep his hands off and let them take care of the baby and drop her off? If he did, they'd be the ones in trouble."

"They'd be in trouble along with him. All that stuff in his office nails him," said Berriman. "And even if it didn't, we're talking someone who's quite a few bubbles to the left of plumb, Sheriff. You saw that letter. We don't think someone with a crazy ego like that would want to, well, share the credit for this. Either he's making a point or he thought he was making a point and now he knows he isn't. Either way, it's not good for the baby."

Before Switch could speak again, Ben Cappadora stepped up and thrust his shoulder back. He said, "What is all this conferencing about? Is my daughter up there or not? Is anyone going up there for her? Is there a hunting cabin or something up there or isn't there?"

"It's a lot bigger than a hunting cabin,"

said Blaine Whittier, coming up behind him. "Sam, I'm trying to help, so please forgive me for saying anything. It's a big house, like, not as big as our house back there in Durand, and not on a street. But it's on a real road and it has all the comforts. If my father is there with Stella, she's safe."

"Yeah, right," said Ben. "I'm certain of it."

"I mean . . . I'm sorry," Blaine said. "The house is safe."

Sheriff Switch explained to Ben how the weather complicated what might otherwise be a simple decision to have a look-see. She didn't mention that everyone's fear of what Bryant Whittier might do was a more vital consideration.

Bill Humbly took over again. "Sheriff. What we figure is that the so-called couple who took her either went back under whatever white-collar rock they crawled out from under, where they probably don't have big sunglasses and blond hair, or they're speaking Spanish by now."

"Why?" the sheriff asked.

"Three people doesn't make for a secret," Detective Humbly went on. "They could start blackmailing Whittier right back if they forget they have their own skeletons in their own closets . . . which means he's probably on his own by now and he might have the jits . . . maybe he didn't mean for it to go this far or he didn't know what it would be like if it did."

The sheriff leaned back in what Humbly assumed must be a form of repose taught only to people who grew up in the mountainous West, her thumbs hooked in her belt.

"That makes sense," she said. "But I still don't get the fired-up need to go right now. I don't get why you presume that the person who abducted this child and who owns a virtual mansion down here in town and another one up in the San Juan Diego Mountains and has the means and know-how to get there through this much snow is too clueless to buy formula or change a diaper," she said. "If he's even up there. Or ever was."

"Sheriff, please," Humbly began. "I'm not saying for sure. There's a good chance though. What if she's crying nonstop? What if he flips out?"

Switch pursed her lips and fiddled with the end of her thick braid. Finally, she said,

"Well, what we can do is a hasty search of this immediate area, see whether any vehicle has passed through here in the past week. I can get the forest service to help, but they're shorthanded because of that case with the campers who got stranded in the snowstorm a few days ago," she began. "You read about that. And we have a group of Eagle Scouts trained in Operation Find."

Eagle Scouts, Humbly thought. Okay, this was going to be a kid movie. It needed only a Baldwin brother.

"I'm going to have to assert . . ." Berriman began.

"Stop," Humbly and Switch said together.

Switch went on, "The weather is unstable, of course. And that's what worries me. Bryant Whittier has been away from home for what, nearly a week? He may have gone in with her twenty-four hours before the first snowstorm, not the one we're having now, which, by the way, isn't even a snowstorm by our standards. The campers were found two days ago. Those people who took the baby, back in Los Angeles, if they were working for Whittier, might also have brought supplies up there. They might have brought the baby up here. But since the snow, maybe they're not sufficient. He may not be able to get out, even with that big honking truck he bought." She paused to think as she leaned over the topographical maps that were laminated on the ranger's desk. "Now from what Blaine here said, presumably he has some kind of water source. It's not a little shack. There's plenty of water up there. That's really all he needs. A day isn't going to make a difference. Let the weather settle down. And no one said we wouldn't try to get someone to fly over. I'm just not sending anyone up there on a foot search. Or a snowmobile either." She turned to the FBI agent. "And sir, I am the sheriff of Cisco County. I assign the case number. I decide if and in what way a search will proceed. I decide what manner of and how much help we request from federal agencies or other jurisdictions. I welcome you here, but let's be clear on this. We have one tracker, our best pro, who we thought was going to lose two fingers from exposure because of that camping rescue . . ."

"What does that have to do with us? Why didn't he wear gloves?" Humbly asked. "This is a helpless baby! If the god-damned sheriff's deputies up here don't know how to keep warm, who does?"

The sheriff then made the threat gesture of the primal female. She shoved up her sleeves and crossed her arms. They were considerable arms, with tame, tended oval nails stained a whimsical sparkled bur-gundy color but muscles that Humbly was sure she could use to knock a door off a small refrigerator. She said, "It wasn't a matter of the rescue tracker wearing gloves, sir. The team took every necessary safety precaution based on known predic-tions. No one could have predicted the drop in temperature to ten degrees."

"I'm not insulting him," Humbly said. "I know shit . . . stuff happens."

"Her," said Switch. "Our team leader on that rescue was Lorrie Sabo. She spent a full day in the hospital. I put her on manda-tory rest for a month."

"Or her! For the love of Mike. This guy Whittier is a nut! It doesn't matter what *he says he is* in a letter! His own wife thinks

he's snapped his cap! We aren't just talking about a water shortage. Or not having
diapers. If you send a helicopter up there,
you might as well send a marching band.
He'll hear it and he could kill the baby if he
panics."

Pat held Beth against his chest as she
began to sway.

Candy and Vincent gripped each other's
hands—Candy grateful that Eliza, who
could not stop crying, had agreed to stay
back in Durand at the Lone Star Inn, where
they would all sleep later.

"The intelligence we have is shaky. Mrs.
Whittier is sure, but we don't really know if
anybody's up at their house. You have the
word of a civilian who has, well, a right-
eous obsession with this case that this
might be a place where Bryant Whittier
would go. That it's his family refuge. His
guy cave."

"And now her daughter says the same
thing," Detective Humbly reminded the
sheriff. "Blaine Whittier is manifestly men-
tally robust and got a wacko call from her
father earlier this week." He gestured at
the crowd who stood a few paces away,

inside the ranger's building—all the Cappadoras except Eliza, Candy, and George, as well as Claire and Blaine Whittier.

They all stared at the sheriff.

"You've done more with less," Berriman said. "We all have."

Switch stubbed at the floor with her boot and admitted, "That's true."

Straining to hear the words from inside the huddle, Candy realized she was hungry to the point of nausea. That morning, realizing she hadn't eaten anything but coffee for more than forty-eight hours, Candy had gone to breakfast with Beth and the others. She had tried to eat. She had made a concentrated effort to break her toast up into bites she could chew and she chewed them as her mother had told her and Belle to do when they were children, twenty times each bite. And yet the sight of her key chain—with a picture of Stella's first smile, given to her and Beth by Eliza just a few months after Stella was born—closed her throat so that no matter how much juice she chugged, the bread was like a wad of wet paper jammed in her gullet. Finally, Candy had to slip into the bathroom and throw it up. A fifty-one-year-old bulimic. She drank the rest of the juice. People could live for weeks without food.

On the other hand, Beth hadn't even tried to eat, beyond a cup of tea.

Candy felt lucky that they had let her come along, on her solemn promise not to abruptly act like a police officer. But she couldn't help asking, "Bill, so who was the woman who mailed the package from Canada? Was it someone else that Whittier found?"

"I'm guessing it was the same woman who actually took Stella, but dressed to look older," Humbly said. "But with no priors, nothing, I'm guessing we'll never know who she really is or the connection to Whittier." He tightened his lips.

Beth sat quietly, watching the men and wishing she could cry. She craved the relief of the scooped-out, limb-heavy exhaustion and deep-nasal-pool feeling that tears would bring. Instead she was hollow, light, and dry as a seedpod. Tears would not come. Losing Stella was outside the fence of sad. There was nothing animated within Beth except a hot, pale column of rage, like a third rail threaded through her torso.

Still, she tried everything to make herself cry. As she lay cradling Eliza earlier that day, while Vincent and Humbly conferred about the trip up, Beth tried to prompt her own tears. She thought of the moment she had first seen Ben, after nine years, when he came to her door to drop off a handmade flyer offering Lawns MoWeD $5! She thought of Ben proudly cradling Stella in the newborn nursery at Our Lady of Mount Carmel Hospital, or talking to Vincent through the Plexiglas when the theft of the coach's car landed him in juvenile hall.

But Beth's eyes remained so dry it was as though they were coated with a film of plastic wrap. She saw through them as through a cataract and realized later that this was because she had barely slept and hardly blinked.

Finally, Bill Humbly turned to the rest of the group. "Well, you heard her. We won and we lost. The sheriff is going to organize a hasty search, a perimeter search around the trailhead where the road goes up that leads to the Whittiers' house. It's an established road. Hikers and campers and people drive up it all the time in most kinds of weather." *Except this kind.* "They'll see if there's any sign of anyone having gone in there with a vehicle, which she says there will be, even with the snow. And if there's no sign, she's agreed to let Berriman pull strings to get some military guys to take a helicopter up there for a look-see. Which," Humbly said, "is a risk considering what we know about Bryant Whittier's mental state. But I don't think we have a choice."

"God, I'm so sorry!" Blaine cried. "This is all our fault!"

"No," Kerry said. "It's because you were brave enough to tell us the truth, you and your mother, that we have a chance to bring Stella home."

"I can't believe you don't want to kill us," Blaine said.

"It must be terrible to know something like this about your own father," said Kerry.

"It makes me wonder why he was so sure that Jackie wanted to kill herself," Blaine said softly. "And even worse, it makes me wonder why he thought she did."

"I want someone, somehow, to go look

for my daughter. Time is passing fast," Ben said. "She can't last . . . like this. If you won't go, I will."

"We will," Vincent said.

"Give her a chance," said Humbly. "She seems like a good woman and a good cop."

"And she's all we have," said Candy. "No hospital or church has reported finding a baby."

Humbly said slowly, "That, too."

CHAPTER FOURTEEN

At dawn, Sheriff Switch's "hasty search" was called off when the snow, which had stopped briefly, began again. She brought the few volunteers back off the road leading to the Whittiers' summer home.

They came back in, slipping their cell phones back into their pockets, turning off their radios, avoiding Vincent's eyes, making a wide path around Pat and Beth and Candy. Ben took one of the rental cars and drove back down to Durand to be with Eliza at the Lone Star Inn, all six rooms now entirely filled with the Cappadora family. Vincent sent his parents after Ben.

Sheriff Switch had shown them a detour around the reporters blockaded two miles from the original trailhead.

Before he left, Pat got hold of as many of the volunteers' hands as he could and shook them.

"I want you to know how much this means to my family," Pat said. "We all know you gave it your all."

No one could fault such earnest, decent people.

The weather had made for a few near misses with the Eagle Scouts, who fell on slippery places under the snow. The only grace was that they had young, elastic bodies that could bend the wrong way and leave nothing but a bruise in the morning, a bruise that would vanish in days—unlike the memory of having failed, which would last. But those falls were enough for the sheriff. Under the new frosting, older snow had melted and frozen again, slickening the rocks and even the paths. And then, for some reason, in the wishbone between the two nearest peaks, Blind Bear and Parker Rock, a slight fog settled like a perfect wedge. The place was called Clear Canyon; it was now a perfect irony.

Before noon, Berriman had called in the troops, literally.

A helicopter from Moffett Field had used the coordinates Sheriff Switch provided to find the Whittiers' big mountain house and land in a clearing in front of it. Except for Claire and Blaine, Sarah Switch was the only person to have actually seen the Whittiers' summer home, and that had been years before. She'd been after someone her former boss believed was an arsonist threatening to start a fire in the area one dry August day—it had turned out to be an eighth grader mad at his father. Sarah Switch remembered accepting a cool drink from the Whittiers and meeting both daughters, then gangly young girls. And she recalled thinking that this was a magnificent post-and-beam house to be seen by only four people—and the occasional friend or family member.

Bryant Whittier had said something about the house being nothing and the view from it being everything. That, and the fund-raising dance she had mentioned to Mrs. Whittier, were the only times Sheriff Switch had ever spoken to Bryant Whittier, though he was a familiar figure in

Durand, striding down from Paramount Street in rain or sun to his office above the Peak State Bank.

Within an hour, the helicopters were back emptyhanded.

The officer in charge said that his squad initially drew their guns. As they approached the house, a light went on. But after they circled to the back, they realized it was only a motion sensor. The officer had made the decision to break a front window and then he swore that people in Utah could hear the alarm until one of them figured out how to pull the wires.

"But there was nobody in that house," said the pilot. "Judging by the dust inside and the snow outside, there hadn't been anyone there for a long, long time. Not a trace." He added, "We jogged up the road. Those other places were boarded up. Summer people, I guess. This was clearly the biggest house and there was heat on, enough to keep the pipes free and such."

Vincent rode back to Durand with the sheriff in her truck. Sarah Switch was so pretty and sad that at any other time he would have made some kind of move on her. The thought might have belonged to another man, in another lifetime.

To his shock, Sheriff Switch stopped in front of the Whittiers' house.

"You can stay in the car," she told Vincent.

"Could I come in?" he asked her.

She shrugged. "You can imagine what I'm going to say to them."

But Vincent could not have imagined what Claire and Blaine would say in return. So he winced when Switch told them that the search was skunked and that there was no one up at their summer home. But Blaine Whittier's eyes flared to life.

"The bill in Dad's office for Small Shelters, Mom," she said. "Did you tell them about that?"

"No, I assumed they would search your father's office," Claire said, and Vincent had a strong, transitory urge to clip this slight, vague, older woman on the jaw.

"Well, I looked up Small Shelters to find out what it was," Blaine said.

"I'll bite," said Switch.

"My father spent . . . come and look," Blaine said, leading the way to her father's office—which she had torn apart, over her mother's protests. "He spent almost ten thousand dollars on one of these mini prefab cabins. My mom didn't know what it was. She doesn't use a computer that much and when she does, it's my father's laptop. Look at the website."

There were a dozen models—a baby Cape Cod, a tiny ten-by-twelve two-story A-frame ski lodge, a wee Victorian that could have accommodated the three bears without Goldilocks. Inside, these places featured fold-down tables and fold-up beds and were generally a triumphant exemplar of the efficient use of space. Some people, people Vincent assumed were deeply eccentric, actually lived full-time in these houses, which could have had, at most, two hundred square feet of floor space. Others used them as hunting or fishing getaways or even guest cottages.

"If my dad bought one of these, and it is not here in the yard or up at our summer house, it has to be someplace," Blaine said. "He wouldn't buy it and not use it. He's too compulsive for that." Blaine tore through a mass of papers on the huge, varnished desk. "See? He was going to donate his other land to some nature group if he and my mother took off on me and moved to some island . . ."

"His other land?" Switch asked. "What other land?"

"It's a parcel of some acreage Bryant owns," Claire Whittier said, obviously deeply troubled by Blaine's assertion that Bryant's madness would have made her abandon her only living child. "Here is the map of the . . . and the deed if you need it. It's farther up than the resort area where our summer house is. His grandfather cleared lumber up there a hundred years ago. Bryant and his two brothers owned it, but Bryant bought the rights from Cooper and Ames a few years ago."

"Can you take us there?" Switch asked.

"I've never been there," said Claire Whittier.

Blaine added, "Neither have I. He and Jackie went camping up there a few times. They skied in and out. There's only a fire road that goes up there. You know, what the lumber guys used. . . . He always said he'd build a place, for Jackie of course, up there. I loved my sister but she was in over her head with my dad's ideas for her future

and what she'd want. He was, like, pos-
sessed by Jackie."

"Well," Switch said. "I know where that
road is. It's a track, not much of a road.
Still, we could ask the helicopter folk
again . . ."

"I know you could never set a helicopter
down there," Blaine said. "Look. This is a
picture of Jackie up there." She held out a
photo of her sister, taken two years before,
an elfin figure mugging on her skis with
her hat pulled down over her eyes. "It's
all treed up. See? They camped in a little
clearing that was . . . well, clear. I guess
my great-grandfather died or something
before he could log it out. It's just there."

Vincent and the sheriff exchanged wide-
eyed glances. Neither of them could believe what they were hearing or that they
hadn't heard it before.

"I'll take this property description," the
sheriff said. "I don't know that there's anything we can do with it. But thank you. And
we will, of course, be needing access to
this office. So, Blaine, if you would, don't
keep digging. I'm glad you did . . ."

"It's like I think he's here," Blaine said,
tears springing to her eyes, her long pale

fingers clenched. "It's like if I keep searching, I'll find him. I'll find whatever made him this way in here." Sheriff Switch reached out and quickly hugged the younger woman. Vincent could feel the force of her pity.

"You did the right thing, Blaine," said the sheriff.

Back in the vehicle, she shook her head and set the map on the seat between them as she drove. "Twenty miles of rough country between the beginning of that fire road and what . . . some itty-bitty cabin that maybe isn't even there? And this weather? It's twisted. Seems like it wants to warm up but the cloud cover means the sun can't get down here. Up there, back on the ridges behind those hills, it's probably clearer. But I can't send my paid deputies, much less other people's, much less the SAR volunteers out looking for . . . what? Maybe a piece of land that looks like a hundred other clearings? Maybe a guy who could be in Thailand or wherever that was she said by now?"

"Malaysia," Vincent replied. "But he wouldn't take the baby away, far away. Sheriff . . ."

"Sarah," she said.

"Okay, Sarah, he said she would be returned. Berriman says that means he'd drop her off at a hospital or a church someplace."

"Vincent, we don't know that. His word isn't exactly his bond, is it? He told his wife of twenty years that he was going to a conference . . ."

"I know. I know. But my niece is just a baby. I'm responsible."

"I know you feel that way, but you're not. And believe it or not, I feel responsible too, in some way that's probably also twisted. I feel like hell about this. People from all over the place, from as far away as New Mexico and Oregon and *Chicago,* for Pete's sake, want to come and help."

"Don't you want to accept their help?" Vincent asked.

"It makes me look as effective as a cartoon character," said Switch. "I don't care, but the sheer traffic defeats the thing, you know? There are reporters out there from places I've never been. Baltimore. New York. Pittsburgh. The dispatcher is losing her mind. She's getting calls at home from the BBC. I've had deputies from other counties come up here and look for people in dozens of households anywhere near this place and either there's no one around until summer or no one saw anything. I've had the public roads blocked off now for two days and there are people who need those roads to do their jobs."

Vincent said, "I know. It's a mess."

"Do I let the press in? If I do, I mess up anything there might be here. But I have to tell you, I don't think there is anything here. If a guy built some kind of shelter up there, like one of those little houses on that website, either he did it with a ghost crew or someone would have seen or heard something in the way of materials going in."

Vincent said, "About the press. I'm sorry. If this had happened a week ago, I would've just been some moke. Another guy."

"Apology accepted. If you had been another guy, there wouldn't be so much press here," she said. "This is the biggest boom in Durand since Miss California came from here thirteen years ago."

"I'm sorry," Vincent said.

She sighed. "No, that's not fair. I guess with the resident genius, because that's what Bryant Whittier was, and his daughter being lost, and then you and your poor little baby niece and your Oscar, and the goofy letter, there still would have been everybody from Katie Couric to Katie Mulhone from the *Cisco County Register,* who went to high school with me. Maybe that's who'll help you. Maybe those pictures will be what will find her. Maybe Whittier gave up when he saw the snow and changed plans. Maybe someone will see her in . . . Chicago. Someplace. Maybe he really will leave her in a hospital, still."

Switch unlocked the door to her office, sat down, and poured herself a cup of coffee, the number of cups of which Vincent had lost count of hours before. He'd seen people drink coffee—his family was renowned for it—but nobody drank coffee like Switch, who also seemed to have the bladder of a camel. Her deputy, a guy called Jackson, didn't even bother with the pot. He put his mug right under the percolator spout. Detective Humbly was in the second, smaller room of the office, using Jackson's desk for some paperwork.

"Where're your folks?" she asked Vincent.

"At the little inn, in town. My sister-in-law, Eliza . . . needs a doctor. She can't really sleep or eat. They all wanted to get her settled." He paused. "It's my job anyhow. It's my doing."

"You did this?" Switch said. "Pretty bad guy, I'd say."

"You know what I mean," Vincent said.

Switch motioned to Vincent to take a coffee cup. He refused, smiling, having drunk so much Cisco County coffee that he feared he'd have to have part of his stomach removed surgically. The way the sheriff drank it down, without even blowing on it, like a kid drinking lemonade, made him think that people up here had different DNA. Nothing, he noticed, however, erased the gray fingerprints at the inner corners of her eyes. A sudden gust of gratitude shook him, making his fingers tremble even more than the Cisco County coffee had. She had done all she could and more. Detective Humbly called out, "I heard the helicopter."

"Yeah," said the sheriff. "But you didn't know about the secret property." Humbly was at her side within seconds, as she explained the visit to the Whittiers.

"Maybe Whittier went from the other side. There is another side?" Bill Humbly asked.

"There's always another side," said the sheriff. "But it's probably . . . wow, it's probably almost in another state."

"Still, Sarah, it could have happened that way," said Vincent. "He would be smart enough to know that his wife would tell people to look for him here if his plans went off the track."

"Mr. Cappadora . . ." the sheriff began, weariness in every syllable, as if she were saying his name on a slowed-down recording.

It was his turn to say, "Vincent."

"Vincent, you LaLas . . ."

"I'm from Chicago," Vincent said. "I've only lived in California for three years."

"Then I'm sorry. People from SoCal come up here and think it's just like where they live only with trees and big pretty hills. But this is dangerous country. There are bears up there and a lot worse, crevasses you fall into and you don't get found until you're archaeology. I grew up here. My father was sheriff here. The other side is up near redwood country. It would be another hundred miles at least to get to this place . . ."

"Could the roads be better on the other side?"

"Not as steep maybe but . . . Vincent, if you go to another part of the state, it starts all over again. New sheriff. New case number. Even the FBI guy, if he wants to get more people up here, he has to get clearance and that takes time. Frankly, and this kills me to say, much longer and we're looking at a recovery. . . . And we might be already."

"You mean you think they're dead," Vincent said. He felt, rather than saw, Humbly brace himself for some kind of explosion.

Switch said, "I don't know. If Whittier provisioned himself for three days, even four days, and the fuel is gone, and he's melting snow for water . . . If this were TV, you'd be asking me now, who's the fastest gun in Dodge? But this isn't TV."

"Who is the fastest gun in Dodge?" Vincent asked.

The sheriff paused. She had removed her hat and sunglasses and shaken her hair loose from its customary tight braid and was now using her finger to do it up again: Vincent had noticed this before. She braided when she was nervous, when she failed to find precise or commanding words. She looked from the Los Angeles detective to Vincent and then back again. Finally she asked, "What do you mean?"

"A rescue tracker who's extraordinary. The best. In any state, anywhere."

Switch didn't hesitate.

"She's here. Lorrie Hanna Sabo. The tracker who led the search for the family that got stranded camping. The one I said was in the hospital for a day. Her dog Roman has done some amazing stuff. Spooky stuff. He found a little girl last summer who hid herself in a cave and put rocks in front of her and stayed in there two nights. She was four miles from where her parents camped and had climbed up over terrain that would give me pause. But Lorrie just got out of the hospital a few days ago after that camper rescue and, uh, recovery. She's on leave. She's a volunteer but I rely on her. She teaches SAR at Snowy Mountain Community College, for people who are doing Outward Bound training."

"Can I hire her?"

It was as though he hadn't spoken. The sheriff said, "I'm going to have to call off the formal search until this fog clears off."

"The FBI guy said maybe they could authorize more," Vincent said.

"I hope he does," said Sheriff Switch. "Let them come. As long as they let me organize them, I welcome them. This is a tiny county with limited resources. This is only our second numbered case that wasn't a broken mailbox or a kid with a bag of pot this whole year. The other one ended in a tragedy. It will take time, though, to put this together."

"Could I hire her?" Vincent asked again. "This Lorrie Sabo?"

"She's on leave." The tall sheriff got up and stood looking out her window in the little office that reminded Vincent of every place he'd ever waited to have his oil changed—old-mustard walls and cast-off furniture, the tabletops invisible under layers of long-outdated magazines and strange tracts that called attention to everything from youth baseball to Bible study. She kneaded her lower back and Vincent noticed how slender she really was. Half a head taller than he was but

probably didn't weigh as much. She finally said quietly, "I will say this. If it was
my niece, I'd pay Lorrie anything she
wanted and get anyone else who had
brains and any sense of the wilderness to
go with me and I'd be out there myself
right now. It's not the right thing to do, but
I would. And if she gave up, I would not. I
would keep going."

CHAPTER FIFTEEN

The sheriff herself drove him to Lorrie Sabo's house, and waited with Vincent while he called his father. He asked Pat to call Ben. Then they went inside together.

Lorrie Sabo was making soup. It was something she did every Sunday with her daughters—putting away meals for the week. To Switch, Lorrie Sabo said, "Sarah. I was wondering when you'd come."

"It's up to you," the sheriff told her.

"I have two daughters, sir," said Lorrie, a small, compact woman younger than Vincent's mother, but not by much. "So yes, of course, I'll try. But on my terms. And that means no one except me goes . . ."

Vincent said quietly, "I have to go."

"Absolutely not. I go alone, and in this weather, I might take my buddy Greg, or have him come in if I need him . . ." Switch nodded. Apparently, everyone knew who Greg was. "No one else."

"I need to go. And my brother needs to go. Stella is his child."

"When was the last time you climbed slick rock in the snow?"

"I've never climbed any rock in the snow. But I have to go. Her father has to go." Vincent added, "You're lucky his mother-in-law isn't insisting on coming. She's a police officer too."

"I'm not going to put up a tent with an air mattress and cook eggs and bacon. I'll eat meals you add a little water to to get them to taste like crap. Most of what I carry will be for Romy . . ."

Vincent leaned against the wall. Okay, he thought. He'd spent a lifetime faking his way out of most things he'd stumbled into. And he could do this too. He waited until the woman had wound down, her last shot involving something about chocolate and buffalo jerky.

Then he told her, "You might think looking at me that I'm some spoiled little boy from palm-tree land but I grew up in a neighborhood where you wouldn't last ten minutes even with your trail mix and your big old deer rifle over there." This wasn't even remotely true but he had a feeling that Lorrie Sabo would buy the bluff. Already, he saw something in her eyes lift a lid. "I know it's not a matter of strength or how many hours I put in at the gym. I know it's about skill I don't have. But I'm not an idiot and I won't say a word to you or do anything but what you tell me. But this is the bottom line. Where I come from no one would let a stranger take a risk for his family he wouldn't take himself."

The sheriff and her tracker exchanged looks.

"Go on, Sarah. Leave him here. I'll call you," Lorrie Sabo finally said. "I guess I have compadres here."

That had been four hours and about a gallon of sweat ago.

Lorrie Hanna Sabo taught Ben and Vincent to walk on snowshoes—although it took her two hours.

Ben caught on right away. He began marching around as though the big webs were some kind of appendage he'd been born with that had grown along with him until he happened to need them. On winter breaks and at college in upper New York State, Ben had hiked and skied with friends. He and George had taken trips to Colorado and northern Minnesota. Ben already knew how to walk on snowshoes in a rudimentary way and the two pairs Lorrie gave them made it easier. They were common bear-paw snowshoes—without the tails used on flat land that could droop and drag on a leg trying to dig a toe for purchase on a steep grade or rock pile.

But after forty-five minutes, the best rescue tracker in California—according to Sarah Switch—looked ready to throw her entire five-foot-one-inch, hundred-pound body on Vincent and pummel him.

Instead, she sat down on her porch and pulled her thick stocking cap down over her eyes. "Breathe, Lorrie," she said. "Breathe deep." Finally, she got up. "You'll have to be able to do this like a person," she said. "This isn't a Sunday picnic."

"I never acted like it was," Vincent answered grimly. "Give me a minute here."

All of the family group was gathered in Lorrie Sabo's yard. Each snowshoe was forty-eight inches long and twelve inches wide, but they were beautifully light and supple and sturdy, handmade by Lorrie's husband, Doug. He used a straight-grained wood that wouldn't crack or buckle on a half-buried stump, the cross bars painstakingly mortised tight. He strung them with lightweight lamb's hide. Doug skinned those lambs, too, Vincent learned, while he wasn't working as an economics professor at San Francisco State.

The ewes would be lambing any day, Doug said. Vincent looked at the pregnant sheep and thought, You'd better run for it.

Meanwhile, he had a hell of a time with the snowshoes.

He figured it was nerves. By midafternoon, precious time had passed.

The need to get up to the land Bryant Whittier owned—its location now confirmed by the other Whittier brothers, Cooper and Ames, and pretty well located on Sarah Switch's big topographic maps—before another second of daylight escaped them . . . it was overpowering. In his haste to adapt to this way of moving quickly, Vincent's natural athletic grace deserted him.

In sports, everything had always come easily. Speed made up for a lack of size. He'd even mastered surfing, first try. But now, although he was twenty pounds lighter than Ben, Vincent seemed made of some kind of gelatinous stuff that hefted to the left or right like water balloons in a sack. If the situation had been anything but what it was, he would have laughed at himself as, repeatedly, he clomped around the Sabos' front yard and fell over backward or got one shoe trapped under the other. Pat had come up and stood watching him, shaking his head, and Vincent knew that Pat might have laughed too, had he not felt the way he so visibly did. Pat had chewed his nails down to bloody stubs with crescents of something at the bottom that didn't look like it belonged on a man— especially a man like Pop. Pat usually had his nails buffed in perfect squares, as a man of business should. He was wearing the tracksuit again. Vincent realized that it was the only "sports" clothing he'd ever seen his father wear. On Sundays, when he didn't have to work, Pat wore a silk-blend shirt and Mantoni slacks to turn on the automatic sprinkler, fifteen minutes before it would have turned itself on anyway.

Pop didn't go without eating.

Pop didn't go without calling the restaurant five times a day.

Since the Oscars—just a week ago today—Pat's skin seemed to have slipped so that what once sat high on his cheekbones now hung from his jaw. So far as Vincent knew, Pop had taken only one call from Grandpa and talked for about five minutes. The rest of the time, he spent looking at Vincent as if he could twist him or turn him some way and a window would appear that read, "My sources say yes."

Finally, Vincent got the walk on snowshoes down enough that Lorrie put her hands on her hips, sighed and said, "Good grief, it's not going to get any better." Then she added, "At least you're young. Geez, though, Vincent. Listen. I've taught five-year-olds to do this more easily. Tell me there's a way I can talk you out of going with me and Romy. I'll give you some of your money back."

Roman was a 170-pound smooth-coated Saint Bernard, a trained air-scenting dog to whom the family had not yet been introduced. But they had heard about him.

No ordinary tracking dog was this.

Ordinary tracking dogs would imbibe a smell off an article of clothing or a shoe and then put their muzzles to the ground and follow a single smell. They would do what the motley pack of searchers' German shepherds and border collies had tried to do after they nosed the house slipper of Bryant's that Claire Whittier had given the sheriff. They tried to pick up one person's particular scent on the ground. But they had run in circles around the verge of the road up to the summer house. Roman apparently could detect any sign of human scent in the air, no matter what human the scent belonged to. Roman had been trained for three years in a complex game of hide-and-seek known only to him and Lorrie Sabo.

Not even trackers who trained air-scenting Search and Rescue dogs knew exactly what the dog was scenting: It could be human hormones or skin drafts, the tang of evaporated perspiration, respiratory gases, or, in the case of cadavers, the bacterial action on human skin or tissues that created the unmistakable overripe lily stink of decomposition. Whatever was out there and human, living or dead, the Saint Bernard would find it. He worked off-lead, looping in large parabolic areas of terrain, his trainer literally making tracks behind him.

"I'll take your brother," Lorrie said now, trying to placate Vincent. "Stella's his baby. And he's got this walking thing down."

"I'm paying you," Vincent told her, tramping grimly. "I'm not trying to be a jerk, but I have to go or I have to find someone else."

"No one else will be able to find her," Lorrie said. "I'm not trying to be a jerk either, but that's the fact."

Ben said nothing.

Vincent and the small muscular tracker took each other's measure and Vincent marveled at the wild circumstances that had brought him to this place.

He sighed and so did Lorrie Sabo.

"Let's get the packs stuffed and go. What the hell," she said.

Pat and Beth had swept through the aisles at Pitch's Sporting Goods and the local Walgreens, which were going to have to restock their goods based on purchases made by the Cappadoras alone.

Beth was distressed that she could find no wind pants anywhere near small enough for Vincent's slender frame—except pants made for kids, which would be too short. Reluctantly, she bought an extra-thick pair of fleece pants for the outside layer, knowing as she did so that this layer would soon be wet. She fretted and yet, for the first time in more years than she could count, she felt like a genuine mother—as she had when the children were small, before Ben was taken from them. She was provisioning them, protecting them from harm, harkening back to a time when being a mother was more than sending checks or presents, when it required gear and hands-on time.

This much, she could do.

Even Agent Berriman accompanied the family back to Lorrie Sabo's house. Eliza, who had barely left the Lone Star Inn, was bundled in a child's parka, as none of the adult sizes at Pitch's would fit her. Like a child also, she held Ben's hand as long as he let her, then held Beth's when Ben had to move away.

Beth watched them as Lorrie Sabo directed the assembly of the long, aluminum-framed backpacks—the little woman dividing the load between the two brothers. She threw aside half the stuff that Beth and Pat had purchased and said, "You might as well not waste your money on this. Tell Jesse Pitch to take it back at the store. Unless I die—and if I do, I give you permission to rob me," she told Ben and Vincent, "we won't be needing more than one ax and one big knife. But they can both have pocketknives. And a mirror. And whistles. Definitely whistles."

Unable to bear the inactivity, Beth squeezed in beside Ben and used the

memory of her teenage days as a super-
market checkout girl to make a square
load—endless sealed aluminum bags of
tuna and other bags of what looked like dehydrated powder. Surprised, Ben glanced
up at her and smiled. Boldly, Beth gently
touched the cheek she'd slapped and Ben
reached up and let his own fingers rest on
his mother's for a moment so brief it might
not have happened, except that later, Beth
would summon that touch over and over to
give herself courage.

Lorrie had been specific about their
buying a Jetboil stove because hers was
acting up and they couldn't count on dry
wood, at least all the time. While she was
at pains to explain that she would not personally need hot food, she was sure that
the men would. Hoping they would find dry
wood, she added to Ben's pack one pan
and several empty film canisters stuffed
with cotton balls saturated with Vaseline,
which she said worked better than any
heavier tinder. Pat asked what the dry
foodstuff would be when she added hot
water.

"Wet protein," Lorrie told him briefly.

"They call it chili or stew but it doesn't taste like any chili I'd ever eat."

Lorrie then gave Ben lengths of rope and plastic groundsheets to top off the large pack. Into the "head" of the pack that zipped on top ("Easiest to get to . . ." Lorrie said) she asked Ben to cram small silky bags of peanuts and M&M's ("Plastic will rip . . ." Lorrie said). To Beth, she gave power bars, two big canteen-type cups, spoons, flares, and matches wrapped in plastic bags and clipped into a solid hard-plastic case. And Beth packed these.

As Lorrie watched, Vincent stacked his own pack with the tent he and Ben would share, their sleeping bags, and Lorrie's first-aid kit. Candy helped Vincent shove things down deep and lay the kit on top.

"You guard that kit with your life," Lorrie said. "I don't think we'll need the bee-sting stuff but I'm bringing it anyway. And I hope we don't need the SAM splint or the pain pills but I have a funny feeling. Blisters can kill out there, if they get infected. So you're both going to pad your piggies with mole-skin like ballerinas." She whipped through their clothes, discarding and approving layers, nodding at the Sorel boots Ben had borrowed from Rob Brent, making a face at Vincent's Timberlands but saying they would have to do. She muttered darkly about Vincent's lack of an outer lower layer and went into her house to get two rain ponchos for them to squeeze into a large waterproof "stuff sack" along with an extra pair of wool-blend socks and wool-blend shirt they would wear under a parka shell.

Then she sent them in to dress.

"They'll have blisters in an hour," Lorrie said to Beth. While she waited, Lorrie Sabo asked Beth, "Do you have a family picture?" Beth shook her head.

"Your key chains," said Kerry, who was already crying, wiping her tears away with the chapped backs of her hands.

Beth ran back for her purse and Candy dug into her pockets. They unclasped the identical charms they carried with Stella's picture.

When Beth handed them over, the tracker said, "Well. That's Stella. Yeah. Okay. If she's up there, we'll bring her down."

"I feel sure you will," Candy told her, the

quaver in her voice betraying her. "If anybody can."

"How long will it take?" Eliza asked
softly. Kerry put her arm around Eliza.

"I don't know, honey," Lorrie told her. "I
would love to say by tonight. But I know
there's no man-made meadow within the
distances I've hiked from here with my
kids or even with my dogs. I packed for
three days and spare change. If we don't
find her by then . . . we'll get my friend
Greg to drop food for us and the dog."

"How will you reach him?" Eliza asked.

"Cell phone," Lorrie said.

"You can use cell phones? Up here?"
Kerry asked.

"You can use cell phones on Kiliman-
jaro. They just don't work when you need
them. I bring three, charged, anyhow. The
trees are hard to plug into." Beth quickly
held out her own cell phone, as did Eliza,
who then turned and ran to bring Ben's
from the car.

Vincent and Ben emerged, suited, and
the tracker went inside her house to dress
and assemble her own gear.

Awkwardly, the two brothers stood facing the others.

Sharply, Berriman turned and walked away, opening his truck and rearranging imaginary stuff inside.

"Well," Pat said.

"It's all good, Pat," Ben told him. He wore a tight wool cap with a thick padded headband around it. The headband was the only one Pat could find in early April and was luminous hot pink. "Only thing is, I thank God nobody who knows me can see me in all this."

"Just be careful. Look where you are. Be careful," Candy told them. She studied Vincent's gloves and his Blackhawks stocking hat. "Neither one of those is insulated." She pulled off her own stretchy woolen gloves. "Take mine at least."

"They only had one pair that was insulated. Dad got it. Sam should have it. He spends more time inside." Ben and Vincent didn't look at each other. "And I have a band like that, too, from my father. I'm just not secure enough in my masculinity to wear it."

Ben snorted.

"You have to stop fighting, Sam," Eliza said quietly.

"We're not fighting, baby," Ben said.

"You're not speaking," she said. "You love Vincent, Sam. What are you doing here otherwise?"

Then Lorrie was back. As she attached "camelbacks," water bags with hoses, to one side of each of their packs, securing the hoses so they would hang over their shoulders, allowing them a drink whenever they needed it, she said, "We have a good four hours if we go now. I just have to let Romy eat. He's getting his regular raw stuff and some oatmeal too. He's going to be on thin rations for a while." With metal rings, she attached the snowshoes to hang from the other side of each pack.

"Let's go, then," said Vincent.

The tracker demonstrated how to get down on one knee and roll the pack onto her back. First Ben and then Vincent did the same thing.

"You have sunglasses? Lip balm? No? Well, great." Lorrie shouted to Doug, her husband, who, after a minute, brought out what he could find. "Plenty of sunscreen. Flashlights. GPS for me and one for you two . . ." She turned to the family. "Is there anything you want to give them?"

Beth gave each of her sons the little

framed photo of Stella. Then Pat unzipped his coat and removed his gold Italian horn pendant, which, to Beth's knowledge, he had never removed, even to shower. He nodded to Ben, who opened his coat and let Pat place it around his neck. Pat gave Ben a hard hug and took off his glove. To Vincent he said, "You already have my high-school ring back at your place." Pat removed his ancient, thin wedding band. "This was Grandpa's. You bring it back and I'll let you have it when you get married. If anyone will ever have you."

"Okay, Pop," Vincent said, and kissed his father.

Beth placed her hands on Ben's shoulders and then on Vincent's. "You're my boys. I haven't said this. Not when I should have. Maybe not at all. But I bind you together. I bind you together. Whatever separates you is foolish. It means nothing. Promise me you'll give me at least the respect of hearing what I say."

"I will, Ma," Vincent said, and Ben nodded.

Eliza turned her face into Candy's lapels and wouldn't look up when Ben asked for her.

Lorrie made a low two-note whistle and the dog stepped out.

Beth caught her breath.

Roman's head would have grazed Beth's waist and was the size of a football helmet. He walked paw across paw, as a lion walks, and wore no collar or chain. Almost entirely white, except for irregular patches of red and black along his flanks and a half-mask that covered his blunt, handsome face, he looked up intently into Lorrie's eyes with an eerie, human-like entreaty. Removing a ragged bandana tied around what seemed to be a tennis ball, the tracker let the dog take it in his giant mouth and then jerked on the corners as Romy playfully slung his own great head side to side. Lorrie threw the bandana and Romy bounded back with it, dropping it at Lorrie's feet and lying down beside it.

"This is our contract," she said to Beth. Lorrie removed a sliver of what smelled like spoiled salmon from one of two zippered wallets around her waist and gave it to Roman. "This is his stinky salmon. The rag and the salmon are his reward. Now he knows what we're going to do. No matter when we find her, I'll stop for a minute and give him his play."

"Doesn't he pull it out of your hands?" Pat asked.

"You can't roughhouse with a dog this powerful," Lorrie Sabo answered. "Romy's the gentlest boy on earth but he's too big to ever get the idea that anything but gentle play is okay. He learned that a long time ago." The tracker knelt at the door to hug her little girls and her husband. The little girls hugged the dog. From behind the children peered a second Saint Bernard that Lorrie introduced as Noble, a one-year-old pup in training. The last two things Doug handed his wife were what appeared to be a small Bible and very large handgun. As the three of them set out, the dog trotting ahead at a hand signal Lorrie gave him, Candy put both arms around Eliza.

"That's a .45 Glock," she said. "Think she intends to run into bears?"

"Would it work?" Beth asked.

"Yeah, pretty much," Candy said. "This is the time for bears to come out, isn't it?"

"I don't want to think about any more dangerous shit than I already am," said Pat.

Beth's sons, walking steadily at least three feet apart, were already visibly smaller. Turn, Beth thought. Wave goodbye. But they didn't, and soon a stand of trees obscured them.

CHAPTER SIXTEEN

Austere and silent, the landscape at the foot of Blind Bear Hill was Christmas-card exquisite. A tiny waterfall had frozen in midstream, its pool a ruffle of ice at the base. Ben stopped for a moment.

"Don't lose sight of me," Lorrie called back, "and please try to stay within my tracks. We're going to have to come out of here someday and we're not going to be stopping to look at the scenery."

"Why aren't you looking for signs?" Ben asked.

"You've seen too many TV Westerns," she answered. "No tracker looks at the ground. Whatever made a track down there made a sign of some kind up ahead. You look up in front of you."

Ben said, "Fine," and Vincent knew he would have pulled a wry face at him any other time in their lives.

They hiked another hour in silence. The sun sank and the snow was deeper.

"We can't post-hole it like this anymore," the tracker told Vincent and Ben. "It'll wear your legs out. Time to snowshoe up."

Once the snowshoes were secure, the two men sat on slippery rocks and devoured handfuls of nuts and chocolate. Lorrie seemed to have some internal fuel source. She settled herself in the sun in the cleft of a rock and pulled the leather cowboy hat she wore over her ski band down to cover her eyes. Ben and Vincent sat in silence for fifteen minutes, listening to the snores of the dog, which had thrown itself over Lorrie's legs.

Suddenly, as though she had heard an alarm sound, Lorrie sat up and slipped into her own snowshoes. "Did you sleep?" she asked.

"Were we supposed to?" Ben answered.

"I sleep whenever I can. You'll get pretty

tired otherwise. You can eat and drink walking but you can't sleep walking, although I've seen people try," the tracker said. "Are you drinking?" Neither of them had. Neither of them wanted to stop to pee. "This is serious. You have to drink all the time. From now on. Enjoy that good well water while you have it because you're going to be drinking water purified with iodine or strained through sand we dig for pretty soon. If I can find any sand under this. Snow melt is more likely . . . and that will have to be warmed up or it'll just add to how cold you feel when the sun goes down."

Another half hour brought them to the foot of a rocky slope with a fringe of trees at its crown.

"How do we get around that?" Vincent asked.

"Around it?" Lorrie said, laughing, as Romy dug in his claws. "We're going up. There's still light up there. We'll get there and camp."

"It doesn't look too steep," said Ben.

By the time they got to the top, both of them were heaving for every breath and bent over, hauling on saplings. Sweat sprang from pores Vincent didn't know he had and he tore off his hat, stuffing it into his pocket.

"Got here faster'n I thought," Lorrie said. "Roman's doing good. We'll keep going."

Vincent sighed.

"You want to go back? Go," said Lorrie. "No new snow. Just follow our track."

Vincent said, "No. We just don't do this every day."

Lorrie bounded off into the trees, where the boughs that clasped overhead erased the waning sun—thrusting them into a tunnel where the honeyed light stippled the ground in front of them. "I'm going to look for a clearing. Stay in my tracks. There's a spring that runs down along here. It could be a trickle now but you never know. I sing to pass time. It doesn't waste as much energy as thinking."

As Ben and Vincent struggled up what had seemed from the bottom to be a gentle grade, their thighs began to ache and then caught fire. Even Ben swore violently under his breath. From up ahead, they could hear Lorrie singing Irish songs, from "Gentle Annie" to "Red Is the Rose," songs they knew from their Irish grandfather, Bill

Kerry, Beth's dad. But when Lorrie began, "Tim Finnegan lived in Walkin' Street, a gentle Irishman, mighty odd . . ." Vincent said, "That's enough of this shit."

He tried to think of any song he knew that would distract him from the elfin dissection of his hamstrings—any camp song, but then he had never been to camp. Any folk song, but he'd never had any idea what Bob Dylan was actually saying. Finally, he began to hum, then to sing, "If a body catch a body, coming through the rye . . . if a body kiss a body, will a body cry? Everybody loves somebody . . ."

"Everybody *has* somebody," Ben corrected him. To Vincent's surprise, he sang, "Everybody has somebody, nay they say have I . . ." and they finished together, "Yet all the girls, they smile at me, when coming through the rye." And then they began again, pushing with their legs, digging with their toes.

If a body catch a body
Coming through the rye,
If a body kiss a body . . .
Will a body cry?

Everybody has somebody,
Nay they say have I.
Yet all the girls they smile at me
When coming through the rye.

"Forgive me and don't answer if you don't want to," Vincent gasped out. "But do you remember when Beth . . ."

"I don't remember, in fact, but it's definitely one of the great Cappadora legends," Ben answered. Vincent was gratified to notice that even Ben was winded. In fact, he was more embarrassed than irritated, sort of faking annoyance to cover up the fact that all those days at the restaurant had him a little out of shape.

"If you don't remember, then why does Eliza sing it to Stella?" Vincent asked.

"I never heard her."

"She sings it all the time. And she sings it like Mom did . . . Mom, as in *our* mom . . ." Vincent added, his rage suddenly a spear sharpened in the burning of his muscles. He realized his feet were nearly numb, the new boots at least a size too small. "She sings it, 'If a bunny catch a bunny . . . '"

"I don't remember!" Ben roared, as, with a horrible slowness, he slipped off the path, down a slight grade, coming to rest on a frozen crest of snow maybe three feet below Vincent.

"Don't move, Sam. Don't move an inch. If we're lucky, that's a stable shelf of snow . . ."

"Okay," said Ben, his eyes blank with dread. Vincent could see his brother's shoulders shaking. He knew what it would mean to hit water, here and now.

"I'm going to lie down on my stomach, in case it won't hold both our weight, and hold out the snowshoe." Vincent ditched the pack and was unlacing one snowshoe when he heard a soft, horrible shushing.

Just as Lorrie shouted, "There's a good clearing up here, and it's nice and flat. Come on, about fifty yards more . . ." the crest where Ben stood began to sink, in-substantial as a meringue. While Vincent scrambled down toward him and Ben clawed for Vincent's hand, Ben sank silently through into water as deep as his chest.

"Jesus Christ!" Vincent yelled. "Help us! He fell in." They heard Lorrie come schussing down the slope. The dog came huffing in front of her, lithe, sure-footed and human-eyed as he drew level with Vincent.

"Don't move any closer to him," Lorrie said in a voice so quiet it had the effect of literally slowing Vincent's heart. "You'll both go in and then neither one of you will survive. If we don't get him out of there, his chances are slim to none anyhow." Pulling a set of straps from her pack, she buckled it around Roman's shoulders, tossing knotted whip ends to Ben who scrabbled to catch them in his gloves. They slipped away, and Ben pulled the gloves off. "Ben! There's genius for you. Now he'll lose a finger. Plus, I hate that he has to do this."

"Me, too," Vincent said. "Hurry, Lorrie. He's not only freezing, he's scared to death."

To Ben, Lorrie said, "Drop your pack. Try not to let it slide underwater. Just shove it into the bank." Ben did. "I mean I hate that Roman has to do this. It's a strain on him. Roman, up," Lorrie said and the huge dog clenched his massive hindquarters and stepped backward. Ben, visibly trembling, came stumbling and crawling up the bank. Vincent thought his brother's face looked gray as modeling clay. Lorrie broke off a branch and snagged Ben's pack with it. Then, ripping off the harness, Lorrie headed back up the path.

"Where the hell are you going?" Vincent howled.

"I'm going to throw the tent up in the clearing and hope to God I can find enough wood that's dry enough to start some kind of fire!" she said. "Get him up here!" By the time they stumbled up to where she was, Lorrie had laid a platform of flat logs she had struck from a single bough and hacked apart with the ax. She'd snapped off low boughs she called "squaw wood" that were bare of snow, stripped off the bark, and used one of the Vaseline balls to start a fire that roared up, although it also smoked like a chimney that hadn't been cleaned in years. Somewhere, she'd also found a big rotten dry stump that was dead and that she split into six pieces, all in about five minutes. "Get him out of his clothes," Lorrie barked.

Half-dragging his brother, Vincent said, "Say again?"

"Get it all off, everything. Look at his face. His eyes. He's sleepy. He's already hypothermic. The wet clothes have to be hung to dry and we have to get him warmed up. We should quit this right now and go back. I tried for a cell phone signal and there's nothing." Lorrie's mouth formed a grim line. "We're on our own."

Vincent began pulling Ben out of his layers. Ben was groggy, shuddering like a guy in a spasm. Under the first layer, Vincent found wet silks. Water had seeped in through the waistband of Ben's wind pants. Lorrie shook out Ben's sleeping bag. "Get this in the tent," she told Vincent. Ben nodded, swayed, sleepy-eyed.

He said, "Fine. I'm good. I'm warming up."

Lorrie said, "Shit. That's not good."

"He said he's warming up."

"People who are too cold feel warm. Get his bag in the tent and get him in the bag. It's probably twenty degrees up here and the wind's picking up. I have to find a better way to shield the fire. I built it in the open like a fool." Vincent was amazed at her prowess. She'd kicked away the snow for three feet around the fire so it wouldn't go out and lugged a couple of big rocks to mount around a silver-coated shield—like a tiny version of some Japanese screen in a fancy living room. "I'll add every bit of wood I can strip to it once we get him figured out. First, I'm going to warm up some hot chocolate."

Once Ben was in the bag in the tent, Vincent asked her for the chocolate. "I'm letting it cool. You ever hear of guys pulled out of the ocean and were walking and talking until they took a hot drink and dropped dead? He wasn't that bad off but I'm not taking chances. You have to give him something warm first." She stared at Vincent. "What are you doing? Strip off."

"I did. He's in the sleeping bag."

"I mean you!" Lorrie said. "Strip down to your underwear now."

"Me?"

"Pull your boots off and leave them outside the tent. I'll put the poncho over them. Strip and get in the bag with him."

"What?"

Lorrie sighed. "Your human warmth is going to do more for him than anything I

can do. He's your brother, and I'm not getting in the bag with him. I have too much to
do out here. I mean it! Now!" She'd thrown
a rope around the two closest trees and
flipped Ben's wet clothes over it.

"Can I pee first?" Vincent asked.

"If you hurry up about it," Lorrie said.
"We'll dig a hole later. Try not to get too
near to the fire. I don't want a bunch of crit-
ters nosing around. When he's warmed
up, we'll pull the food up off the ground in a
bear bag . . ."

"Can't he just lie down close to the fire?"
Vincent asked.

"Sure, but it could kill him if it takes him
that long to warm up," Lorrie said.

Vincent pulled off his clothes down to his
underwear and threw them into the tent. He
set his boots just inside so Lorrie wouldn't
see how wet they already were. Then he
got down on all fours and crawled into the
mouth of the tent. Lorrie zipped both open-
ings behind them and pegged down the fly
to cut the wind. Ben seemed asleep but he
began to thrash when Vincent started to
slip into the bag.

"What the hell are you doing?" Ben's
skin was like the outside of a cold glass

on a summer day, before the surface beaded up.

"It's not my idea. You're . . . you have hypothermia. I have to warm you. I'm warm from all the hiking."

"Get outta here!" Ben mumbled, shoving weakly, his words coming slowly and slurred over each other like a song on a record with the batteries on the player about to run out of juice.

"Come on, Sam. Cut it out. If I don't do this, you'll really be bad off." Vincent wiggled in next to his brother. "I'm not going to make a pass at you. Come on. Lie still." Ben finally stopped thrashing. Vincent could feel his arms, smooth and cold as the rocks outside. He wrapped his own arms around Ben's back and held him close and slung his leg over both of Ben's. The inert chill of his brother's body poured over him like a fluid. "There. Now, um, try to relax." Vincent blew on the back of Ben's neck, the only exposed part of him.

Within a few minutes, Ben's shivering began to slow down. "There you go. That's good. Just push up close to me. It's working."

"Great. Okay. Imagine how this looks, with our pink headbands," Ben said, and Vincent's heart took off. Thank God. If he was okay enough to be sarcastic . . .

The zip opened and Lorrie, in her silks and her fleece pants, slid into the tent with a cup of chocolate and something on a spoon. "Sit up, Ben. And Vincent, you too." Both of them struggled to a sitting position, like two caterpillars in a cocoon. "Get your hands around this." Ben did. He drank the chocolate and Lorrie fed him a spoonful of peanut butter by bits. Then she said she'd stay outside to build up the fire. "I didn't want anyone to see us, especially Bryant Whittier if he's out here with one of his hunting rifles. But there's no way around having the fire." She gave Ben and Vincent each a power bar. "Stay here. We'll eat more in the morning. I'm just going to put up my tent and let Roman sleep with me. It'll get colder. But at least the wind's going down. Normally, I'd think it was pretty. It's all stars." She looked back at them. "Sleep tight. Thank God for good dogs."

Ben slept, and though the sweat rolled off Vincent, so much that he had to pull one arm outside the sleeping bag, Ben stayed dry.

Vincent tried to sleep. He thought, Ben was that close. Ben nearly bought it. Ben was so cold that it's stifling in here and he doesn't have enough warmth or fluid in him to sweat.

A few hours later, Lorrie woke them and gave them some warm Jell-O in liquid form. It nearly gagged Vincent but Ben drank it all down as though it were some kind of magic potion. They lay back down.

Vincent imagined he heard things. He imagined he heard Bryant Whittier's voice, saying some villain thing, like *What have we here?* He imagined he heard snuffling and coughing and told himself, it's only a raccoon.

When Vincent finally slept, or thought he slept, a twitching version of sleep, through which sounds and cold swam readily, he saw things in his dreams. Once, he was almost sure he cried out, at a vision of red eyes in the darkness. But when he woke, the fly of the tent was still tightly shut.

"What?" Lorrie called.

"Nothing. I'm good," Vincent said. "Nightmare." He slipped out of Ben's bag and pulled his own from Ben's pack—which was back in the corner where Lorrie had stowed it. The groundsheet crackled with cold as he wriggled down into it and slapped his arms and thighs to warm himself, finally pulling out his extra wool shirt and struggling into it. But Sam was unprotected in there now, with nothing on but the bag. "Sam?" Vincent whispered.

"Yeah?"

"I got your dry clothes. Can you put them on in there?"

"Yeah," Ben said. "Hand 'em to me, okay?"

"You got them?" Vincent asked in the dark.

"Gloves," Ben said.

"They're still drying out." Vincent pulled off one of his layers. *Whoa!* Had the temperature plummeted or was it just that he was alone? Maybe moving over hadn't been such a good idea. He handed his gloves over to Ben and put his own hands between his knees. "You warm now?"

"Are you?"

"Not so much." Vincent scooted his bag over until he and Ben were back to back.

"Come back in here then."

"Now I'll freeze you," Vincent said.

"It's okay. Come on." Vincent wiggled back out of his bag and into Ben's, a cold dollop of fear coating his stomach as he realized how very badly prepared and provisioned they had been for this accident. And as much as they were was only because Lorrie had insisted. He and Ben would have brought Kit-Kats and sports drinks.

After a moment, Ben said, "I do remember her singing that. Beth."

"Yeah. I figured."

"But it was like they wanted to own me. I hated them for that. She kept looking at me all the time. Like she wanted to devour me. Those big eyes."

"Yeah," Vincent said.

"And they probably felt like I feel now. Like if I ever see Stella again, I'll never let her out of my sight. I'll never put her down or let her go to school. And they waited so long and gave up. I never got it," Ben said.

"How could you get it? You were twelve. Anyhow, it doesn't matter. You get it now, and I'm sure Mom and Pop wish you had no idea how it feels. They felt just exactly like this."

"I never knew," Ben said again.

"It's not your fault."

"Basically, I treated them like crap. I didn't know who they were. I only knew they wanted me because they produced me. I was their possession. Like I was a . . . crop. I didn't know how you would feel because I . . . didn't know."

"They don't blame you."

"Vincent, if they felt like I feel about Stella . . . the morning she was born, I felt like I was going to explode. Like go up in the air like a hot-air balloon. I felt like nobody ever felt like I did, like you could die from loving a person. I wanted to get on my knees. Why didn't they tell me?"

"You didn't want them to, Sam," Vincent said carefully. "They didn't want to make it worse for you. It's okay now. Go to sleep."

"Great. I'm an asshole. When I said that

to you . . . at the hotel. I didn't really . . ."
Ben began.

"People say things. Go to sleep."

"She's so little."

"We'll find her."

"What if we never find her?" Ben asked.
"What if I'm one of the parents in the
movie?" Vincent rolled over on his back
and studied the clear plastic window in the
roof of the tent. He saw a single shooting
star among the broken crystal of all the
rest. He wished, squeezing his fists and
closing his eyes, like some stupid kid.

"It's so dark," Ben said.

"Sam, go to sleep," Vincent said, reaching over to pat his brother's back. "Go to
sleep now." He felt Ben's shoulders shaking and was about to ask if Ben was cold
again, when he realized that Ben was crying. He withdrew his arm and looked up at
the stars until they began to spin. He
closed his eyes for a moment. When he
looked up again, the sky was gray.

They could get up and get on the move.
Vincent felt like he had a hangover but felt
oddly energized too.

He burst out of the tent. Lorrie said, "It's
almost six a.m. I thought you were going to

sleep all day. Sam, you survived and now I don't have to lie to your daughter when I tell her her dad's a very brave man. Not to mention a very foolish one." She glanced at Vincent. "And her uncle's worse."

CHAPTER SEVENTEEN

What they ate in the morning looked like what came up after a long night with a Mexican meal and too many margaritas. Vincent forced himself to get it down, chasing it with two cups of tea and five or six spoonfuls of sugar.

"Okay, this is why we stay on the path," Lorrie said. "Suck the tea down and pee or whatever it is you have to do. If whatever you do is more than pee, dig a hole and cover it up. Leave no trace."

"We're being eco-friendly while my niece is out there?"

"Why not?" Lorrie asked. "It's just as easy."

"I thought we were going to sleep three hours and race through the night or something," said Vincent. He thought then, Why am I arguing with her about pooping?

Lorrie said, "We would have except for your brother's little dip. It took all night to dry his clothes. I had to keep moving them around while you snored. Thank you very much. Just hang the tent up to air a little and get dressed," she told him, turning to the dog. To Ben she said, "Are there any parts that feel funny? Hands or feet?"

"I'm good," Ben said.

"So drink a lot today and watch it. I'm shocked that the boots dried out," Lorrie said to Ben.

Vincent didn't mention that his hadn't. He slipped a plastic bag over each dry sock and heard the small squish as he laced his boots up.

Within an hour, they were packed up, Lorrie rearranging their packs with some magical ability to get them square and squat when Ben and Vincent could barely manage to get them closed. Before they did, Lorrie asked them to wait and stand with her as the sun came up. She read, "I will lift up mine eyes unto the hills, from whence cometh my help. . . . The sun shall not smite thee by day, nor the moon by night. . . . The Lord shall preserve thy going out and thy coming in from this time forth, and even for evermore."

"Did you think we were religious?" Vincent asked.

"Why would I care?" Lorrie asked, as she fed the dog. "I'm doing what makes me feel strong."

They hiked in silence for four hours. Lorrie stopped for her usual unannounced siesta. Then, still in silence punctuated only by their gasps, they slogged on. An hour, then two, then three, when suddenly Lorrie stopped. Without hearing her saying so, both men knew that she thought the dog had seen or smelled something. They pulled up short behind her.

"What?" Ben finally asked.

"There was a wood fire," she said. "Recently."

"Ours," said Vincent.

"No, up ahead. Can't you smell it?" They tried and Ben said he caught a whiff of something like the bonfires they lit when he was a kid. "That's it. It's up there to the left. Maybe just campers. But I don't think so. There can't be more than one idiot on this ridge right now. It smells like more than a campfire, though. Good wood. Cedar, maybe."

Lorrie struck off where the track divided, following Roman, who suddenly seemed to have brightened up. Back and forth, the huge dog worked, like a needle in and out of a cloth, crashing out of the scrub trees to a large cleared area. "Stay back here a minute."

While they watched, Roman veered to the left and looped back slightly to the right, then headed straight on. Lorrie signaled for them to follow, quietly. Roman continued for what Vincent imagined would be the equivalent of a few city blocks.

Then he stopped and raised his head and tail. Telling them to stay put, Lorrie approached the dog, knelt and pulled out the bandana, pulled it back and forth in his great mouth and then ruffled his neck and ears before she gave him a handful of treats. She motioned to Vincent and Ben.

"If you look closely, you can see the little house," she whispered.

It was like a reclusive goblin's hideout from a fairy tale—a peaked roof with green shingles and a green door, almost concealed by tall pines. No smoke came from the chimney, but they could definitely smell smoke by then.

"I can't let Roman go up there, because whoever is in there could shoot him if he has a gun," Lorrie said. "So, I'll try to come in from the side. Don't either of you move. Promise. No matter what you hear."

Even the trees maintained silence as Lorrie used her snowshoes to leap quietly over the faint tracks toward the little house. Ben nearly started forward as he saw a movement from inside . . . or was it a trick of the sunlight on the glass? Lorrie, out of the line of vision of the front windows, edged closer, slowly removing her gun from its shoulder holster and steadying it in both hands.

Then they heard the blast of the gunshot.

Ben screamed, "No!" And both of them stumbled forward.

CHAPTER EIGHTEEN

Beth, Candy, Kerry, and Pat wandered through the streets of Durand, searching for somewhere to eat something even vaguely urban. A scone. A muffin. In Durand, such a place didn't exist. There was a diner, but even the condition of the window, so smeared with grease and handprints it was impossible to see whether it was open or closed, deterred them. There was a shop that sold exquisite rock-based jewelry, two gas stations, three bars, Pitch's Sporting Goods, the Walgreens, and probably ten restaurants of varying ethnicities—all closed for the winter. The owner of the Lone Star thoughtfully gave them tortillas and cheese and there were peanut-butter crackers and milk from the drugstore. One boutique displayed luxe men's and women's clothing. It was called Darandella's.

"The town's single Italian," Pat said.

At the same moment, they all noticed in the window the slight smattering of children's things—quaint Elefanten shoes, tiny smocked and flowered Oilily dresses with polka-dotted tights, sturdy yellow-and-green spring corduroys for boys. Quickly, as if pulled by one string that joined them, they turned away from the smocked dresses and bright spring rompers.

All of Durand was composed of four streets, with the residential portions arrayed around the square like layers removed from a cake. During their second tour, they decided to ascend Paramount Drive, which was steep, and walk for a while. It kept them warm and no one could bear the silence of the inn—broken only when Eliza woke and wept behind the door—or the silence of the single cell phone that they had left, which was Pat's. As they tromped along, although they first imagined it to be a trick of the wind, they heard someone calling them. "Pat! Beth!" Whirling around, expecting to see the sheriff or Bill Humbly, they saw Claire Whittier, a white cardigan hugged around her, gesturing to them from the door of a massive stone-and-cedar house. Following Candy, who took a step toward her, they found themselves on Claire's doorstep. She said, "Please come inside. Let me make you something to eat at least. I have bread and eggs and Blaine is a good cook."

In the kitchen, surrounded by drawings painted and framed by the lost Jacqueline, they drank French-pressed coffee and ate slices of sourdough with Blaine's spitfire cheese-and-salsa omelet. Pat noticed that Blaine didn't eat and mentioned it.

"I can't," Blaine said. "My father spent my whole life telling me not to eat so I wouldn't get fat and now I can't. I can't stop thinking about what's happening up there. Sarah hasn't heard a thing."

"No news is not necessarily bad news," said Candy, who, strangely, had some appetite for the first time in a week. "It just means slow going."

"I feel like all I want to do is sleep," Blaine said.

"My sister-in-law, Eliza, is the same way, Blaine," Kerry told her. "Now that the doctor gave us Valium for her, Eliza sleeps and sleeps. She just gets up to brush her teeth. Sleep knits up the raveled sleave of care."

"Was that Dr. Slaughter?" Claire asked.

"Yes," Candy said. "Quite a name for a doctor."

"When we're awake, we just talk about it all the time and around and around it goes. There's not a thing you can do," Blaine went on, ignoring Claire.

"We know," Candy said. "We absolutely know."

"My father held a grudge. Obviously against whoever took my sister, but it was more too. He felt responsible for what happened to Jackie."

"You do," Beth said. "Even if you aren't. I did. I was . . . well, basically, I was nearly catatonic for at least a year after Ben was taken. I never once believed Ben was alive. In itself, that's not so strange."

"He never once believed Jackie was alive!" Blaine said. "Not from the first moment. He convinced both of us. And I wanted so to hope. I think that was what pushed me over, into a real depression. I had to have medication, and gained weight, and of course . . ."

"That infuriated Bryant, although it wasn't Blaine's fault," Claire said. "He wanted us to keep shipshape, like a military troop."

"What a thing to think about at a time like that," Candy said. "That wasn't fair to you."

"I distracted myself. You grasp at anything," Pat said. "For me it was, let's start a restaurant. Let's start a great theme restaurant, like an Italian wedding, only every night . . ."

"That was one distraction that worked out well, at least," Beth said gently.

"Yeah, it let me avoid how my wife and my kids were falling apart. So I guess you could say it was successful."

"Pat, honey," Beth said. "I'm lucky you didn't leave me."

"You sure?" Pat said. No one laughed.

"We saw your shopping center," Candy broke in, politely. "Your one clothing store, besides the sporting-goods place."

"Oh, Darandella's been an old friend for years. I'm sure my friends and I have kept her in business," said Claire. "Bryant never had time to go shopping. I bought a good many suits there for him, and had shirts made. And of course, when friends had babies . . ." She literally clapped one translucent hand across her mouth. "I'm so sorry."

"You didn't mean anything by it," said Candy. "It's okay, Claire. We should walk back now. My daughter's alone at the inn."

"Let me walk with you," Blaine said. "I can't stand to sit here anymore. Pictures of my sister. My father's . . . lair in there."

"I'll come too," Claire said.

"Mom, you don't want to do that," said Blaine as though Claire were a much, much older woman.

"Yes, of course I do. It would do me good to get some air. Just let me grab a coat and my boots."

In the end, the six of them walked back down past the imposing faces of the homes on Paramount Street and around the corner where Darandella's Boutique faced both the main thoroughfare and the ascending residential road. As they shook hands, Claire said suddenly, "Wait for me here. Just for a moment." And it didn't take more than five minutes for her to emerge, with three white bags, tufted with golden tissue, looped over her arms. "Here," she said, handing them to Beth, and when Beth couldn't hold both with her mittens, to Candy.

"What are these?"

"Spring clothes. Please take them. I thought, nine months? Babies are bigger now than the age they put on the clothes. I've often thought it's so mothers can feel pride in their children getting so big. Dresses and a couple of little coats . . ."

"We can't take these," Beth said gently.

"You mean, from us," Blaine said softly.

"No, I mean . . ."

"Please take them, for luck," said Blaine, and Claire nodded. "Please believe she's alive, for us. Because I know my dad is crazy but I don't ever think anything would make him hurt a baby. Please help us believe she's safe."

"They'll be the first things we put on her," Candy said. They watched as the Whittiers made their way slowly back up the block to their haunted house. "Jesus," Candy said.

"I'll keep them in my room," Beth said.

"I was just going to throw them in the trunk of the rental car," Candy told her. "I don't want to look at them."

"That wouldn't be right," Beth said. "She's trying to help us believe. I . . . threw away everything everyone gave me for Ben, back then. Now, I don't know if I should have shoved hope away from me so hard." She remembered how she had thought of the little pagan gods, how the Chinese believed the opposite of Westerners, that it was best to have those bored little gods catch sight of something shiny—elsewhere—than to notice a healthy child, good fortune made flesh. She thought for a moment of all the pagan ones that scarpered in these mountains and the ancient people who had prayed to them and tried to placate them. Would the bored little gods turn impassive eyes on this street where the meltwater torrented down the drains and nod?

The group finally caught sight of the awning that announced the Lone Star Inn. On the steps, they saw a figure in white, waving and leaping. Whatever she was calling was torn away from their ears by the steady push of the wind that came down from the mountains.

"It's Eliza," Candy said, and she and Pat began to run, the bags slapping against their legs. Beth stood in the snow, her hands clasped under her chin. Had she let herself hope too much? Had she let herself hope enough?

CHAPTER NINETEEN

It took Vincent's and Ben's combined strength to shove the door open against what was blocking it.

They glanced down when it finally budged. It was a man's leg, in denim with a flannel cuff.

"Jesus Christ," Ben murmured.

Bryant Whittier lay sprawled where he had fallen. He was dead.

Lorrie Sabo knelt and said, "I'll look for a pulse."

Vincent said, "I'm thinking that won't do much good." What had been the back of Bryant Whittier's head festooned the coat racks and one arm of the built-in benches that circled the one main room of the house.

Quickly, they turned away from the sight and examined the room. A ladder rose to a sleeping loft. Ben and Vincent nearly vaulted up. "He put the fire out first."

"Where is she? She'd be crying if she heard me!" Ben said. "Where's Stella?"

They clambered back down from the loft.

"Wait, wait," Lorrie said. She opened the door and with a cluck of her tongue, summoned Roman inside. He immediately took up his peculiar stance in front of a deep bank of recessed kitchen drawers. One of the drawers was open perhaps an inch.

Vincent pulled it out all the way and Stella kicked her feet and smiled.

"Stella bella. She wasn't afraid," Ben said, scooping up the baby, holding her close. "Stella. My baby."

"Of course she wasn't, were you?" Lorrie cooed. "You knew your dad was coming. You're a smart chick, isn't ya?" To Ben, Lorrie said, "In another life, I was a nurse. Let me just have a look at her quick." After a few deft presses and peeks, Lorrie said, "Heck, she's fine. She's not even dehydrated, though I'd like her a little bit warmer."

Ben opened his parka and shirt and tenderly zipped the baby inside, unconsciously humming the denied old song, *If a bunny catch a bunny.* . . . "My little girl. My little girl. Daddy's here. Daddy will never let you go ever again. My little heart. *Mio piccolo cuore.*"

"You don't speak Italian," Vincent said.

"What do you know? For a guy who won an Oscar, you don't know that much," said Ben. His face was childlike with rapture.

Quickly, Vincent turned away and examined the panes of glass on the windows of the little house, each a prism in the morning light. The carol of Stella's steady stream of rolling nonsense vowels made him weak; her face was a beacon of contentment. Vincent stared around the inside of the little house—trying to take in the genius of its economy, from the built-in beds to the fold-down table. Bryant Whittier's body, with its achromatic face, took up much of the floor space.

Lorrie pulled a plastic tablecloth from the head of her pack—she called that piece a "cranium," perhaps in deference to the scene—and said, "Let's see how much propane he had left." She pumped the levers to get the stove going long enough to warm water in a pan. "There we go. I knew there was a reason I kept one of Mariel's old bottles."

"What's that?"

"Ah, that would be baby formula," Lorrie said. "I fed some without iron to a mouse my daughter Dana found last winter. Now I have the fattest mouse in California. Then I just kept the formula. Who knows why? Anyhow. You think it's just your B.O. that's making her cry? Think she might be hungry?"

"Where're the bottles Whittier had?" Vincent asked.

"In the trash. They're disposables," Lorrie said. "I looked first. They're the kind they have on planes."

"We didn't think of bringing a bottle," Ben said.

"Among so much else," Lorrie said with a radiant, mischievous grin. "We have enough for one, anyhow."

They sat on the built-in bench, keeping their feet away from Bryant Whittier's corpse, while Ben fed Stella and changed her into one of two remaining disposable diapers in the cabin. Then he found an absurdly light stretchy suit, one that Eliza had brought to L.A., and dressed her. With Lorrie directing him, Vincent searched the loft and the bags for anything they could wrap around Stella. Her little hands were pale and chilled. There was a snowsuit, perhaps an eighteen-month size, that was too big, so they stuffed the legs and the feet with burp cloths and a baby blanket to make it snug. Vincent turned up the brim on his Blackhawks cap and pulled it down over Stella's black hair, leaving his own pink headband in place. Then Ben picked up his child, holding her cheek close to his own. "Do you think she's deaf?" he asked Lorrie.

"Why the heck would you think that?"

"She would have heard that gunshot."

"That drawer was probably her bed. It was lined with blankets. She probably startled and then went back to sleep. Babies don't startle that easily if they feel safe. He probably made her feel comfortable here." At that thought, Ben exhaled a long breath and rubbed his forehead. "I'll never figure this out if I live a hundred years."

Lorrie began marshaling the troops. "You don't have to. Now, Vincent, Sam, listen. I'm going to go back for help and you're staying here. You fell once and you can't fall now. We're at least fifteen miles in over rough country. But it's country I know like the back of my hand. If I hike as fast as I can, which is a lot faster than you, and given how much the snow has melted today, maybe I can make it out by sundown. There's a good chance of that. The sky's still clear. That's good as far as the likelihood of there being no more snow, but it also means it might get cold. Too cold to take a chance with Stella."

"How long?" Ben said. "Why can't we all go?"

"Your job, Ben, for your baby, is to stay here. Stay right here until I send help. I will have the FBI guy send a helicopter for you three. This is the safest place you can be. Shelter and light and water. At least enough."

"Sit here? With Whittier's body?" Vincent asked.

"Push him outside. Turn on the heat . . ."

"For as long as it lasts . . ." said Ben.

"You have wood," she said. And glanced at the tiny stove. "Well, a little. You have your sleeping bags too. You know how to zip them together. Get in together. Put her in the middle and just huddle if it comes to that," Lorrie said. "But it won't. You hired me to find her, didn't you? And bring her back safe? This is the only way I can do it." She stepped just outside the door for a moment and tried her cell phone. "Shoot! Nothing."

"Lorrie, just go," Vincent said. "I'll make the deciding call here."

"We can't even let Eliza know!" Ben said.

"I'll call as soon as I get a signal. That way, help might be on the way before I even get to the trailhead," Lorrie insisted. "The sooner we do this the better. I'm going to unload my pack to travel light. I'll leave you everything I don't need for an emergency. I'm going to take my phone and a few power bars. I'll take my gun. You . . . obviously have one," she added, looking down at Bryant Whittier. "Let's, ah, pull him outside so that you can . . . it's just better."

Lorrie held Stella while Vincent and Ben gingerly hauled the body outside the little cabin. They laid him a few feet from the door. Before they used one of the blankets from inside to cover him, Vincent looked down at Bryant Whittier's placid, businesslike face, the hole in the back of his head invisible. He had aimed the rifle up through his mouth and apparently used his toe to pull the trigger. Inside, he had set his boots carefully to one side. They were nice Merrells. Whittier wouldn't have wanted to splatter them. Vincent thought briefly of Jackie's ballet slippers. He and Ben pulled the blanket up to cover Whittier's face.

Back inside, Vincent wondered If the boots would fit him. He used the toe of his own lousy boot to bend back the boot top and see the label. They were yet another size too small.

Damn. Whittier could have done some good in death he hadn't done in life.

What had this guy's life been? Vincent wondered. What had his thoughts been?

Back inside, Lorrie was hurrying to get ready to leave. She said, "Just promise me you won't move. *Promise* you won't leave here. Nine of ten times that civilians go with you, they get all excited or worried and they can't wait. They go off thinking, Hey, I made it here, I can make it back. Don't. It always has a bad result. Sometimes a really bad result."

"How many times have you let civilians come with you?" Vincent asked.

"Twice. This is the second time. The first time I swore I would never do it again."

"So nine out of ten times was really one out of two times," Vincent said.

"Every tracker I know says the same thing," Lorrie told them, her mouth a grim line. "No one listens to good sense."

She began to remove items from her pack—the harness, the disgusting bags of dried goop, her little stove, one of her water bags. "Boil snow for water. This far up, you probably won't even need iodine to purify it. There's enough formula left for a couple more bottles. I'd say cut up some cloth and tape it on her for diapers. Save the one disposable. If you get a chance, cut more wood. I'm leaving you all the food I have. Romy and I will go as fast as is humanly possible. And caninely possible. You'll hear that helicopter whomping by tonight. There's more of a clearing here than I thought from what Sarah said at first."

While Roman ate the last of his high-energy kibble, Lorrie instructed the brothers, "Show me your mirrors and your lights." Dutifully, they dug out their headlamps and flashlights and mirrors. "You could use those to signal if you had to. But that's crazy. It's not as though they won't spot this place. They have super-spotter lights on helicopters, particularly the military kind. The tree cover here won't mean a thing to them."

Vincent wondered if Lorrie was talking to them anymore or to herself. Her voice seemed to have slipped down a register, into a deeper key. "I've got my groundsheet and my sleeping bag and *my* mirrors and headlamp. I've got water. That's it. All I ever needed and all I need now. If I get hurt, Roman knows how to go for help. But I won't get hurt. That's it."

Lorrie stood up, kissed Stella, who was now asleep, with her lips furled around the nipple, and hugged each of the brothers.

"Godspeed, Lorrie," Ben said. "I owe you everything."

"Thank you. Remember what I said,

now. Stay put. We got off lucky with Ben. We got our prize here. Don't rush it, now." Vincent raised his hand in a parody of the Boy Scout pledge. "If, God forbid, you had to leave, it's straight south. *Straight* south. You have your GPS. But don't. Wait, no matter what."

Together, with Ben straining against Vincent's hand on his arm, they watched Lorrie and the huge dog take off out of the trees and into the sunlight.

"She's something else," Ben said. They dug chocolate bars out and ate them. Stella wakened and they took out spoons for her to play with. Within ten minutes, she tired of them and began to fuss. Ben fed her the last of the bottle and mixed another with the dregs of the water from his carrier. "I wish we could set her down to play," Ben said. "But the floor's not exactly . . ."

The blood on the floor had begun to freeze, crystalline and black. Stella seemed sweaty, so Ben took off the snowsuit. The two men made a cave in which Stella could crawl back and forth between them on the padded bench. Her father would pull her to her feet when she reached him, to Stella's instant hilarity.

When she got back to Vincent, he would do the same thing. Her laughter sounded to Vincent like wind chimes on a summer afternoon. Finally, she visibly ran out of steam, and crawled into Ben's lap, popping her thumb into the side of her mouth. He swaddled her close. Vincent said, "It's getting cold. Let's start a fire, and put the snowsuit back on."

Ben agreed, then said, "Geez, if we had cards, we could play gin. How long has it been?"

Vincent looked at his watch. "An hour. Maybe an hour and ten minutes."

"Long time to go," Ben said.

"Six hours, easy, even if she only stops once or twice."

Suddenly, Ben asked, "What's that? Look outside the window. It looks funny . . . like metal, silvery."

Vincent stepped outside, closing the door behind him.

Out of nowhere, a curdle of cloud had darkened the sky.

And it began to snow.

CHAPTER TWENTY

For something that looked to have been built by the Three Little Pigs, the eight-by-twelve-foot cabin was startlingly well-insulated: Heat poured from the little woodstove so quickly that soon, beads of sweat curled the dark tendrils along Stella's forehead and Ben loosened her snowsuit yet again. The brothers could feel their shoulders relax almost instantly: Vincent's began to throb with a steady ache. He hadn't realized how much he had been protecting himself from the cold by holding his back rigid.

"He came all this way to do this," Ben said, as he glanced outside, pointing to how the snow began to cover Bryant Whittier. It was falling faster now. Vincent noticed that the blanket soon looked like a mound . . . like a grave.

Vincent answered, "He didn't mean for it to get like this. He meant to get back down and leave Stella in a safe place, make a phone call, probably. Or have someone make it for him. Whittier obviously had a lot of checks he could cash, a lot of favors out there he could call in. My guess is that he gave it up when the snow forced him to stay up here. He's a lawyer. He would have known that if it went this far and he was found, he was in prison for life. Kidnapping is a capital crime. From what his wife said, I don't think it meant all that much to him anyhow."

Ben asked, "What?"

"His life. He didn't care."

"Then maybe he did mean for it to get like this. How the hell did he get all this stuff up here?" Ben said.

"Fucking beats me. Over from the other side."

"What other side?"

"Sarah Switch said there's always another side."

"Why'd he wait until he heard us then, if it didn't mean anything to him?" Ben asked.

"If I had to guess . . ." Vincent began. He stopped then.

"Go on. What?"

"So he knew for sure that Stella would be safe."

"Oh, Jesus. Thank God. How could somebody be that crazy and also that, like, good?"

"He loved his little girl too, I assume."

"We should probably put up some of these red blankets and make some kind of sign out there so that somebody can come up here and get him," Ben said.

"I don't know if anyone will ever end up seeing it," Vincent said. Unspoken, between them, was the reason. The snow was falling too fast. Anything they laid down now would be covered in thirty minutes. "We'd better stay inside, conserve the heat. I'm going to try to catch ten while Stella's asleep. You should too."

"I'm too wound up."

"Kerry told me once that when she had to grab a nap before a performance, she would just lie down and listen to some sound far away and she could pass out for fifteen minutes, wake up ready to go," Vincent told him. "Try that."

A few moments later, when Vincent glanced at Ben, he saw that his brother was already asleep, Stella cuddled like a doll between Ben and the back of the bench. It was surprisingly easy for Vincent to pillow his head on the coat he found (okay, it was Whittier's, but who cared?) and blink out too.

The sound that woke him was howling, distant, insistent. The wind was rising.

Determined not to wake Ben, Vincent slid to his feet and laid his hand on the woodstove. It wasn't cold, but his hand was comfortable against it. He looked inside and used a long fork to poke the ashes. The nylon log carrier Whittier had used was empty but for a few chips. Vincent stepped out and dragged in what wood he saw stacked against the wall. It was soaking wet. Next, he turned to the cooking stove. He lifted the ten-gallon propane can. It was empty. In turn, he lifted the other three he found outside lined up against the cabin—willing to hear a slosh inside one, just one of them. Nothing.

Nothing but hollow steel.

Nothing.

The single light above their heads blinked out. What was this? A generator of some kind? What ran it? Where was the box? Vincent could barely see the outline of his brother, huddled on the bench. He began to search the cabinets and the loft for an electrical box or another propane tank, making no attempt to be silent. He climbed up into the sleeping loft. The only thing left was the little tank for Lorrie's portable camping stove. How long would the cabin hold the heat?

As Vincent descended the ladder, a beam pierced the murky daylight. Ben was sitting up, wearing his headlamp and looking at Vincent.

"What in the hell do we do now?" Ben said.

"We have to go down," Vincent said. "It's dark. No helicopter. She had to stop."

"You don't know that," Ben said.

"You know it has to be me and you know it has to be now."

"How do I let you do that?" Stella woke and began to cry. Ben recovered the bottle and quickly, the baby sucked down the last of the formula and began to cry harder. Ben filled the bottle with water. Stella took it, but whimpered. "Vincent, that's all the food I have for her."

"The water's good. You can give her some . . . crackers."

"I will," Ben said. "But she's not used to eating food."

They secured Stella by a blanket strip around the waist to the only chair, and she began contentedly banging spoons on the table and throwing them against the wall, laughing when they fell back down in front of her. Her absurdly long legs in the snowsuit danced like blue puppets.

The cabin was still warm but Ben and Vincent had contrived to hook up the canister of stove gas to the stove. They agreed that no one would turn it on until the cold was mortal.

"I'm uneager to go," Vincent said. "Believe me. I don't want to go out and stumble around in that muck. I'm not the hero. That's you."

When Ben muttered, "Yeah, right," Vincent's heart stepped up a rung.

He said, "I won't go all the way down. I'll stop at the big clearing. Halfway. I'll call for help on the phone and get them to come and get you."

"You first. I have shelter here."

"You have Stella here," Vincent said.

They waited a few moments—Vincent unable to think of an encouraging word, Ben unable to think of an argument.

"Well," Vincent said, "I'm going."

"Take at least half this junk. Take the sleeping bag to wrap up in. Put on a double layer of socks," Ben said. "Here are some wool socks. Clean in the package. He didn't wear them. And this vest thing."

"You sound like Ma," Vincent said.

"And don't take that huge backpacker thing. There's this little pack, like a school bag. The sleeping bag's at the bottom if you get cold. And I'm putting in some of this trail mix and a water bag. I found some Coke . . ."

"Don't make it too heavy, Benbo," Vincent said. He realized too late he hadn't said that word for ten years or more.

Ben said, "Shut up." Vincent heard the gravel in his voice. Ben was trying not to cry.

Hurriedly, Vincent went on, "I've got my compass and my miner's light and every other gizmo on earth. I'd have to be a deef to get lost."

"Which is why I said it," Ben told him. Stella was waving a cracker in each of her mittened fists. "I just stuck in some of those little stadium warmer things you crack open. Just in case. Whittier had them too."

"Hey," Vincent said. Ben looked up from stuffing Vincent's pack. "You're good. You think about cracker face here. I'll be okay, Sam."

"If you get fucking lost out there, I'll kill your ass. I'm on the level here," Ben said, standing up straight.

"I'll take that into consideration," Vincent said. He pulled the pack onto his back, slipped the light over his head securely, and affixed the snowshoes to his boots. Then, without waiting to think it over, he stepped out into the clearing and shut the door behind him. Instantly, he was in a cloud, a moving cloud that pelted his face. When he flipped on his light, the cloud became a dancing, gossamer curtain, silver and crystal, dense as fluttering fabric. He looked down at his GPS and then at his feet and took his first sliding three steps due south.

"Vincent," Ben called. Vincent looked back. He could see only a faint outline of the little house. "I'll find you!"

"Dude," Vincent answered, and the wind pulled away his words. "No worries!"

The flare of the headlamp disappeared as Ben ducked back inside.

Move forward, Vincent instructed his feet. One foot in front of the other. Push, sink, slide. Push, sink, slide. *Ben,* Vincent said without sound, *I can't feel my hands. Thank Christ I took the hat off Stella's head before I left. I can't feel my feet either.* Push, sink, slide. How, he thought, am I going to feel the rocks when I get to them? Easy, fool. The rocks mean you're going down to another flat place. Through the snow, he thought he could sense a slight lowering in the path, a depression, the remnants of Lorrie's trail.

Push, step. Push, step. Vincent held his arm up to the headlamp so he could see the hands on the dial of the watch. He had been moving for an hour. Or a minute. He could scarcely see where the hands stood.

It must be an hour. Under the vest, his two layers of shirting were soaked with the sweat of his effort. *Talk,* Vincent said. *Stay alert. Stay alive. Who said that? He had! He and Rob said that in some PSA ten thousand years ago. Stolen it from someone else . . . Why didn't I put my goggles on, Ben? Ma, can you believe this is California?*

Vincent stumbled forward in the darkness. He counted his steps. Twenty. Eighty. One hundred and nine. Two hundred. Five hundred and five.

Miraculously, the snow began to thin to wispy pinions of flakes, whirling among the trees. Then there were no trees. Vincent turned on the big flashlight and panned around him. Cautiously, he began the descent from the high meadow to the trail. From this vantage, he thought he could see faint marks of the deeper trail they had made going up and Lorrie's trail going down. Next to him, just below and to the right, was the creek where Ben had fallen. To his left, behind and above him, then back in the trees, must have been the shelter of their hasty campsite. Look ahead, Vincent told himself, look ahead and not down at your feet. He began the descent, balancing steadily. Step. Step two. Step three. One more step down. Vincent grounded himself on the snowshoes and reached for the last of the incline, glancing up toward the path, over which he would fly to the next and gradual descent, the last one before the big clearing, the halfway mark. His right foot was on the path when the toe of his left snowshoe caught something and tugged. Vincent stumbled and went down hard, to the unmistakable stomach-churning bite of a twisted ankle.

Hell, no!

Don't worry, Ben, Vincent said, *I'm okay. I'll lace the boot tighter. Goddamn boots are so tight, at least it won't swell.* He lifted his leg out of whatever little hidden crevasse had trapped it and concentrated on his injured ankle. He didn't dare remove the snowshoe. There was no telling if he would get it back on, for, as he fumbled with the laces, Vincent tried and failed to ignore how his fingers really were as cumbersome as little stubs of lumber. When he moved his gloves, it was as though he were operating a robot claw. Shit, Vincent then realized, no wonder. He had begun with two layers of cheesy gloves, given one to Ben forever ago in the tent and forgotten to get it back. Jesus, where was his mind? He knew that Ben didn't realize he still wore Vincent's woolen layer under his own insulated gloves.

But Ben was in the middle of the epic crisis of his life—to which he'd added enough guilty realization about his childhood and their parents to last for the next forty years. How would he have thought of such a little thing? It was Vincent's own fault.

Vincent leaned back and jerked the laces tight. A red band of pain exploded between his calf and his wooden foot. His breath came faster and his mouth filled. He leaned over and puked his chocolate into the snow. Scrabbling in his pocket, Vincent found his phone and flipped it open. He had bars! Desperately, he punched in his father's number.

"Hello?" Pat said. "Vincent? Son?"

Vincent tried to answer.

"Vincent? Vincent? It's his number but nobody's there! Where . . . ? Somebody tell Candy!" The screen went black. Pat couldn't hear him. Vincent tried again. This time, the phone didn't even make a connection.

Other phones, Vincent thought. The other phones.

He had left them behind, in the big reinforced pannier pack, stuck only the one into his pocket.

Why?

Ben had no use for them! He wouldn't get squat up there. Lorrie didn't. But maybe he would. Ben would try.

Ben should try.

Vincent knew he would try, at least.

So, for now, Vincent would handle it. Was there a choice? Didn't he hear once—hadn't he read that you rubbed snow on them? On frostbitten fingers and toes? Vincent stripped off his gloves and gasped at the sight of his fingers. They were waxen, like Halloween dummy hands, despite all the time they'd spent in the relative warmth of the cabin. When the hell had this happened? Reaching down, Vincent pulled off the gloves, then rubbed snow between his palms. Carefully, he stowed the gloves in a pocket and stuck his hands inside his shirt under his arms, where he felt their stiff cold bash into his warm core and, distantly, like the sound of fireworks far away, he also detected a slight prickling in his palms and thumbs. Vincent kicked off his left snowshoe and was unlacing his right when he slipped back on his elbows. The pain in his ankle growled once more and then bit hard. Vincent fell over onto his back. The pain was a howl, keening.

The stars above him steered a hard right and disappeared.

At eight p.m., as the last light faded above the tree line, the canister of propane from Lorrie's little outdoor stove breathed its last. Ben had finally found the tracker's Jetboil, but it had burned no more than twenty minutes. So the little house fell into darkness and the cold curled against the windows like a waiting thing.

From his experience of the past five hours, Ben knew he had a good hour or more of heat left and an hour after that of relative chill.

It must have been harder going for Lorrie than she first thought, the new snow adding another layer, literally, to an already difficult situation. And as for Vincent . . . Ben was scared as hell for Vincent.

Tucked back in her blanket nest in the drawer, Stella slept quietly.

Glancing at his baby, Ben thought, What the hell? Why not try? Because it will kill me if it doesn't work? I can wait. I can do anything, he thought. Grabbing one of the phones from the pack, he stepped outside into snow that swept over his ankles and crowded his knees in drifts. He closed the door behind him, first testing it to see that it would open again. Looking down, he could see a vague green smudge of lights, distant as a planet. He breathed a prayer and flipped the telephone open. He had a connection. Not daring to move, barely daring to inhale, Ben dialed his wife's number.

"Eliza?" he said.

"Sam . . ." she answered, her voice blurred. "Sa . . ." She was gone. Two further calls yielded nothing but the red FAILED notation on the screen.

Ben went back into the cabin and chafed his cold hands. Stella slept on. Back outside, Ben faced the opposite direction and dialed Pat's phone.

Someone picked up, but the only sounds were static, with the rhythm of speech. Damn it! The top of the line, when it came to cellular phones, was about as good as two cans and a string.

He dialed again.

"Hello?" Pat said, as clearly as though he were standing beside Ben in the darkness. "Who's this?"

"It's . . . it's . . . it's Ben, Pat. Pop. Dad. I have Stella. Send help. Send . . . anyone you can. Come to the trailhead."

"Who is this?" Pat demanded. And then Ben was holding a dead phone. He almost shrieked from frustration, but was fearful that Stella would hear him, even through the door, and awaken. Then, nearly immediately, the mobile phone in his hand rang. Pat demanded, "Who is this? Is this some kind of joke?"

"It's me. It's Ben. Really. It's Ben. Sam."

"Cut it out," Pat said.

"You were named by a nurse who took care of Grandma when Grandpa was on the road. Her name was Bridget and she named you after Saint Patrick. Grandpa was a cook in the war. Kenny shorts the shots drinks after the first three drinks," Ben said.

"You are Ben. Where are you?" Pat asked. "We thought Eliza was high from the sedative when she told us you called her . . ."

"I'm up at this little cabin. Over fifteen miles in. And up. Isn't Lorrie Sabo there yet? At the trailhead?"

"*We're* not there," said Pat. "We're at the inn. We were waiting for the sheriff to call. The only one up there at the trailhead is the sheriff, Sarah . . ."

"Lorrie didn't come in yet?" Ben asked.

"Not that we know. Sam, stay on the line. Candy is calling Sarah . . . wait. Candy says Sarah has contacted . . . somebody. They'll be there in . . . what? She says an hour if there's a place to set it down. To set the helicopter down. Is there?"

"There's a clearing about a hundred yards from here," Ben said. "It would have to be a helluva good pilot. Is Eliza there?" There were more thumps and rustlings as more people crowded into the room on Pat's end. Pat shouted to them at large, "They got Stella! Lorrie's on her way to the trailhead. They got Stella!" There were cries and cheers. "Liza, it was Ben! It wasn't a dream."

Then Ben heard Eliza's voice.

"Is she with you? Our baby? Sam, sweetheart? Did you find her? Are you holding her? Is she alive? Is she breathing?"

"She's right here, Liza. She's safe and sound," Ben said softly. "I love you and she loves you."

"Oh, Sam! Oh, Santa Maria, Santo Antonio, Santa Anna, forgive me my foolishness and greed and all my sins . . ." Eliza wept. "Oh, thank God."

"She's fine, Eliza. We're fine."

"Sam, I love you so much!"

"And I love you . . ."

"I never really believed . . . oh, I can't wait to touch her! Please come now!"

"Let me talk to my father, honey," Ben said.

"He's not here. I'll have to call him," Eliza answered.

Abruptly understanding, Ben told her

gently, "I don't mean George now. It's Pat I have to talk to, Liza."

Eliza said, "Hurry back, Sam. Thank you, Sam. I love you. It all sounds so artificial. I can't wait to see you." She handed off the phone.

"Is Stella okay, Sam?" It was Pat's voice again.

"She's fine, but someone has to get here soon. But listen. Pat . . . first, someone has to find Vincent."

Pat said, "What . . . Vincent? Where's Vincent?"

"He left because the little cabin . . . Whittier's cabin . . . it was getting dark, the firewood was wet and we ran out of formula. There's no heat, but we're safe. We're out of the wind."

"Whittier? Where's Whittier now, Sam?"

"He's . . . Lorrie will explain. Or I will. I have shelter. You have to find Vincent first. And Lorrie," Ben said. The line went dead. Ben grabbed another of the phones and punched in Pat's number.

"Pat?"

"Yes?" Pat said. "Sam? Listen, the helicopter is coming for you . . ."

"Not me! Not yet! They have to find Vincent and Lorrie!"

". . . on another trip, Sam . . ." Pat said, as the line began, ominously, to crackle, whatever momentary magic that had permitted the connection about to be snuffed, like a match flame guttering. Hearing Stella's cry, Ben whirled toward the door, into the wind.

"What do you mean, Pop?"

"I'm here!" Pat's voice came faintly. "Can you put a light on out there? Can you hear me, Sam?"

"I will! I'll put all the flashlights out in front! That's all I have."

"Okay," Pat said, fainter now.

"You can call me Ben, Pop," Sam said, suddenly, softly. But no one was there.

Ben found six flashlights and set them heads up, in a line that ended in an arrow, on the shred of ornamental porch to the left of the door. There was barely room on the floor of the porch thing for a stool but there was less snow under the tiny overhang. Why had Whittier even bothered with it? Back inside, Ben wrapped Stella close against him in a cocoon of blankets, pressing the last of the chilly water to his daughter's roseate mouth. As she drank, hungrily, Ben reached for a Coke and drained it in a single draft.

Barely thirty minutes later, he heard the whop-whop of the helicopter's rotors, first indistinct but growing louder, closer. Then a light as blessed as morning swept the clearing with a mighty eye and a magnified voice spoke his name.

CHAPTER TWENTY-ONE

The helicopter carrying Ben and his baby set down a good distance out into the clearing, away from the trailhead.

"People are going to run out here," the pilot said to Ben. "They always do. I don't want them to get hurt."

As the pilot slowed the blades and a soldier held Stella while Ben climbed down, it took his dulled mind a moment to recognize what he had glimpsed as they swept closer and closer to Durand. There were lights—lanterns swinging like pendulums, lights from filming crews mounted on cranes above him, lights like a necklace of yellow pearls from cars snaking up a road that must extend back two miles past Durand. As Ben marched closer, and shielded his eyes, the murmur he heard built to a roar. Everyone behind the police line was cheering. He picked out George and Elena in the silly matching red parkas they'd bought for their honeymoon. He spotted Kerry jumping up and down. Lorrie had her goggles pushed back and Roman raced back and forth in front of her. Then, one slight dark form broke away, skipping neatly out of the grasp of a tall man and running straight for him like a sprinter. His whole life sprang into his throat. Only Beth heard Ben when he swallowed and croaked, "Ma."

She stopped. And then she nodded, rushing forward.

Eliza was suddenly there, too, her arms around his waist, holding Stella between them. Ben pulled them close and thought, Now I can stop. I can relax and sleep forever. It's over.

But reality snapped its finger under his nose and dragged him back out into the darkness under the whorl of gathering stars.

Lorrie was safe now but Vincent was still out there.

The helicopter surged to life and lifted again, this time with Beth climbing in beside the soldiers. The searchlight began to sweep the direction that Lorrie had pointed out. Holding Stella close, Eliza followed Sarah Switch to the waiting squad car, as reporters and people from the town and beyond closed around them.

Ben kept his place in the field. He was cold, but not so cold as Vincent must now be. After it was obvious to Candy that he would not follow her back to the warmth of the other car, she and Pat stood beside him.

"I'll wait here for Vincent," Ben said.

Candy said, "Makes sense."

It was the phone's insistent ringing that woke him. Where was he? Where was the phone? Vincent scrabbled for it on the ground and finally found it in an inside pocket of the vest.

His ankle was pulsing, a hot little nova, threatening to break the leather shoelaces. With the aid of his headlamp, he examined the ugly bulge of swollen flesh curling over the top of his boot under the sock. He was grateful at least that he could feel it, the ankle. Struggling to his knees, Vincent tried to stand, but the ankle shrieked and he fell back down. His pants were soaked through and he was shuddering as if he were having a seizure. Vincent shrugged off the pack and scattered the contents in the snow. Sleeping bag, he thought, pulling off the layers of wet pants. He ripped the wrapper off a peanut-butter bar and stuck it in his mouth. And then he pulled the bag around him. Lying back against a hummock of snow, Vincent fumbled for the stadium warmers, cracking one, then two, then three of them open. He tucked them down into the recesses of his sleeping bag and felt them begin their warming but dimly—as though they were down the street, in another person's house.

His cell phone rang again. This time, Vincent caught it in time, holding it between his palms.

"Vincent? Vincent!"

"Vincent," he said. "Yes."

"It's Mom. Are you okay?"

"Okay. Yeah."

"Ben's here with the baby. Your words are slurring," Beth said.

"I'm cold. I'm only cold."

"Hold on, Vincent. The helicopter's here. Can you hear it?"

"I can hear it. I'm not up on Everest, Ma. I'm cold is all."

"I can hear you like I was standing next to you," Beth said.

"I wouldn't be so unpleased if you *were* standing next to me."

"They're fast. We should be there any minute," Beth said. "Okay, I'm getting in the helicopter now . . ."

"All good, Ma. Let's let them bring me in, in style. For the news cameras. I am an Oscar winner."

Beth's voice was drowned by the thickering of the blades but Vincent heard her say, ". . . a signal?"

A signal.

Vincent needed to think. He held his mind out and shook it like a box of nickels and fishhooks.

Well, his headlamp was one. It was a signal.

And the mirror.

Vincent placed the mirror on his chest and began to tilt it back and forth, back and forth. When the phone rolled out of his hands and disappeared beneath the snow, he watched it as a dog might, curious but unable to act. He tilted the mirror once more, back and forth.

"Stay on the line, Vincent," Beth called from the snow. Unaccountably, that seemed funny. "Vincent? Vincent?" Beth called again.

"I see a reflection down there," said the second pilot. "Look. At two o'clock. I see someone shining something . . . there, just above that big clearing. I'm going to sweep it again. See it?" The medic riding shotgun nodded.

"I see it. Either it's random glass . . ."

"No, it's moving. Somebody's moving it."

"He's not answering anymore," Beth interrupted, leaning over to see, her stomach heaving at the sudden cant of the aircraft. "Do you think he's conscious?"

"Either he's moving it or the wind is," the pilot said. "Could be the wind. But I just picked up something with the searchlight for a second that's bright blue . . ."

"His sleeping bag is blue!" Beth said. "Did you hear me? He has a blue sleeping bag!"

Vincent lay in the snow and thought of summer light streaming through trees. He was riding his bike past the red house. Ben was shooting hoops but he saw Vincent and turned and walked toward him, growing taller and older as he walked. "Hey, Vincent," he said. "Hey. Wanna play Make It, Take It? You scared?"

"Not scared exactly," Vincent said slowly.

"Don't be scared. We're going to just lift you onto this board and start a line and get some fluid in. . . ."

"Why?" Beth demanded. "Why not just put him in the helicopter?"

"We'd start a line in hell, ma'am. And we don't put him on the board until we do a flashlight check to see if there's anything going on with his spine and his brain. . . ."

So, excruciatingly slowly, the medics did just that. "Looks good," the woman said quickly. "Okay, buddy. Here we go." Vincent looked up at the person shining lights on him. It wasn't Ben. Green guys with double lights above their eyes were lifting him onto a bed and carrying him. One held a full bag of fluid above his head.

Cool.

This was also pretty funny, considering.

The Martians were landing.

Thoughtfully, they had brought his mother. She looked pale but she smelled so clean.

The pilot told her, "We're going directly to St. Luke's in San Francisco, ma'am."

"We're ready," Beth said evenly. As though Vincent weighed nothing, the soldiers strapped him to a board and loaded him like lumber into the aircraft.

"His hands and feet don't look too, too bad," said the medic, gingerly removing Vincent's gloves and touching his fingers, removing his sodden boots and socks. Beth could tell that the medic was lying. "Can you feel my hand, Vincent? Can you feel this?"

"What?" Vincent answered. The medic was pinching his finger as hard as she could.

One of Vincent's feet was huge and red and one was small and shriveled, but both looked diminished, poached. Beth breathed in and out slowly.

As they sped over the hills toward the gold-beaded net that was the lights of San Francisco, Vincent told Beth about Bryant Whittier's desperate, hopeless death, about the small house and the eerie clearing.

Doctors were waiting on the rooftop at St. Luke's when the helicopter set down. They hurried through the doors and down the elevator to the ER. Three nurses rushed Vincent through the double doors while another ushered Beth into the treatment area partitioned off by a bright yellow curtain. Beth stepped outside while the team cut off Vincent's clothes and doctors began the slow warming process of his limbs. When Beth stepped back inside, Vincent was wearing a brightly patterned blue hospital gown. He still smelled of smoke and sweat and his cheekbones reigned over a face so dirty and gaunt that only the grin and the game face he put on for Beth bore a resemblance to the son she knew.

Eventually, the ER resident said, "You're

a lucky guy. A few degrees colder and you'd have been way worse off than you are. This goes fast. You'll be practically as good as new, with a little luck, in six weeks or so. So, you going to make a movie about this, huh? Who's going to play me?"

"Not for anything in the world," Vincent said. "I'm thinking romantic comedies, although my girlfriends have told me I'm neither funny nor romantic."

The doors closed.

Beth retreated to the cafeteria, where she ate something off every glass shelf, from toast to a grilled cheese to chocolate pudding. She read a magazine article about fitness after forty and gave up when she got to the lunges. Then she spent fifteen minutes in the washroom cleaning her own face and putting on lipstick and mascara. Finally, she called Pat and learned that the family were all on their way to the Marlborough Hotel on Powell Street. Some of them were in Sarah Switch's truck, others in Bill Humbly's car. The twenty miles from Durand to the city might take an hour, Pat said, mostly because the reporters' trucks combined with San Francisco traffic had the road backed up like the Eisenhower Expressway in Chicago on the night of a home game.

"I thought they would put on lights and sirens," Pat said, sounding as disappointed as a kid who'd missed the parade. There was a huge whoop then, as Humbly and Switch did exactly that and began to muscle their way through the parallel silver grid of cars.

Beth relaxed. Tonight, their lonely room at the Lone Star Inn would be empty.

She walked past the hospital room, 112—the one to which a floor nurse had said Vincent would be moved. There was a cushy reclining chair inside and someone bustling around, setting up stands and affixing what looked like wings to the bedside. Beth wandered on, covertly glancing at half-opened doors the rooms of which seemed nearly empty. Thankfully, a quiet hospital night.

Having killed as much time as she could, she went back to the door of the emergency room. She asked, "Is Vincent Cappadora awake?"

"You're his mother. We met before," the nurse said. "Well, he is sort of. He's groggy. We've kind of knocked him out on purpose. They have a lot of work to do. But you can wait in his room for him. I'll get another chair in there. Or a cot if you like."

"That's okay," Beth said. "I can sit in the chair that's in there. I peeked inside. It looks pretty comfortable."

From one of the hospital's tiered windows, Beth glanced down at the street. It was nearly midnight, and news trucks and throngs of reporters clogged the street in front of the hospital. She supposed there would be more back at the Marlborough Hotel as well as back in Durand. Beth had already heard about a one-hour special planned by Katie Couric that would include an interview with everyone from Bill Humbly to, Beth supposed, Roman the dog.

Briefly, Beth thought of Claire and Blaine Whittier and whispered the tag end of a prayer for them.

"The one chair is fine," Beth said again.

"For both of you?" the nurse asked.

"Both of who?" Beth asked. "You aren't getting Vincent to sit up tonight?"

"I meant you and his brother."

"His brother's in there? Are you sure? I just came past," Beth said.

"So did he, the other way," the nurse told her.

Beth walked back down the hall to the door and leaned in through the small opening. When she let her eyes adjust to the gloom, she saw that the big leather chair indeed was now occupied. Ben sat there quietly, his hands in his lap. He still wore his dirty wind pants, but his shirt was clean, his hands and face washed, his hair wet-combed.

At that moment, she heard a gurney rattle up behind her.

Vincent was wheeled past, a white sheet pulled up to his bare chest, the blue-flowered hospital gown over his shoulders. Both hands were wrapped in gauze and secured to individual boards and his ankle was suspended on a thick, formed foam block. The doctor with him explained to Beth that the fracture on his ankle was serious, but would mend. The packs on his hands and feet would bear watching and would be changed throughout the night. "We'll hope for the best," the doctor said.

"Meaning?"

"Meaning that your son could lose a finger or a toe. Or more. I hope not," the doctor admitted. He and the nurse began to guide Vincent toward the room. For a moment, Vincent opened his eyes.

"We did it, Ma," he said, his voice something above a croak and below a squeak.

"You did it," Beth said.

"*Now* you can be proud of me."

Beth smiled and said, "Naaah." She kissed Vincent's forehead but did not follow him into his room. She heard Vincent cry out as he and his structure were shifted onto the bed. Still, she hung back.

Beth listened as a nurse told Ben, "We'll bring you a pillow once we get him situated. And a blanket."

"Can I help?" Ben asked.

"When he wakes up, yes," the nurse said. "You! Hey, you're the dad of the little baby. How is Baby Stella?"

"She's great. She's with her mom at the hotel and she's just great. Perfect. Thank you," Ben said.

"I'll bet you can't wait to run back there and cuddle her," the nurse said. "She's beautiful. I saw her picture on TV."

"I can't wait. But I'm going to stay here tonight with Vincent," Ben said. "I'll stay here until morning."

"Your mom's here . . ."

"I have to be here too," Ben said.

"You guys must be close."

"He's . . . uh, well, yeah. He's my brother. Stella wouldn't be here without him," Ben said. "Come to think of it, maybe I wouldn't either."

As Beth watched, unseen, Vincent grimaced and wrinkled his nose, tossing his head in opiate sleep. Ben leaned over and brushed his brother's face, as though to banish whatever disturbed him. Then Ben sat back and put his feet up on the railings of the bed, his eyes watchful, flicking between Vincent's face and the blue screen of the monitors. Quietly, he said, "It's okay, Vincent. Shhhhhhh."

Beth's eyes blurred. She fled for the elevators and grabbed a cab to the hotel.

"Where's Ben?" Eliza asked as soon as Beth ducked into their adjoined rooms. "He just . . . left."

Eliza lay curled on the bed with Stella sleeping between her and Candy; Pat had passed out on a kind of cushy chaise in one corner.

Candy looked around. "I don't know. I

didn't hear him say anything but about wanting a cheeseburger. And somebody brought about fifty cheeseburgers from the Air Force base. Those should be luscious."

"He's at the hospital," Beth said. "He's with Vincent."

"How is Vincent?" Candy asked.

"His ankle will be fine. They're not sure about frostbite and if he'll lose . . ." Beth glanced at Eliza. "Toes or fingers."

"No!" Eliza said and the baby cried out briefly. "I'd give up my own fingers!"

"It's what he wanted to do," said Candy. "You married into kind of a good family." Eliza smiled.

"Where's Kerry?" Beth asked.

"Well, she's decided to revive her career instead of teaching high-school chorus and giving up opera," Pat said, suddenly waking with a broad yawn. "She told me if we found Stella she'd never let anyone take a photo of her, except you, Bethie. For the rest of her life. But she just took a long shower and said she was going down to the lobby to have cocktails courtesy of CNN."

"She looked beautiful, like the old Kerry," Eliza said.

"You're might pretty, baby," Candy put in.

"She's the prettiest thing I ever saw. She's the most beautiful baby on earth. And thank you for the sweet dress, Mama."

"That was a gift from someone," Candy said. "And I meant you. But I hope they're okay tonight. Blaine especially."

Beth said, "It's going to be a long time before they're okay."

The next morning in Durand, after she'd stood next to Lorrie Sabo while she introduced Roman to TV audiences all over the world, telling them that it was "absurd" to think that she would let Vincent pay her for finding Stella, Sarah Switch slipped away to the trailhead that led up to the little house on Bryant Whittier's land.

Despite her stealth, news crews caught sight of her.

They had already put two and two together when a helicopter churned over them toward the mountain field and made ready for whatever they could catch on film when it returned.

Claire and Blaine waited with Sarah Switch as soldiers gently handed out a red-blanketed stretcher with straps firmly holding down a motionless form. From the top, a thatch of Bryant Whittier's dark chestnut hair whipped in the artificial wind. The morning was soft and spring-like. Claire Whittier covered her face and wept. Beside her, Blaine stood tall, her dry eyes impenetrable. Claire confided in Switch that, beyond her relief over the baby, she was unable to think of anything except that this might have been the moment of her twenty-fifth-anniversary toast in Tuscany.

Whittier had the right wife, Switch thought. She wondered again if she should have honored Claire's plea to bring her husband's body down before police visited the crime scene. It would be a choice she would regret and a lesson she would never forget. The sheriff would not again accept that something that seemed unambiguous and unequivocal actually was.

As they waited for the ambulance to finish loading her father's body, Blaine

Whittier said, "Mom, Dad made a choice. And you do have me."

Alone, later, although she wept at the unbearable details of his lonely death, Blaine Whittier hated her father for torturing her and Claire. She would hate him even more a week later when the snow melted.

Then, police and recovery volunteers, headed by Switch and Humbly, searched and dismantled the little house. Beneath it, they found a cross, handmade from logs and bound with rawhide thongs, crushed deep into the soil. Under that, swaddled in a nearly disintegrated white wool blanket, were remains quickly identified as those of Jacqueline Whittier. The coroner's opinion was that Jacqueline had died by misadventure, although no one could say for sure, after two full years in the ground, how she got the blow that fractured her skull.

The story that had ended in cozy glory took a sinister turn and exploded.

Blaine decided to take her junior year abroad, in Italy, where eventually Claire would visit her.

When Claire opted to sell the house in Durand and return to Chicago to be near her parents, she asked Blaine what she should do with the mountain summerhouse. Blaine suggested her mother donate it to some children's charity, in Jacqueline's name.

And she wondered if her junior year abroad might turn into forever.

CHAPTER TWENTY-TWO

"Bye," Beth said to Pat, who was headed for his first night back at the restaurant. They had come back from California several days earlier but Pat had taken his time about going back to work. "Is it going to feel weird?"

"I wouldn't have thought so, but kind of, Bethie," Pat said. "I used to think of it as my second home. Hell, I used to think of it as my first home sometimes. But now, it's like, it's my job. I'll probably stay there for a while. Dad can close. He's only been back a week. Hasn't seen any of the crowd. Except Charley Two. Those guys practically threw a parade for us."

"That bother you?" Beth asked. "All the fuss, I mean."

"I'm not looking forward to it, after seeing this mug of mine on TV for the past two weeks. Then again, who wouldn't be happy? We're lucky to have friends like the friends we have."

"We are."

"What I'm scared of is women, to be honest." Pat paused to glance in the hall mirror. "I'm wearing suits I couldn't fit into for ten years. Nice ones, too. I could get mobbed. Tragedy's good for weight loss."

"So I hear. But don't even joke about it, Paddy." She smiled then. "On the other hand, go ahead. We should smile. Go out and get 'em, stud. I'm just going to sit here like a lump of flesh."

"Kerry home?"

"Recital practice. Coming up. It's nice they let her be in it, considering that she'll graduate later," Beth said. "Vincent's coming."

"They're lucky to have *her.* I can't wait to see her. I know what she's singing," Pat said, his eyes suddenly misting. "I heard her upstairs."

"'Un Bel Di, Vedremo,'" Beth agreed. "One fine day. The saddest song in the world. I don't know if I can handle it."

"Unless the little boy came back . . ."

"And the little girl," Beth said. "But that's not how it is in operas. In operas, everybody has to die but the bad guys." She added, "You better get going."

Pat bent over and kissed her neck. "'Night, Gram," he said.

"'Night, Gramps."

"Never thought I'd be so glad to hear it," said Pat. "I'd hear it ten more times."

Beth crossed herself involuntarily. "Be careful what you wish for," she said.

She waited until she heard his car round Pebblestone Court and pick up speed. Then she carried her glass of tonic and lime out onto the pool deck. This was the kind of night that made a person want to stay up too late; the kind of night that she and Pat, twenty-five years ago, even twenty years ago, sometimes found the will to wrangle away until they heard the birds cheep or Baby Kerry kick the bells on her crib in the nursery—which was their bedroom closet. The air was weightless, free of the slightest humidity, or bug or breeze, an exquisite texture on her skin. She lay back in her chaise, on new cushions Pat had bought last fall, so thick, with some kind of downy stuff, it welcomed Beth to sleep there. Above her arched a riot of stars. They were not like the mountain stars. When Stella was missing, she had gazed up at them astonished that the spangled heavens' display could share space in the universe with the black hole where nothing seemed to move or breathe. Beth didn't know if she could ever lie on a hill and look up into the pure darkness and wait to see a shooting star, not ever again. Her pulse beat at the thought. But Harrington wasn't yet so spoiled by lights from malls and schools and car dealerships that the stars were blocked entirely.

There was still something that ached with romantic immensity in a starry night. When she was a young girl, and had no idea why the night sky made her stomach clench, when she missed her mother and couldn't bear the noise that even her father's drunken silence beat like a drum,

Beth lay on the lumpy grass in her backyard and comforted herself by thinking,
This is the best night of someone's
life. She thought that now. Tonight, someone learned the lump was only a lump;
someone said yes; the stick had a plus
sign; the call finally came; the smoke from
under the hood was only steam; the kids
won the game that would send them to
State; the mother woke up in her hospital
bed and recognized her daughter; the girl
who had always been just ten pounds over
perfect was voted prom queen.

It wasn't the worst night of Beth's life, either. She sat still and held it gently. Her
whole family—in California, downtown in
Chicago, up here on the North Side, down
in the old neighborhood—nestled in the
cup of her hand. When she arrived home
last week, the mailbox was stuffed with
cards and notes—most without stamps.
And on her porch, under the portico, were
baskets of flowers and candles and picture
frames and crocheted afghans, from
neighbors whose names she didn't know
and who she would have thought didn't
know her name. In fact, they probably
never did know her name until Vincent

won the Oscar. That didn't make them any less kind or noticing.

Vincent hadn't been kidding about a comedy.

He and Rob were working on it now.

Last week, Vincent had called to give her the gist: A woman wants so badly to break up her son and his trashy girlfriend that she pays a hunky jock, a would-be actor, and even the scion of an old Italian duchy to romance the girl at college. Finally, she falls for one of the prop guys and he falls hard for her as well. Then the woman's son comes home for spring break and embraces her with gratitude. To her shock, he knows all about her scheme, but if it hadn't worked, he'd never have met the great love of his life—Craig.

"We're still tweaking it," Vincent said. "We don't want it to be derivative. But we don't want it to be too un-date-movie, either."

"Too art house?"

"Deeply into sheer dough and entertainment this time around, Ma. Art for art's sake when I get the oxygen for it. Right now, I don't have the heart for depth and meaning."

"Speaking of meaning. Am I supposed to get a message out of that plot?" Beth asked, forcing herself not to be the mother—not to ask about the first joint of the index finger on Vincent's left hand, the shard of the index finger on his right, which both had to be removed. He knew now that the tissue might have survived if he hadn't rubbed snow on his bare hands. He knew that the numbness along the arches of his feet would confound him always. The single time they'd discussed it, Vincent said it had been small enough a price and it would remind him, each step he took.

He told Beth, "No, the sleeping bag with Ben was the closest I'll ever get to that kind of male bonding, I think."

Beth nestled back into her lounge, and tried to ignore the phone when it rang.

It could be a reporter.

It could be her brother.

It could be . . . anyone. Whoever wanted her badly enough, they could call back.

Annie's parents weren't strict about her going to school basketball games or anything. They'd let her go to a dance.

But the movies were a different story.
Movies weren't supervised. They lasted
late, after her little brother and sister were
in bed. And they were with girls who didn't
attend Cornerstone Church. But Annie's
mom admitted that, before meeting her
dad, she'd loved being a popular girl too.
Annie Hixon's parents had been true to
each other since senior year in high
school.

So, because Annie would be thirteen in
a few months, and a lot of her friends already were, they said yes when she asked
if she could go see the new animated
movie about the mouse who started her
own ballet company. It was Disney. Annie
and at least three of her five friends loved
Disney, even if they pretended they were
just watching it because of their little sisters. Still, Annie's parents didn't know that
the girls were going to sneak into another
movie, the one about the girl who fell in
love with her boyfriend's younger brother
while the older guy was in the war. It was
only PG-13, but Annie felt guilty.

She usually never lied to her parents, although her little sister, Mary, did. Mary was

adopted, like Annie. But Mary was adopted when she was littler, about three. Mary was seven now, and boy, was she the mischief type. At school, she used the name Amelia, which she remembered having from her foster home. Mary knew that the password on the lock their parents had on the TV armoire was their zip code and she opened it to watch TV when she wasn't supposed to. She was a smart little girl, Annie's father said, but she overheard him say that Mary needed "direction and discipline."

Annie had been older when her parents brought her home. She already had a lot of self-discipline so she never got in any trouble. Her mother said she was "very mature" for her age.

That night, when Lucy's mother picked them up, Annie was so excited she practically danced out the door into Lucy's mom's van. Four other girls—Lana, Mercy, Caitlin, and Gina—were waiting for her.

"Lip-gloss drill!" Gina said. She was the worst of all of them, but in a good way. She dabbed lip gloss on Annie and added a little mascara at the tips of Annie's lashes. "Glam, ma'am! You don't want David Brandenauer to think you didn't dress up for him!"

"I didn't dress up! For him at least! I'm not interested in boys!" Annie said, laughing hard despite the trouble she knew she'd get in if she didn't get to the jar of Vaseline in the upstairs bathroom before her mom saw her.

It was true what she said about boys. She was just enough younger than the other kids in seventh that the whole boy thing hadn't quite kicked over for her yet, and it wasn't just that she went to church Wednesdays and twice on Sundays.

But she had to admit that she *was* more interested this year in looking nice than she had been. She chose her clothes with care, the night before instead of that morning, and was going to ask her mom if she could have her ears pierced next year. All of her friends were going out for pompoms in eighth grade and Annie was already sure she would stick to swimming and volleyball. But not long ago at the Target, she'd stared so long at a shorter skirt with a matching vest that her mom, who usually made all her clothes, broke down and bought it for her.

Lucy's mom pulled up at the front doors of the multiplex.

"Be out here at nine-thirty sharp!" she said. "Lucy Dillon Murray, do you have your phone?"

"I have it, Mom!" Lucy said. "I'll call you the first monster I see!"

They ran up the walk and David was there, along with Cameron and Hanson and two other guys. Was this some kind of setup? But, no. Gina seemed ready to stay and flirt but the rest of them went running inside to buy their tickets.

As they headed down the hall to get popcorn, Annie studied the posters for the other movies. Her family rented DVDs and watched them together—although less often since her younger brother, Ross, had come home. Rossie was only two and he cried all the time, day and night, for his foster parents, the poor little guy. So her own folks were a little distracted, what with visiting the pediatrician and the minister coming over and such. They didn't even want to take Ross to church until he stopped kicking her parents and hiding behind the drawing table and crying for his "my-house Daddy-Mommy." Annie knew every time her parents came back, in the van that had a sunrise over a mountain and the words "Begin Again at Cornerstone" painted on the side, she would hear Rossie crying as soon as her mother opened the paneled door.

It was in that same van that Annie had come to her new home after her birth parents got divorced and her birth father went to jail for something like cheating the government. It had all happened so fast that Annie's mother said that Annie's birth parents were lucky they had an "adoption connection" with Cornerstone. Mom and Dad were able to come and bring her home from some school event or game, just at the moment police arrested her birth father. Annie was spared the pain of seeing him taken away. For the first year, Annie's new mother homeschooled her and taught her almost entirely from the Bible. After that, she went to Christ the King school, down the road in Eagle.

Her sister Mary had come home in the van, too, and later Ross.

Annie felt sorry for Rossie and sometimes went into the room where he slept all by himself in the crib (at least she had Mary!) and patted his sweaty little head. Once, Ross said, "Dada" in his sleep, and for some reason, Annie began to cry. She wondered why they didn't take babies for adoption when they were little and didn't have to suffer so much? Her parents said that older kids were harder to "place" and it was more Christian to do it the way they did, but Ross didn't seem to be getting much happiness out of his "forever home."

But tonight, Annie wasn't going to worry about Ross. Just today, she'd given him six colors of Play-Doh she'd saved up to buy with allowances from the past three weeks. When she left, he was happy, making snakes and pretend pizza.

While her friends ganged up on the concession stand, Annie wandered around. She didn't get to see the inside of theaters too much, so she was enchanted by everything from the flat water bubblers that never stopped gushing to the life-size cardboard figures of movie stars.

There was a poster for that film, *No Time to Wave Goodbye,* the one her parents talked about one night when she couldn't sleep and was eavesdropping. It was easy to listen to them. They always talked at the kitchen table, right under the heat vent in her and Mary's room.

"Of course, I feel that," Annie heard her mother say. "But think of how far removed this is from this child's life as it is now. You remember, the paint and the bikini she was wearing . . ."

In the poster were a man and a woman holding a picture of a little girl doing a movement—it was called a scorpion, Annie suddenly realized—on a balance beam. The little girl had blond pigtails and wore a silver-and-red skirt with a black-and-silver turtleneck top. The man was also holding a teddy bear dressed in the same colors. You almost couldn't see the little girl's face. Annie moved closer. The face was still blurry. Annie moved down to the next poster for the same film; it was showing on two of the screens. This was a different picture—three kids on a beach, walking away on a cloudy day. A banner slapped across it said "Winner of the Academy Award for Best Documentary Film."

When would her friends be finished getting their candy?

Annie didn't have money for extras, especially after Rossie's Play-Doh, but she knew everyone would share their Sno-Caps and Dots with her.

She didn't really feel like eating candy anyhow. Wandering back to the first poster, Annie stared hard at the face of the woman sitting on the couch and again at the little girl on the balance beam. Then she ran for the bathroom, where she threw up all her meatloaf and peas. Annie hadn't thrown up since she was ten and had the flu. She searched her red sweater for any telltale signs and had to rinse her mouth and rub soap on her teeth before she ran back out to join her friends.

"What happened to you?" Gina asked.

"It's so hot in here!" Annie lied. "I had to go splash my face. Aren't you just dying?" Gina thrust a gigantor mug of Coke at her and Annie took a swig. It made her stomach feel better.

But not really.

She had been so excited to go out with her friends. But she was glad her mother said no when she asked to stay over at Lucy's, relieved when she could wave and jump up the six steps into her house, two at a time.

Late that night, Annie made her way down to the office den where the computer was set up so that she and Mary could use it for homework—and homework only, with one or both parents watching the screen. Still, it wasn't hard to sneak down: Annie knew every board in the stairs and could make a complicated slalom to avoid a single creak.

She closed the door softly behind her before she turned on the computer and winced when it made its "ta-dah!" sound.

Quickly, she Googled *No Time to Wave Goodbye.* There were absolutely tons of stories, lots of them about winning the Oscar.

One was a story about what happened to one of the guys who made the movie. His brother's little baby girl was kidnapped and by one of the people who was actually in the film! The guy was scary, scary nuts! They found the body of his own daughter buried up by the place he hid out with the baby. The baby was fine, but the medical examiner couldn't tell how the girl died because her body was so decomposed. And anyhow, it didn't matter because the kidnapper shot himself to death just when they came to rescue the baby. There was the father of the baby and the Oscar-winning guy, Vincent Cappadora, standing next to this little lady with big sunglasses pushed up on her head. Next to her was a huge, really pretty Saint Bernard dog. The small woman and the big dog helped find the baby.

Annie wanted a dog.

It began, "Familiar terrain is often the easiest to walk, but the Cappadora brothers had to fight their way uphill after Vincent Cappadora's Oscar-winning documentary provoked . . ."

Among the other pictures was one of that heavyset man and the little blond woman but a different photo of the little girl. This time, Annie could see her whole face. She was holding a trophy almost as big as she was and peeking around it with this big grin like someone would peek around a tree trunk.

Her name was Alana Cafferty.

Annie Hixon repeated the name. Alana Cafferty. Aly. Aly.

Aly, hurry up! Aly, sleeping beauty, it's French toast!

Annie heard a sound, spun around in her chair and reached back, ready to turn the computer off. But it was only the wind, slapping the branches of the big maple against the roof. Her father was going to trim those branches, he told Annie that night of the big storm, when both he and her mother were so tired after they got back from driving home with Ross, who had thrown up all over the inside of the van.

Annie put one finger on the little girl's face on the screen.

What was the name of that thing people used to find the names of people?

ZuYuSearch. Gina said she used it all the time to try to call movie stars.

Annie scrolled up. She typed in "Vincent Cappadora."

She imagined he lived in Hollywood. But the search found no Vincent Cappadora in Hollywood, not even in Los Angeles. Annie turned back to the story. Mr. Cappadora came from Chicago. Maybe, if he was rich, he had an apartment there, like Oprah. She typed in Chicago, Illinois. Cappadora. There were ten of them, but most of them had unlisted numbers. Angelo. Benjamin.

Patrick.

Patrick and Beth had a phone number.

Feeling like someone was going to come up behind her and stab her, Annie wrote the number down: 847-854-2386. She turned off the computer and tore off two sheets of the yellow pad of paper, in case the pen marks came through. She got up to go back to bed, folding the paper six ways and wrapping it up tightly into a star shape.

Then she sat back down, in her father's huge desk chair, and unfolded it. She turned her father's desk lamp on, just for a moment, and committed the number to memory. Annie was good at that.

Picking up the telephone, she dialed: 847-854-2386.

A recording picked up. "You must first dial a one or a zero before completing this number."

Annie tried again. The phone rang three times. No one answered.

She had to pee now and felt that same grinding in her stomach as at the theater, except now her stomach was empty.

Aly, Adam, come in here. Time to read! What was this voice? Her mother would say it was the devil or something. If she dialed one more time and no one picked up, it would mean God didn't want her to sneak behind her parents' back.

She pushed the buttons again and right away, a woman picked up. "Hello?" she said. "Hello?" Annie couldn't speak. "Hello? Hello? Is anyone there? Who is this?"

"Yes," Annie finally said. "I'm here."

"Can I help you?" the woman repeated, sounding a little annoyed.

"Is Vincent home?"

"Vincent lives in California. I'm his mother. I'm Beth. Who's this?" she asked, not sounding so upset now. Annie started to cry, so hard she didn't know if she could talk anymore, or if anyone upstairs could hear her.

"Do you know some people name Cafferty?"

"Can you tell me who you are?"

"Please. I have to ask you. Do you know the Cafferty family?"

The woman asked slowly, "Why?"

"Please," Annie said. "Are they dead? Is the father in prison?"

"No. I know Eileen and Al Cafferty. They're just fine. They live in Lake Madrigal, Wisconsin. Where do you live?"

"Up in the north woods. I live in Rhinelander, Wisconsin."

The lady said, "No! Damn."

"What's wrong?" Annie asked and almost pressed the button.

"Nothing. The Caffertys were interviewed for my son Vincent's movie. They lost their little girl. She was kidnapped. She was kidnapped six years ago, no . . . seven years ago, from a gymnastics meet."

"I know," Anne said. "I remember."

"You remember," said the lady. "Honey. Don't be afraid."

"I am afraid," the child said, almost wistfully.

"Don't be afraid," Beth said. "Don't hang up and don't be afraid. I'm going to get my other phone out of my purse. Is that okay? Can you tell me your address?" Annie did. Beth went on. "Okay. Blue Lake Terrace. Hixon with an 'x.' Okay. Will you stay right there till I come back? Will you promise not to hang up?"

Annie Hixon's hands started to shake. She cried harder and had to hold the receiver with both hands. But she said, "I promise." She thought of Mary-Amelia and of Rossie, in his sleep, his hair all baby sweat, calling for his daddy. She sat up straighter. "I promise."

And even when she saw the three cars cut their rotating red lights and slide silently up beside the window, Annie didn't hang up.

Acknowledgments

So many experts and friends—and experts who became friends—contributed the facts that form the spine of *No Time to Wave Goodbye.* Wilderness guide Lorri Hanna Sabo does not do exactly what a character with a name much like hers does in the novel, but elements of the trek into the wilderness were taken from the journey she and I made into the Gila National Wilderness, which transformed both our lives. My family and I thank her. Author and Search and Rescue instructor Hannah Nyala West and I are old friends and, with her remarkable dogs, she has performed the equivalent of feats recounted in this story. I have no words big enough to thank Greg Davenport, renowned authority on wilderness survival and the medical implications of exposure; no one could have been so giving of his time and knowledge. SAR expert John A. Carlson also offered trenchant advice. Thank you to Annette Gomez of the Gila National Wilderness staff and Melody Skinner of the San Juan County Sheriff's Department for helping me create the fictional Durand and the fictional sheriff of Cisco County in her mountain juris. Filmmakers Frank Sommers and Frank Caruso, my homies, told me all I needed to know about equipment, and the differences between video and film. Award-winning documentarian Wendy Cramer let me shadow her with a tape recorder. To my friend and slang collector, Carol Ann Riordan, my best loyalty always. Authors Holly Kennedy and John Fetto encouraged me at every step. Thomas Cook generously contributed an essential plot idea that lifted the narrative out of a doldrum. Researchers John Holcomb, Anna H. Reeves, and Maddie Goetter found facts that supported this narrative.

As there are times when the most difficult births reap splendid rewards, I must thank the skilled hands that coaxed this narrative past what seemed insurmountable obstacles. The consummate editor, Kate Medina of Random House, as well as editor Laura Ford, gave me insights, comfort, tough talk, and time. I can never thank them enough. My compliments to Kate Norris and Vincent La Scala for saving me in mid-fall with skillful edits. My beloved agent of nearly twenty-five years, Jane Gelfman, green-lighted a project few would have dared to hope could succeed. My co-worker and pal Pamela English worked with a madwoman during the day; my husband, Chris Brent, lived with her at night. My ever-tolerant children—Rob, Dan, Martin, Francie, Mia, Will, and Atticus—never forgot that the eccentric being in the upstairs room adored them. Most important, I thank you, reader. For fifteen years, at lectures and signings, you asked me what became of the lost boy, Vincent, until finally I knew.

This is a work of fiction, set in an imagined Chicago and an imagined California, where the real and the fictional slip over each other like plates of the earth. The choices I made were composed of the geography of fact and the geography of dreams. All the events are products of the author's imagination, and any similarity to actual localities and events is both the result of coincidence and the sum of my own experiences. Errors are no one's fault but my own. If you have reached this point, I hope they were few enough.

ABOUT THE AUTHOR

JACQUELYN MITCHARD is the *New York Times* bestselling author of the first Oprah's Book Club selection *The Deep End of the Ocean* and more than a dozen other books for both adults and children. A former syndicated columnist for the *Milwaukee Journal Sentinel,* she is a contributing editor for *Parade,* and her work has appeared in *More, Reader's Digest, Good Housekeeping,* and *Real Simple,* among other publications. She lives in Wisconsin with her husband and seven children.

www.jacquelynmitchard.com